Differen

Everett Monaghan

Introduction

Living three hundred miles away from my Grandmother, I was only able to see her once or twice a year. Although she lived in very modest accommodation in a mining village, I loved the times I spent with her. The smell of coal dust in the air, whatever time of year, was familiar and comforting.

Inevitably, my Grandmother would show off the photograph of her father and his brother, wearing their handball kit, and posing proudly in front of the camera. I liked looking at the photograph and hearing her story, but I did not take as much interest, or ask as many questions, as I should have. Theirs is a story that deserved attention and should be remembered.

As my grandmother passed away and time has passed, I realised that the exceptional lives of these two men could easily be forgotten forever. I did not want that to happen. Encouraged by my spouse, I decided to find out as much as possible about the lives of my Great Grandfather and his brother and put pen to paper.

I decided a historical fiction novel would be the best way to relay their story. The basic facts are true, but I did not know my ancestors personally, and my mother, the oldest living relative, only knew some of the people concerned, when they were in their latter years. I do not know the personalities and day-to-day lives of my ancestors. Rather than listing the information I know, I decided to use my imagination to embellish the facts and create a story which I think is interesting, and hopefully close to the truth. The opening letter is an exact copy of the original letter sent by Micky.

I dedicate this book to all the descendants of the Mordue brothers, who are numerous and widespread. I hope they, and you, enjoy reading the story of the lives of Micky and Jacky Mordue.

Chapter 1

August 1915

'Just a few lines hoping you are all keeping in the best of health. I am pleased to say that I am all right myself, thanks be to the Lord. We left our camp to go into action last Friday, August 6th, and I shall never forget it. We had to make a new landing on the Peninsula. Arriving about 10 o'clock at night we found the Turks were waiting for us. They rained bullets at us as we were coming off the boat. Our Colonel and Captain got shot straight away. I am sorry to say that Wilf Belcher got killed about 10 minutes after we landed. We got our orders not to fire, but use the bayonet only. It was just like facing certain death, but our regiment, who were the first to land, never faltered. We got the order to charge, and we did not forget to either. I am the luckiest man alive. I was with Wilf Belcher and another five of our section, and I am sorry to say all of them were shot by my side. How I escaped the Lord above knows. You can tell Mr. Bob Belcher that Wilf died like a hero. We have never faltered since Friday night until today (Thursday), when we are back out of the trenches. I have not much more to tell you. Only tell my mother how I am getting on. Keep your heart up, because I think I am sure to pull through now after the escapes I have had. So now I shall conclude. Give my best love to all.'

Micky put down his pencil and closed his eyes. As the words transferred from his thoughts to the paper, he still could not believe his current situation, yet, he called himself the luckiest man alive. A more apt description would be 'the man luckiest to be alive'. Bodies and filth surrounded him, the stench of death and war, in the stifling heat of the Turkish sun.

The surviving soldiers did not understand why their commanders had allowed them to rest and have a day off when they had finally begun to make progress, and continued momentum could have resulted in significant advancement into the Turkish higher ground. But the rest was more than welcome, battling as they had for almost a week with hardly any sleep, and in scorching

1

temperatures never experienced in their homeland, the North East of England.

Micky was lost in his thoughts — thoughts of his beloved Meg and their five children, thousands of miles away. How had he come to be in this situation? Why the hell wasn't he at home with them? He could smell the warm pies baking on the range; the crackling of the coal sparking in the grate; the laughter and tears of the bairns...

'You're keen to get out the door Jacky, man. Any money you won't be so eager tomorrow once you know what you're in for.' Micky put his lunch box in his pocket and pulled on his tough leather boots, ready to set off for the colliery.

'Aye, this is it Jacky, once you start at the pit there's no getting away from it. You'll be part of the pit and the pit will be part of you,' Jimmy said.

It was Jacky's first day at the colliery, the youngest of six brothers, all who worked at Sacriston colliery in the North East of England. Jacky was keen to be part of the team, hoping his brothers would see him as the man he now felt he had become. He was constantly trying to prove to his brothers that he was as good as them. He had just turned fourteen years old. His enthusiasm for starting work deep underground in the belly of the coal pit was ignited by the frustrations of lagging three years behind everything his brothers did.

'Now, you and Jimmy watch out for Jacky, won't you?' Elizabeth Mordue, the lads' mother, fussed over Jacky as he restlessly stood by the door, waiting to be on his way.

'Don't worry, Mother, we'll look after your bairn,' Micky teased. 'Howay, let's get going.'

'Off you go then, and make sure you bring your bait boxes back,' said Elizabeth tersely, ushering the lads outside so that she could quickly close the door behind them without anyone noticing the tear which had begun to roll down her cheek.

Elizabeth watched anxiously through the kitchen window as the three teenage brothers tramped along the dusty street towards the colliery. Although she was not large in stature, she was strong both physically and mentally. Elizabeth never made any show of emotion, being the rock of the family. She had endured more than her fair share of hardship and loss in her life, and built up a thick skin to help her cope. But Jacky was her youngest son, and she could not help feeling overly fond and protective towards him. She would busy herself throughout the day to stop herself thinking about Jacky, in the bowels of the earth. Being the mother of six lads it was assumed from the day they were born that they would start at the colliery once they were old enough. If they didn't there was a

3

chance the family would lose their colliery house, which was rented to them by the pit owners on the understanding that all the sons would become miners. But to Elizabeth, Jacky, being her youngest, did not seem ready to follow his brothers down the pit.

'Sit down, Mam, and I'll fetch you a cuppa,' said Lizzie, seeing through her aunt's brusque exterior. Lizzie had lived with the family since she was three, following the death of her mother, Elizabeth's sister, during childbirth. Lizzie was now eleven, and when she was not at school, she helped Elizabeth with the daily chores. Collecting water from the communal pump, washing dishes, polishing and sweeping, were amongst her tasks.

Elizabeth had three daughters of her own. Annie, the eldest, lived four miles away. She was a young widow, raising three daughters on her own. The second daughter, Barbara, lived in Newcastle with her family, and Hannah, the youngest of Elizabeth's daughters, had died from eclamptic convulsions three years ago at the age of just nineteen, fourteen hours after giving birth to illegitimate twins. Elizabeth had nursed the twins; one survived for just two weeks and the other clung to life for three months before losing her fight for life. Hannah had been forced upon by the married head of the house where she worked as a servant. He had used her for his pleasure and sent her packing as soon as she could no longer hide her pregnancy. The result of his actions put an end to the life of a much-loved and delightful young woman. Hannah had been a keen sportswoman and had a love for life. She had excelled at football and was in the local women's team — an advocator of the women's game. Since her untimely death, she was sorely missed by all of the Mordue household. A light had been extinguished.

Lizzie passed the cup of tea to Elizabeth, who was discreetly wiping a tear from the corner of her eye.

'Thank you, Pet. You're a good lass,' said Elizabeth.

Lizzie set about seeing to the fire and went out into the yard to fill the coalscuttle.

Elizabeth's husband had died five years earlier, and it was now the sons' responsibility to bring in the wages. Sam, the eldest, and Joe, the third eldest, were family men and both lived in Sacriston with their wives and children, but thirty-year-old Dan, the second son, had taken his father's place as the man of the house and had

4

never thought to marry. His duty was to his mother. He worked a different shift to his brothers and this week he was covering a night shift. As Jimmy, Micky and Jacky went off to work it was not long after that Dan returned home to have his bath in front of the fire, eat his meal, and then fall into the bed vacated by his brothers, which was still slightly warm and bore their indentations.

Jimmy, Micky, and Jacky strode along the cobbled path towards the colliery— the rhythmic pounding of their boots joining the steps of the other lads who were also on their way to start their shift at the colliery. Jacky felt excited to be a part of this crowd; comrades who were united in their mutual understanding and experience of working life as a coal miner.

At the pit, the brothers went their separate ways. After collecting their lamps, Jimmy and Micky stepped into the cramped cage that would take them down into the depths of the mine. They worked as putters, pushing and shoving the loaded coal tubs from the coal face to the bottom of the shaft, and returning the empty tubs to the coal face ready for the miners to refill. This was heavy and demanding work, the lads tugging and pushing the unwieldy tubs along tunnels that were dark and cramped, with low ceilings, having to stoop and bend as they toiled. As the lift descended the daylight diminished, and they were transported into the dark subterranean other-world.

Jacky reported to the overman. As a new boy, he was given the job of a trapper, opening and closing the ventilation doors to allow coal trams to pass through. Jacky was given a lamp and led to the lift where he packed in tight with other workers. Jacky noticed himself trembling slightly, his stomach churning as he was filled with excitement and nerves. The cage dropped and kept on dropping lower and lower — the tiny ray of light at the top of the shaft disappearing above them. With a jolt, the lift stopped. The cage was opened, and the men streamed out. The chamber was large, with a number of tunnels leading off in different directions. Jacky was led through the darkness along a passage. The further he walked, the lower the ceiling became. Jacky tried to ignore the rank smell and the dust filling the air. The mine was larger than Jacky had imagined; the walk was longer than the walk from his home to the mine. By the time they reached the trap door where Jacky would be working, the mineshaft was a long way back. Jacky was given his instructions and left in dark isolation. Adrenalin still pumped through his veins. He listened eagerly for the sound of an approaching tub in order to carry out his duties, and opened and closed the door with a sense of importance and achievement. But, as he closed the doors, he was left alone in the darkness, his lamp illuminating his immediate vicinity, but away from the light it cast there was a vast blackness. Sitting, waiting for the next load to pass through, Jacky's thoughts were taken up with listening out for the movement of another tub, but as the hours went by, Jacky was left to dwell on the gloom and solitude of his situation. The reality of the position slowly dawned on him as the excitement wore off. He thought he could hear someone approaching from the depth of the tunnel and called out sheepishly. As he raised his lamp, the light illuminated the glistening eyes of a rat as it scurried by, searching for food. A beetle ran across his arm making Jacky jump and he almost dropped his lamp. Jacky suddenly felt very isolated, the blackness closing in around him. Just then, two miners approached pushing a hefty tub and Jacky opened and closed the door to let them through, relieved to see their weary faces. Then they were gone, and he returned to silent solitude. Jacky decided that it must be about time for his lunch, so he took out his tin bait box. As he sipped his lukewarm tea Jacky realized how parched he was, and how quenching the tea felt as it passed down his dust-filled throat. He took out his bread and dripping sandwich and noticed coal dust had stuck to the edges, but it tasted comforting and satisfying. His Mam had also given him a small piece of fruit cake as a treat for his first day on the job; he would save that for later. Just then, he heard someone else approaching, so he got ready to open the door, but it was a miner whose lamp had gone out.

'Give us your lamp, son,' said the miner. 'I canna do my job without a lamp. You'll get it back at the end of the shift.'

Jacky did not dare argue and handed his lamp to the miner. As the man walked off down the tunnel Jacky was thrown into pitch blackness like he had never known before. He held his hand up in front of him but could see nothing. The darkness enveloped him, and he felt a loneliness he had never felt before. The scratching and scurrying of the rats and beetles seemed amplified, and his head started itching; was it really crawling with beetles or was his mind playing tricks on him? Jacky felt the tears welling in his eyes. He had never imagined the grim reality of being a miner, the job he had longed to do for so long. The occasional light of an approaching miner pushing their tub lifted his spirits. He longed for them to stay with him and not to disappear back into the tunnel, returning him to complete darkness and solitude. Jacky did not eat the piece of fruitcake. His appetite had gone. He could not control his bladder any longer, and not daring to move from his spot he simply urinated into the abyss. The smell of pee added to the stench which surrounded him. Jacky wanted his shift to end so he could return to the outside world, where even the smoky coal-filled air of the colliery town would feel heavenly compared to the stale rancid air below ground.

At the end of the shift, the brothers walked home together, tired and coated in coal dust from head to foot.

'How did you get on, Jacky?' asked Jimmy.

'Yes, good,' Jacky replied, focusing on keeping his voice steady, but his positive words did not fool his brothers.

'Ah, that's good. I thought it was hell my first day as a trapper,' said Jimmy.

'Aye, worst job there is,' concurred Micky.

The brothers had been careful not to enlighten Jacky before his first day at work.

'When you get to work with other lads it's not so bad. You'll not be stuck as a trapper for long, Jacky.'

The weekend could not come soon enough for Jacky. At the end of his Saturday shift, he had his bath and dinner and headed to the handball alley in the village to practice. He knocked the hard ball with his toughened palm. The ball smashed against the wall and rebounded across the court. Jacky hit it with his other hand and continued to chase and strike the ball. All thoughts of the pit evaporated as he imagined he was playing against a world champion. The older lads would be here before long, and he would be turfed off the court. Jacky darted from one corner of the court to another, the ball hitting the wall with a satisfying thud, before rebounding in varying directions. Jacky was beginning to build up a sweat when Jimmy and Micky turned up with a group of friends. Jacky was expected to make way for them.

'Let us have a game with you, Micky, just for a bit,' pleaded Jacky, knowing what the answer would be.

'You can sit and watch how it's done, Jacky. When you've got a bit of muscle on you, and you can hit the ball as far as the wall, then we might let you join in,' Micky quipped, squeezing Jacky's biceps.

Jacky sat and watched as his brothers breezed around the court, seemingly effortlessly, making the ball speed through the air. Jimmy and Micky were a handball pair, and they were training for an upcoming match. The official games were well organized, with many spectators surreptitiously placing bets on the outcome. Jimmy and Micky had just reached a standard where they felt they had a real chance of winning some big matches. Not only was handball a blessed relief from the hours they spent below ground, but it could also be a way of making some pocket money on the side. Jacky's school friend, Tom Coatman, turned up, and the pair decided to find a less desirable wall on which to have a knock about — the end wall of a row of terraced houses. A few other lads joined them. There were too many to play handball, so they decided to head to the field and kick a ball about. Jacky was happy playing any sport which involved a ball, but football and handball were his favourites. The lads picked teams; Jacky was always the first to be picked. Jacky was a lot faster and more skilful than the boys of his own age; it was just when he was up against his brothers that he looked less proficient. This was due to the age difference, but Jacky was not letting that stop him. He was determined to be as good as Micky and Jimmy and practised his ball skills at every possible moment.

Chapter 2

Thankfully, Jacky had to spend just two weeks as a trapper before he was moved to the surface. His job was as a sorter, picking stones and rocks out of the coal. This was much better work; Jacky could see the light of day and had fellow workers around him, making the time pass quickly. Although all the men in his family were miners, two weeks underground had made Jacky realise that this was not what he wanted from his life. But there was no other local work, and there was a chance they could lose their colliery house unless all the menfolk worked for the owners; it was one of the tenancy conditions. Working long hours did not make Jacky feel that he needed to rest when he had free time — quite the opposite. He relished every waking moment when he was not at the colliery, and spent more time than ever with a ball either at his hands or feet. As the weeks and months went past, Jacky was developing into a naturally muscular but lithe young man, with unrivalled speed over short distances; he was like a whippet.

Micky and Jimmy had played a few minor handball doubles matches against local men, and they had won every game. Now they had a match lined up against two lads from the neighbouring village of Pelton Fell. They practised whenever they could, working on their weaknesses and game plan. Their opponents, Ted Tate and Saul Green were experienced men, a few years older than the Mordue brothers. They were top players in the area, and Micky and Jimmy felt lucky just to be given the opportunity to play against them. The Mordues knew their chances of winning were very slim, but it would be a great experience, win or lose. The match was to be played at Pelton Fell, giving the opposition the home advantage. When match day came Jimmy, Micky, and a crowd of supporters from Sacriston, including Jacky, made the journey along the track, setting off early. The match could possibly go on for hours, so needed to start at a reasonable time, although this particular game was not expected to last too long; Tate and Green should take a rapid victory against such untried opponents. A crowd gathered, and money exchanged hands as bets were placed on the outcome of the match. Jimmy and Micky felt surprisingly relaxed as they warmed up for the game. They were not expected to win, so there was no pressure on them. The money that was riding on their victory was not their concern; they would do their best to win, but they knew anyone betting on them would be taking a huge gamble. As they shook hands before the start of the match, Micky felt his hand being enveloped in what felt like a glove; Tate and Green had palms like shovels coated in leathery skin.

As the match got underway it soon became clear that this would be no walkover. Tate and Green struck each shot with enormous power and had the Mordues scampering about the court, chasing the small ball as it sped in all directions. But Micky was a shrewd player. Even though he was still relatively inexperienced, he seemed to be able to predict where the ball would be hit, and skillfully positioned himself for his return shots. Jimmy was powerful, and his shots were fast and had depth. Tate and Green kept ahead in the game, but not by far. The minutes turned to hours and the game continued. Wooden chairs were brought out, and people from the neighbouring houses brought mugs of tea for the players when they had their well-deserved rest.

'I think we can do this Micky,' Jimmy whispered to his brother. 'If we can make them run around for every shot, they're going to get tired. Their legs aren't as young as ours.'

And that is exactly what they did; instead of trying to kill off every shot, the Mordues placed the ball in spaces which meant Tate and Green had to run for each return. The home crowd became less animated as they could see their men becoming weary. In contrast, the crowd that had travelled with the Mordues raised their voices in encouragement, cheering on the brothers. As the match went into its sixth hour, the legs of all four men were becoming increasingly tired, but it was Green who felt more than any that his legs were made of lead. He struggled to run, sweat pouring from his entire body. The Mordues could sense this, and it gave them the boost they needed, returning shots their bodies defied them to get to, and placing returns in parts of the court that could not be reached. Cracks appeared on Micky's palms, the blood mixing with sweat, but this did not dishearten him. He played through the pain, hardly noticing the sting of the ball as he focussed on each return. Match-point to the Mordues. Green and Tate knew it was over; they just wanted this torture to end and dropped to the floor as Jimmy placed the winning shot in the far corner of the court. Cheers went up from the Sacriston crowd. This was a day to remember, and the Mordue brothers' reputation was elevated in handball circles. Jimmy and Micky slumped onto the wooden chairs, and were handed pints of beer and mugs of tea, which they downed in blissful satisfaction. They managed to hitch a ride back to Sacriston, which was just as well as their legs could not carry them any further. Jacky sat with them, a huge grin across his face.

'Glad to see you're so pleased for us Jacky. You look like the cat that's got the cream,' said Micky.

'I got more than the cream,' Jacky smiled as he produced a wad of cash from his pocket. 'I put a bet on you two to win — good odds.'

'You lucky bugger, I wouldn't have put a bet on us. I can't believe we won. Wait 'til Mam hears about it — you with brass to bet —— she'll be upping your keep,' teased Jimmy.

'No, don't tell her, please Jimmy. I'm going to buy a pair of football boots with it. I can hardly get me feet in the pair I've got. And I'll buy you both a pint when we get back.'

The following week Jacky bought his boots; the first pair of boots he had had from new. All his other pairs had been hand-me-downs from his brothers, which had already been at least second hand.

Chapter 3

Jimmy and Micky's next game was a fortnight later, against the Robson brothers who had won quite a few matches against accomplished players. The Robsons had heard about the Mordue brother's victory at Pelton Fell, and were ready for a tight game. Although the Mordues battled hard and came close to winning, they could not repeat their outstanding performance of two weeks previously, and lost in just under three hours.

'I needed to get round the court a bit quicker. I think my legs hadn't recovered from the last game,' said Jimmy.

'There's always next time. Don't worry, we'll tan their hides before long,' said Micky. 'We just need a bit more experience playing the likes of them.'

'Jacky man, you didn't bet on us again did you?' Micky asked.

'No — no money left from buying my boots. Just as well, eh?' Jacky smiled. 'Are you going to come and watch me play football this afternoon? I've got a call up for Sacriston Rangers, the colliery team; my first game for them, and first for my new boots.'

'You only got the nod because they're short as they knew we'd be too jiggered to play, Jacky,' said Jimmy.

'So what? It still means I get a game. Are you coming to watch me?'

'We maybes will after we've been to The Robin Hood,' said Jimmy.

Jimmy and Micky did not go to watch Jacky. In a way, he was pleased. He could just play his own game, without being criticized and teased by his brothers. He was the youngest player in the team, and Jimmy was right: he had only got the call up as the team was short. Jimmy and Micky would be back playing for the colliery team the following week, as that was their last handball match of the summer, as now the football season got underway.

Jacky had butterflies in his stomach as he took to the field, playing with men rather than lads of his own age, but wearing his new boots empowered him. The manager knew that although Jacky was comparatively small, he was very fast, so put Jacky on the wing. The opposition had finished near the bottom of the league the previous season, and Sacriston were expected to win comfortably. As they kicked off, Jacky ran up and down the wing, being something of a spectator as the men passed the ball to each other, knowing who they could rely on to keep the ball. Jacky had barely had a touch of the ball when Sacriston went one up. Instead of feeling pleased that his team was in front, Jacky began to feel excluded and frustrated, but he did not let his head drop. He knew it was up to him to get involved and show his worth. Jacky could tell that his opposite number was a lot slower than him; Jacky would have no trouble beating him on speed. Jacky called for the ball time after time, but was ignored. He felt it was not worth him being there. That was until a miskick from an opponent went in his direction, and he raced and won the ball. As he had anticipated, he easily ran past their left-back and was able to put a perfectly placed cross into the box, which was slotted into the net by the Sacriston centre-forward. From then on, his own team included Jacky in a lot more of the play, passing the ball out to him, enabling him to sprint down the side-line and cross into the box, time and time again. Yes, the opposition were poor, but Jacky's speed and accuracy stood out even though he was a boy amongst men. Sacriston finished the game-winning six goals to nil.

'You're a canny player Jacky Mordue, just like your brothers,' said the manager. 'There's a place for you in this team, don't you worry. I've never seen anyone run as fast as you, lad.'

Jacky was beaming from ear to ear as he went home. He just wanted to be as good as Jimmy and Micky, and he was getting there; all the practice was paying off.

Micky and Jimmy did not take much notice of Jacky when he was telling them about the game. They thought he was exaggerating to try and impress them. It was only when they did their shift the following Monday, and men were commenting to them on how good a footballer Jacky was that they paid attention, and started to realise that their little brother had grown up without them noticing.

The brothers played alongside each other for Sacriston Rangers from then on, and were a formidable trio. They trained together, and Jacky's boots got plenty of use. But they still excluded Jacky from the handball sessions. Micky and Jimmy were a team. They did not have any matches lined up, but they continued to practise together. Jacky practised alone or with his friends Bill and Tom Coatman.

As autumn turned to winter, the days drew in, and the weather deteriorated — most of the men only seeing the light of day on their day off from the pit. Jacky was content with his job as a sorter at the surface of the pit, and was no longer jealous when watching his brothers descend into the earth's belly, to resurface much later, encrusted with coal dust and grime. As a sorter, Jacky had to stay focused and work quickly — removing stones and rocks from the coal on the conveyor belt as it passed continuously throughout the day. Jacky was earning a lot less than his brothers, but at least he saw daylight.

The Thursday started like any other, with Jacky busily sorting stones, and entertaining the other sorters with his quips when the manager's back was turned. Suddenly, there was a commotion at the top of the shaft, with the overman and some miners hurrying about. There had been an accident, and men were running to assist. Jacky's heart leapt in his chest; miners lived in fear of accidents underground. Jacky could not see what was happening, but was reassured by one of the older men, who reported that it was a minor accident. A coal wagon had come off the track, and careered towards a couple of workers. They had just about managed to get out of the way, but one of them was hit on the foot, and was being brought out. As the miner emerged, Jacky realised it was Jimmy who had been injured. Jimmy was obviously in a lot of pain and had to be carried — his blood-stained foot hanging limply under him. Jacky instinctively rushed over to Jimmy, who weakly nodded to Jacky, urging him to return to his job, and assuring him it was only a superficial injury. Jacky reluctantly returned to his position, knowing there would be severe recriminations if he left his work, but he could not help but dwell on the image of Jimmy's battered foot. Jimmy was taken home. The men rapped on the back door and entered without waiting for an answer. They laid Jimmy on the floor in the kitchen. Elizabeth bustled in but came to an abrupt stop when she saw Jimmy lying on the floor. The colour drained from her face, but she maintained her composure.

'What's happened? Dan, come in here!' she beckoned her elder son.

Dan hurried into the kitchen and gasped when he saw Jimmy's foot.

'Get the doctor, Dan. Hurry up now,' said Elizabeth.

'We'll be heading back to the colliery now,' said one of the men.

'Aye, thank you for bringing Jimmy home.'

'Keep us informed of his situation please, Ma'am. You're in good hands now, Jimmy. We'll see you back at the pit in no time, I'm sure,' said the other man as they left.

Elizabeth quickly poured boiling water from the kettle into the teapot and made Jimmy a mug of warm sweet tea to calm him, but her hands were shaking more than Jimmy's as she passed it to him.

'I could do with a drop of brandy,' said Jimmy.

'Sweet tea is what you need. Get that down you,' said his mother.

Since their father had died from liver disease, five years earlier, their mother had refused to have any alcohol in the house. Thomas Mordue had worked down the pit all his life, but had taken to drinking when the pains in his back and knees had become unbearable. It had started with an occasional swig of whisky to take the edge off the agonising affliction, but as his condition worsened, Mr. Mordue had found the only comfort to be had was when he was numbed by alcohol. The occasional swig became more frequent and copious, eventually leading to him losing his job as he spent his days either drunk or unconscious.

'It's alright Mam; I'm sure it's not as bad as it looks,' Jimmy tried to reassure his mother, but he could not remove his boot and was frightened of what he might see when he did. The pain was excruciating, but he could feel his toes, so that was a relief.

When the doctor arrived, he asked Dan to cut off Jimmy's boot. The boot was mangled and torn, so would need to be replaced in any event. The doctor carefully cut Jimmy's sock away and exposed the badly lacerated flesh beneath. There were cuts and broken bones, but the foot was still in one piece and had not been completely crushed. Jimmy would be off his feet for a while, but he would recover enough to be able to return to work in a few weeks, which was a huge relief. The doctor's bill and lack of earnings from Jimmy would hit the family, but they were fortunate that there were another three workers, Dan, Micky and Jacky, to bring in money.

As soon as Micky and Jacky finished their shift, they rushed home to see Jimmy and were relieved to find that there would hopefully be no lasting damage. Then, as always, their thoughts turned to sport. There was no way Jimmy would be able to play handball or football for months. Just when Jimmy and Micky had started to become a successful doubles pair this had happened.

'That's it. I can't play without you Jimmy. We're a team and I'll wait until you're fit and running faster than ever before I'll play handball again,' said Micky.

'Don't be daft, man. You'll have to get yourself another partner. This foot could take months to heal— that's if it heals properly. The doctor said I should be able to return to work in a few weeks, but there's a chance the foot will never be right,' said Jimmy, his voice faltering through pain and emotion.

Micky sat by Jimmy, sighing and shaking his head. He and Jimmy were a team; they did everything together. How could he even think about doing anything without Jimmy? For days Micky spent every spare moment he had sitting at Jimmy's side. Micky told Jimmy what had happened at the pit, and they played cards and talked together. He could not bring himself to play football or practise handball without Jimmy and just wanted to keep Jimmy company while he recovered. However Jimmy's foot was taking longer to heal than they had hoped. Jimmy knew that he should rest his foot completely but felt he should return to work even if his foot was not completely better.

'Look Micky, it's me that's had my foot damaged, not you. I want you to play football again, and handball,' Jimmy pleaded.

'But how can I play while you're sitting on the side-lines watching, unable to take part? I couldn't do that to you, Jimmy,' said Micky.

'I'd feel a lot worse if you didn't play, Micky. I want something to do, and I'd rather watch you play than waste your talent keeping me company. Promise me you'll play again.'

Micky felt that he would never again enjoy kicking or hitting a ball, but he knew that Jimmy meant what he said, and it would make Jimmy feel better, not worse, to watch him play.

'Alright Jimmy, I'll start playing again. But I'm doing it for you, not for me.'

'And you could do a lot worse than to get Jacky to partner you at handball. He thinks the world of you, Micky, and he'd be made up if you were to play with him.'

16

'Our Jacky? But he's just a lad. He's not got your strength or head on his shoulders.'

'No, but he's fast, and he's still learning. And I bet he's at the wall right now, practising. You couldn't find anyone more dedicated than our Jacky.'

With that Micky put on his jacket, and walked up the street to where Jacky would be playing. Sure enough, there was Jacky, tearing around the court. Micky kept hidden and watched as Jacky chased every ball. He really was fast around the court. He needed to learn to hit the ball with more power and precision, but he could certainly return almost any ball that was played.

When Jacky and his mates had finished playing and drifted away from the court, Micky approached Jacky.

'Jacky. Do you want a quick knock around before you go?' asked Micky.

'Micky! Why aye. Of course, I would,' said Jacky, trying not to sound overexcited about the prospect.

Micky and Jacky knocked the ball against the wall. At first, it was a little awkward. Micky had a feeling of guilt as he had only asked Jacky to play as Jimmy was no longer able, and Jacky felt somewhat nervous, knowing his brother was used to a better partner. Even though Jacky knew Micky was only playing with him due to Jimmy's accident, he still adored his brother Micky, and wanted to win his approval in everything he did. As the two frantically ran about the court, Micky trying to catch Jacky out, and Jacky trying to impress Micky, their somewhat stilted relationship began to soften. Whilst they were playing, their thoughts were concentrated on the game, but as they walked back home afterwards Micky started to consider Jacky as more than just an annoying little brother who was there to be ridiculed and mostly ignored. Jacky's enthusiasm and eagerness to improve his game came through as, being Jacky, he talked all the way home. Micky just listened and threw in the odd word, as was his way.

Jacky and Micky were not ready to take on opponents just yet, but they continued to practise together. They needed to practise as a team, so found lads to play against, but it was soon evident that few pairs in Sacriston could give them a match worth playing. Micky and Jacky jelled almost immediately. Micky had to adapt his game; he had been used to Jimmy dictating the game, while Micky had

17

followed his lead. It was Micky who now called the shots, and he was proving a very canny player, using his and Jacky's strengths to their best and adapting their game accordingly. They played in a different way — much faster and unpredictable than most players. Micky and Jacky approached their games with a freshness and altogether different approach to the standard players. They were lighter on their feet and did not just use brute strength to return the ball. They were precise and clinical. It soon became clear that Micky and Jacky were the perfect partnership. As the football season came to an end, handball matches were organised, and although the brothers faltered at first due to their lack of experience and sometimes Jacky's over-eagerness, they improved with each game, and had a self-belief that could not be broken. They could see each other's strengths and weaknesses and supported each other completely. Jimmy was pleased to see his brothers gel and succeed. And their neighbour's daughter, Betty, had been paying him a lot of attention since he was injured. She had completely taken Jimmy's mind off his troubles. Why had he not noticed her before? Although over time Jimmy's foot had recovered, and he was once again able to run, Jimmy did not want to spend every spare moment he had playing sports. He had found a different kind of happiness. He returned to playing football, as this was not as intense as handball and over time, slowly regained most of the strength and movement he had in his foot.

Chapter 4

On a wet Sunday morning in September, Lizzie returned home after attending church with Elizabeth. She looked dejected and upset. The lads were gathered around the kitchen table, discussing football, but stopped when they saw Lizzie.

'What's the matter, Lizzie?' asked Jacky.

Lizzie threw off her wet coat and boots and slumped onto the cracket by the fire.

'It's Mam. She's been talking to Mr. Crossley again. She even told me to go on ahead without her. She's paid him far too much attention since he lost his wife.'

'Don't talk about Mother like that, Lizzie. It's none of our business. You know she promised the late Mrs. Crossley, when she knew she wouldn't live much longer, that she would look out for him and their children. Mother is just carrying out her word,' said Dan.

'Well, he's been widowed over a year and got a lass of his own who can look after him and her brothers,' Lizzie protested.

They heard their mother's footsteps approaching the back door and dropped the subject, trying to act nonchalantly. Elizabeth entered the back kitchen.

'Ah, champion, you're all here. There's something I want to tell you. I'll just take off my wet things. Pour me a cup of tea, please Lizzie.'

The family waited expectantly. Their mother had never addressed them in this way before. After what seemed like an age Elizabeth sat at the table and took a sip of tea.

'I'm to marry Mr. Crossley,' she said.

There was stunned silence. They dare not question their mother but were eager to know what had brought about her decision. It was Jack who could hold his tongue no longer.

'What are you doing that for, Mam?'

'Don't you go asking questions like that, our Jacky. It's none of your business. I'm just telling you all now so you can prepare for the move. We'll be leaving this house and moving to The Crossleys'.'

Dan stood up, threw on his cap, coat and boots, and headed out of the house without saying a word. He had assumed his place as the man of the house but would soon be living under another man's roof. He felt cheated. Jimmy, Micky, Jacky and Lizzie all looked bemused and were lost for words.

'Well, you needn't all sit there catching flies,' said Elizabeth, getting up from the table and going over to the fire to give it a poke.

The youngsters shook themselves back to reality and got on with what they were doing.

A few weeks later Elizabeth Mordue and Joseph Crossley were married. It was a quiet service with only close family present.

Afterwards, The Mordues moved with the new Mrs. Crossley, just a few streets away to the Crossleys' house, which Joseph shared with his sons, twenty-four-year-old Gilbert and twelve-year-old Fred, and his twenty-year-old daughter, Sarah. The lads all packed into the larger of the two bedrooms. Lizzie had to share a bedroom with Sarah; they were lucky to each have their own bed. The new Mr. and Mrs. Crossley slept downstairs in the front kitchen.

Before the wedding, Sarah had looked after her father and brothers. She had recently begun courting a local lad, and it was inevitable that before long she would want to marry and leave the family home. With the arrival of her stepmother, Sarah was able to find employment at the colliery. Sarah and Lizzie also helped with the daily chores; with ten people living under one roof, there was always work to be done. Most houses in the village followed the same daily routine, with washing day being on a Monday and other jobs being carried out routinely on other weekdays. Sunday was a rest day when the family would put on their Sunday best, some of them attending church. This pattern remained the same from household to household, so the general way of life did not alter greatly when the households merged. All members of the families quickly adjusted to their new housemates and living conditions. Dan, who had been the most apprehensive, found Joseph to be amiable. Joseph had no interest in stamping his authority as the head of the house. He liked a quiet life and was happy to do his own thing, seemingly oblivious to what was going on around him. As long as his clothes were washed, he was given his meals and his favourite chair was always available for him, he was happy. He worked hard at the colliery, being very fit for a man of fifty-two, but he did not have the energy of the younger men. When he was not at work, he spent most of his time reading his bible, relaxing in his chair. Joseph appreciated Elizabeth and was happy for her to take over the finances and the running of the home. He, Sarah, and Gilbert handed over their pay packets to her, as did her sons, and Elizabeth gave them each their spending money for the week. In return Elizabeth ensured they all had decent meals, a warm home and adequate clothes.

Chapter 5

Jacky continued to spend time with his friend, Tom Coatman. Tom and his brother Bill practised doubles handball with Micky and Jacky. Sometimes they would play in Sacriston, where Micky and Jacky lived, and other times they played at Kimblesworth where Tom and Bill lived, just over a mile away. It was good to play on different courts, as they were all slightly different. The main village court was reserved for official matches. If an individual or pair felt they were good enough, they would put in a challenge for a match on the main court. This would become an organised event, with referees and bookmakers becoming involved. The practice courts were scattered all over the villages; some were specially built walls, whereas most were areas at the end of a row of terrace houses, the wall being part of someone's home. After a knock-about at Kimblesworth, Tom invited Micky and Jacky back to his family home.

'Howay, me Mam's made a meat pie. I am sure she wouldn't miss a bit,' said Tom.

The back door was seldom locked as family and friends frequently came and went at all times of the day. The fire in the range was always burning, with a kettle of water and pot of broth bubbling gently all through the day. The lads went through the back door and poured tea from the pot by the backfire.

'Sit yourselves down,' said Tom.

They sat on the bench next to the large kitchen table. Susannah and Martha were sitting on the other side, practising their spellings. The Coatman's house was always bursting with activity. Mrs. Coatman had nine children, ranging in age from twenty-five to just four years old. The eldest daughter, Anne, had married and flown the nest and was now living in Sacriston with children of her own, but she often called in on her family. Adam, Bill and Tom all worked at Kimblesworth Colliery. Adam was courting a local lass and was planning on getting married as soon as he had some money saved. Meg stayed at home helping her mother with the chores; since Meg had left school her mother had had three more children, and Meg's help was invaluable. Martha, Susannah and George-

Robert all attended the local Catholic school, and the youngest, Teenie, stayed at home.

'You'll get wrong if you eat anything our Meg has baked, Tom. She told us we couldn't have any of it,' said Susannah.

'Aye, well she's not here and it'll be too late when it's in my belly,' said Tom.

He was just about to cut them each a piece of pie when Meg entered the back kitchen.

'Get your hands off that pie, our Tom, that's our supper tonight,' Meg shouted, running over, taking the pie from Tom. 'Get yourselves some stotty or some broth if you're hungry.'

It was only then that Meg looked round and noticed Micky and Jacky sitting on the bench. She was slightly embarrassed at her outburst in front of company. She was used to seeing Jacky at their home but had never met Micky before. Meg blushed and straightened her pinny, turning away and covering the pie with a cloth. Micky smiled. In the short time he had been there he had seen two sides to Meg; the forceful, no-nonsense woman and the shy, vulnerable young woman. As she left the room their eyes met, and Meg quickly looked away. There was a chemistry between the pair that neither had experienced before, a strange magnetism. Meg hurried out of the room; Micky's eyes following her as she went. The other lads were oblivious to this spark that had momentarily lit the room for Micky and Meg. Micky was deep in thoughts as the conversation continued around him and had to be woken from his daydreams by the other lads.

'Micky! Do you want a bit stotty?' said Tom.

'Oh, no thank you.'

The lads carried on their conversation and finished their tea before Micky and Jacky headed home.

As Micky lay in bed that night he knew he had to see Meg again. He could not get the vision of her brilliant blue eyes out of his head. But Meg must be a few years older than Micky. Would she really want anything to do with him? This thing that had stirred in him, which he had never felt before, was not going to go away. Micky was quiet, but he was not shy. He was not frightened to approach Meg. He had to approach her; there was no other option. The spark was not going to die out and was burning him inside. But how would he be able to talk to Meg without the others knowing?

Micky and Jacky continued to practice handball and kick a football around when there were a group of lads to join them, but the weather was turning colder, and with it came the first snow of winter. Jacky took the opportunity to give his boots a good clean, but Micky was still struggling with thoughts of Meg. He needed to get out of the house and have some time on his own to think. Micky put on his boots and wrapped his coat around him and headed out of the back door. He would walk down the lane to Kimblesworth. Just heading in the direction of Meg would be a start. As his boots crunched on the fresh snow, his footprints leaving evidence of his route, he walked in silence looking over the blanketed hills around him and the trees with their branches weighed down with the fresh snow. Micky cleared a tree stump of snow and sat looking at the world around him. It was something Micky had never really done before. He was always coming or going. He noticed the blackbird happily pecking at wild berries. He noticed the clouds, thick and grey, ready to deliver another load of snow. He noticed the smoke rising from the chimneys in the distance; becoming part of the clouds themselves. He noticed the silence. There was a change happening in Micky. He was looking at things in a different way. Maybe this was what it was like to be a man? To start taking in the big picture and looking at the world from the outside rather than being in the picture at the centre of all things. Micky breathed in the icy fresh air and felt the peace around him. But there was the nagging, smouldering feeling inside him that made him restless. Meg Coatman's eyes shone from within.

A monthly dance took place at Kimblesworth village hall and Jacky and Tom were going to attend it for the first time. Bill Coatman regularly went to the dance. It was a good opportunity to see the local lasses dressed up in their best clothes, without their pinnies. And besides, there was not a lot else to do on a Saturday evening in the village. Micky had never been to the dance. Dancing just was not his thing and, up until that point, he had not been interested in the girls. But Micky did not take much persuading to go with the others; hoping that Meg might be there. He could not ask Bill outright, as Micky didn't want to let him know that he had a thing about his sister. It was strange dressing up to go to a dance. The lads only had one set of "good" clothes, so there was not any deliberation as to what to wear. Bill was his usual rough unsophisticated self, but Tom preened himself like a peacock. His clothes immaculately pressed and not a hair out of place on his head. Jacky did not give his appearance a second thought — he just dressed as he would on any Sunday, whilst Micky combed and re-combed his hair and scrubbed his hands and fingernails until they were raw. Micky and Jacky walked to Kimblesworth and knocked on the Coatman's door, before letting themselves in. Bill was stood in the back kitchen ready to leave. They waited for Tom to finish primping himself and join them. Micky looked around but could not see Meg. It was then Bill called out.

'Howay Meg; we're off.'

Meg came hurrying into the kitchen, pulling her coat around her. She was obviously surprised to see Micky and Jacky standing there and became flustered — fumbling with her coat buttons and lowering her eyes. Micky was stunned. He had hoped to see Meg at the dance, but it had not occurred to him that she would be coming with them. But then a lass would not go out unescorted. He was aware that he was staring at Meg and tried to avert his gaze, but it was difficult. Meg lit up the room and drew Micky's eyes like a moth to a flame. Micky had thought Meg was the most attractive woman he had ever seen the first time he saw her, but this was another side of Meg. Her dark brown hair shining against her porcelain skin enhanced her sparkling blue eyes. Meg's looks were not those of a classic beauty, but she was enchanting. Looking at her face transformed Micky to an unworldly place and stirred his emotions. Micky had looked at other girls, pretty girls, but they had not had this strange effect on him. It was both unsettling and exciting to Micky. He could not understand why he suddenly felt very warm and was shaking slightly. He had to compose himself and appear nonchalant. What had got into him? The group left the house and walked the short distance to the village hall. When they were there Bill bought a round of drinks. Meg soon spotted her friends on the other side of the room and left the lads and joined the group of young women. The eyes of many of the lasses in the room had turned to inspect the group of men with whom Meg had arrived. They were fine-looking lads. Micky's eyes followed Meg. Now what? He was not sure of the etiquette of local dances and did not want to look a fool. Jacky, on the other hand, was just enjoying being out amongst men and held his pint with pride. As the evening went on, it was evident that the only way for Micky to be able to talk to Meg would be to ask her to dance. The problem here was that Micky could not dance. Why hadn't he thought about that before he came? He had not known what to expect. And then again even if he could dance, there was the chance she would say no. She might even find it amusing that a lad three years her junior would ask her to dance. But then if he did not ask Meg to dance, he might miss his chance; Meg wasn't short of dance partners, and she might take a shine to someone else. The more he thought about the many scenarios that could play out over the evening, the more nervous and restless he became.

'What's up Micky? Are you going to ask some lucky lady to dance?' said Bill.

'I'd love to Bill, but I haven't got a clue how to dance. I'll end up tripping over the unlucky lady,' Micky replied.

'Our Meg's a good dancer. Why don't you ask her to show you how to dance, then you can amaze some unsuspecting beauty with your moves?'

'Your Meg wouldn't want to do that; she's here to enjoy herself, not take a dance lesson.'

'Look; she's sitting there doing nout. Come on, I'll get her to show you the ropes,' said Bill, grabbing Micky's arm and leading him in Meg's direction.

It would have looked rude of Micky if he turned and headed back to the bar at this point, so he went along with Bill — although he felt scared witless.

'Meg! Micky here doesn't know how to dance, so I told him you'd show him what to do,' said Bill, thrusting Micky in Meg's direction.

Meg smiled and stood up, taking Micky's hand, and leading him towards the dance floor. Micky was quite red in the face. He tried to apologize to Meg but tripped over his words.

'Just follow what I do, Micky. You won't be the worst dancer in here tonight,' Meg tried to reassure him.

Micky suddenly exhaled deeply, and then it occurred to him that he had forgotten to breathe. He took a few deep breaths and tried to calm himself down. He followed Meg's lead and soon his legs stopped feeling like blocks of wood and started to move freely. He did not have a clue what he was doing, but Meg put Micky at ease. Micky's face was a picture of concentration, while Meg smiled with amusement at Micky's terror and with happiness that she was dancing with him. After Micky got used to the few basic moves he needed to know, Meg thought he might now be able to manage to talk as well as dance.

'So you didn't really want to dance with me, Micky; you just want me to show you how to dance?' Meg teased.

The horror that Meg should think that immediately put Micky off his step, and he trod on Meg's foot.

'I'm so sorry Meg. Are you alright?' the colour was returning to Micky's face.

'Yes, no damage done,' Meg smiled.

They returned to silence as Micky continued to focus on which foot he should put where and try and look at least slightly competent. When he played sports he did not have to think about where his feet moved; they just danced around the court or the football pitch with skill and dexterity.

'It's just practise, Micky,' said Meg as the dance was coming to a close.

Just then Arthur Bateman, a fellow miner five years Micky's senior, approached Meg and, giving Micky a disdainful glance, took Meg's hand and lead her to the centre of the dance floor. As the music restarted the pair seamlessly glided across the room, and Meg was all smiles. She was in her element; in her best dress and shoes she felt liberated and free; losing herself in the music and the steps. Micky returned to Bill at the bar. The inane grin on his face had been replaced by a look of frustration. A beer would help.

'My shout.'

Chapter 6

Micky could not get thoughts of Meg Coatman out of his head. He recollected her sweet smell as they had danced together. Her smooth skin, bewitching eyes and full lips. The curves of her body and her small hands that he had held for such a brief time as they had floated around the dance floor. Well, maybe not floated; stumbled around the dance floor. Nonetheless, they were visions he could not erase and did not want to forget. But it was clear that Meg and Arthur Bateman were more than just dance partners. Meg had looked a picture of happiness when she danced with Arthur. Micky wanted to know if Meg had any feelings towards Arthur, or whether he himself stood a chance with Meg, but he could not confide in Jacky or Meg's brothers, as he did not want them to know how he felt about Meg. Micky had to see Meg. He could not just blatantly go around to see her, but he could call in on Bill Coatman.

Jacky and Micky were working different shifts, and Jacky was at work, so it was the ideal time for Micky to go to the Coatman's. He took his handball and set off towards Kimblesworth. Micky was going over in his mind what he might say to Meg should he have the opportunity to speak to her. He rehearsed his lines and carried out an imaginary conversation in his head — oblivious to what was going on around him.

'Hello Meg. It was a pleasure to dance with you the other evening.'

'Why thank you Micky. You are the best dancing partner I have ever had. '

'Well Meg; that's because we're made for each other — like…jelly and dripping.'

Micky chuckled to himself as he continued his fanciful conversation in his mind.

'Would you like to dance again, Meg? Here in your back kitchen?'

'Oh yes, Micky.'

'Micky. Micky.'

Meg's voice sounded so real; it felt like she was next to him.

'Micky!'

28

Meg patted Micky on the arm bringing him abruptly back into the here and now.

Micky turned with a jump almost knocking Meg off her feet.

'Meg! Oh, I'm so sorry. I was miles away,' Micky flustered. Had he been talking aloud? Had Meg heard everything he had said?

'You looked like you were somewhere nice; you had a big grin on your face,' smiled Meg.

Micky tried to act with calmness although his heart was pounding, and his palms were sweating. He desperately wanted to tell Meg how he felt or say something sagacious, but his mouth had other ideas.

'Aye Meg,' he said, with an inane look on his face.

Before Micky could compose himself and let Meg see that he was actually very articulate and polite, their conversation was interrupted.

'Hello, Meg. On your way to the shops? I'll walk with you,' said Arthur. It was more of an order than a request.

Meg looked surprised to see Arthur, but quickly said goodbye to Micky and walked away with Arthur in the direction of the shops. Initially, Micky was once again frustrated at Arthur's appearance, but then on reflection he began to wonder why Arthur had suddenly appeared from nowhere. And now not only had Micky shown Meg that he could not dance; he also appeared to be unable to speak.

Micky made sure he attended the next dance held in the village hall. He went along with the lads as before, and Meg accompanied them. Micky was too embarrassed to talk to Meg with the brothers around. He felt almost dizzy in her company and found the simplest tasks difficult — even walking. He did not want to put a foot out of place. Never before had he been so self-aware.

The smoky hall was like an oasis in the village. Young people left the hardship of their daily lives behind them and immersed themselves in their few hours of release. Protocol was followed, but eyes flashed across the room; expressive faces revealing hopeful intentions.

Meg sat with her friends; however, Arthur was showing her a lot of attention. He was dancing with her more than anyone else, but Micky was determined to have at least one dance with Meg. When Arthur was at the bar ordering drinks, Micky seized his opportunity.

Meg had been surreptitiously watching Micky and made it easy for him to approach her.

'Would you like to dance, Meg?'

Meg and Micky kept their dance simple; Micky did not want to step on Meg's toes again. Micky was not good at making small talk, but the lack of conversation did not feel awkward. Their smiling eyes said everything to each other. As the tune too quickly came to an end the pair were abruptly interrupted by Arthur. He glared at Micky and took Meg's hands. Micky was happy to have had a dance with Meg. As much as he would like to believe it, he did not think that Meg would go for a lad like him.

The following day some of the lads were having a kick about on the field. Micky and Jacky and the Coatman brothers were joined by anyone who wanted to play. Arthur Bateman and a few of his mates joined in. It was just the usual game, nothing serious, just knocking about. Arthur gave Micky a few malicious looks which Micky ignored. Micky was not going to be intimidated by Arthur, and as far as Micky could tell he had not done anything to suggest he was a threat to Meg's affections, unless she fell for gormless idiots. Micky gathered the ball and made a run up the left of the field and was just looking to see who might get on the end of the cross he was about to deliver when he felt his leg being taken out from beneath him. Micky tumbled to the ground. An acute pain ran up his shin and his ankle throbbed. Arthur had lunged into him making no attempt to play the ball. There were angry shouts from the other lads who quickly ran to surround Arthur. Arthur's mates went to his defence and a scuffle broke out. Jacky was lashing out at Arthur; his fiery temper ignited. After a spate of thumps and abuse the altercation was soon over, but Micky still lay injured on the grass. Only he knew the reason Arthur had made such a wild tackle on him, but he wasn't going to let the others know. Luckily, Micky was able to get to his feet. The ankle hadn't been broken; it was just badly bruised. Micky hobbled home. Instead of feeling angry with Arthur he felt an inner glow; Arthur had seen him as a real threat to Meg's affection. If Arthur felt that way then surely Meg must see Micky in a positive light?

Micky was keener on seeing Meg than ever. Arthur had given him a reason to believe that he was a serious contender for Meg's affection. As soon as his ankle was better he went to the Coatman's home. Once again he would take his handball and see if Bill wanted a knock around with him, but hopefully see Meg in the process. Micky rapped on the open back door and strode into the kitchen where Meg was busy baking — hands covered in flour. She quickly wiped them on her apron and beckoned Micky to sit down.

'Would you like a cup of tea, Micky?' she asked.

'Aye, that would be champion,' replied Micky, taking a seat on the wooden kitchen bench.

'Everyone's out,' said Meg.

'Oh, I'll not keep you then,' said Micky, getting to his feet.

'No, sit down. I was hoping to see you,' Meg fiddled nervously with her apron strings and looked down awkwardly. 'I wanted to say sorry to you for what Arthur did the other day.'

Micky smiled. 'It's not for you to apologise for him Meg —— unless you asked him to do it?' It was an idea that had never crossed Micky's mind until then.

'As if I'd do that!' said Meg defiantly.

'No, I didn't think you would have. In truth I was quite flattered — that Arthur might think you'd actually be interested in me,' said Micky.

'Of course I'd be interested in you,' said Meg, the words leaving her lips before she had time to realise what she was saying. With that her cheeks went crimson, and she busied herself pouring Micky's tea.

As Meg passed Micky the mug of tea their hands brushed each other's. It was as if a spark had ignited at their touch, and they fleetingly looked into each other's eyes. Micky felt the passion rise within him and wanted to gather Meg in his arms, but he controlled himself and sat with his mug cupped in his trembling hands.

'Meg.'

'Yes, Micky.'

'I was wondering...'

Just then the back door opened again, and Meg's younger brother and sisters poured into the house, amidst laughter and chatter.

'What are you baking, Meg?' asked Susannah.

And that was that. The moment had passed. Micky quickly drank his tea and left.

Chapter 7

As Micky and Jacky's relationship improved on and off the
handball court it also improved on the football pitch. They both
played for the colliery team and were like arrows darting up the
wings; one on each flank. The defence would pass the ball to either
lad who would then make dashing runs with the ball at their feet
and then cross the ball to whoever was the centre-forward at the
time. With lightness on their feet, they would dance around
opposing defenders with ease. They were always the first players on
the team sheet. Micky and Jacky were becoming outstanding
sportsmen. If they were not at work at the pit they would be
practising with a ball. The brothers wanted to play for better teams
and tried out at Spennymoor United. Jacky was just a little too
young, but Micky was taken on. It was disappointing that they
would be playing for different teams, but Micky reassured Jacky
that it would not be long before Spennymoor signed him up as well.
Micky fitted in well at Spennymoor. He was the fastest player on
the team and ran up both wings — racing past the opposition to put
in crosses to the centre-forward. The team got behind him, and all
upped their games. Jacky and Micky still played handball together
and were getting harder to beat. More competitive matches were
arranged, and the brothers had to travel further afield to play better
opponents. Runners surreptitiously took bets for illegal bookmakers
at all the contests as men enjoyed betting on everything and
anything — adding a buzz of excitement to the games.

As the weeks passed Micky thought about Meg and knew he
had to see her again, but his time was taken up with matches and
training. He had missed an ideal opportunity to ask Meg if he could
court her, and now he just had to hope he would get another chance.
He had called at the Coatman home a couple of times, but Meg had
been out or been busy with her household duties.

One Sunday morning in January the brothers had planned to
play football, but they woke to a thick blanket of snow. The snow
continued to fall, and the clouds looked heavy. The lads headed to
The Robin Hood at midday. Pints were already lined up on the bar

as the landlord expected a busy trade that wintry day. They sat at a table with a couple of other friends and drank, chatted and played dominoes. Tom Coatman came up in conversation, and it set Micky on thinking about Meg — his mind wandering.

'Howay Micky, it's your turn,' said Jimmy.

Micky was brought back to the present but continued to think about Meg. Having drunk his pint he felt relaxed and confident. He made up his mind to pay her a visit. He got up and put on his coat.

'Where are you off to?' asked Jimmy.

'Just fancy some fresh air. I'll see you back home for dinner,' said Micky.

As he left the other lads looked at one another; perplexed. Micky trudged through the snow towards Kimblesworth. There was less snow on the path through the woods as the trees formed a wintry canopy. He had a spring in his step and was oblivious to the cold. On arriving at the Coatman's house, Micky rapped on the back door hoping it would be Meg who opened it. There was a shuffling from within and sure enough; it was Meg standing in the doorway, a picture of beauty, however, she did not return his smile.

'Micky! Hello,'

Before Micky could reply Meg continued...

'Sorry, Micky, but you can't come in right now. The bairns have gone down with the measles. It's bad; Susannah, George Robert and Teenie — they've all got it. I can't stand here with the door open, sorry.'

And with that Meg shut the door, leaving Micky standing in the back yard, covered in snow. Micky turned and left. He was disappointed; he had rehearsed what he would say over and over in his head and had not even uttered one word, but he was more concerned for the family. Measles came and went every few years taking with it innocent lives.

The measles epidemic swept through the villages. Households kept their curtains closed, darkening the rooms to protect the eyes of the sick. Some curtains remained closed as death had knocked at their doors. Nobody in Micky's household developed the illness as they had all had measles before and developed an immunity. Micky saw Bill and Tom the following week. Snow still lay heavy on the ground, but the lads had gone up the hills to watch the whippet races. Rabbits were released and dogs were held by the tail and scruff of the neck before being launched forwards. As soon as the whippets' feet touched the ground they were off in pursuit of the panic-stricken rodents, darting off towards the scrub, trying to find a place to hide from the blood-thirsty dogs. A few rabbits escaped the jaws of the hungry beasts, taking refuge in the undergrowth, only to die from fright and exhaustion. These would be searched for the following day; rabbit stew a reward for the appropriators. Proud dog owners and lucky gamblers collected their winnings — others counted their losses.

'Hello, Bill. How are the bairns?' said Micky.

'Not good. I needed to get out of the house. Teenie and George Robert are on the mend, but Susannah is still bad with it. Mam had the doctor out, but she doesn't seem to be getting any better,' said Bill.

'Sorry to hear that Bill,' said Micky. It did not sound good.

A few days later Micky heard that Susannah had lost her fight against the disease. Her death had been caused by encephalitis — inflammation of the brain, caused by measles. She was nine years old. Micky knew how upset Meg would be and wanted to be there to comfort her, but this was a time for privacy and mourning. Susannah had always made her presence felt as she was an outgoing and lively lass; she would be sorely missed by the heartbroken family. Even though money was tight, Susannah would have a worthy funeral and a beautiful, large white headstone. The curtains would remain closed in the Coatman household for some time.

Chapter 8

Micky did not get many opportunities to see Meg during the spring as most of his free time was taken up with football. He had managed to see her a few times when he called at the Coatman's home but hadn't had an opportunity to talk to her alone. Spring turned to summer. In mid-July it was the day of the Durham big meeting. It was a warm and sunny day, without a cloud in the sky. The Mordue family packed a picnic and joined other families outside the Sacriston working men's club. Chosen workers, two union members, held aloft the colliery banner, and they led the crowd, on foot, towards Durham City. The colliery band was amongst the procession, their music filling the air, as everyone marched with pride and excitement. Micky, Jacky and all the family marched behind the flag — walking the four or so miles to the city. Elizabeth had packed them a picnic but opted to stay at home, not feeling up to the walk. The sun was shining, and everyone was in good spirits. Families from collieries all over Durham ascended on the city in celebration of their unity. The congregated crowd slowly marched through the streets of Durham. Many proud miners carried their colliery banners aloft, surrounded by fellow workers, each with their colliery bands following their banners. Families and friends joined in the parade and lined the streets, cheering and waving. The marchers made their way to the racecourse, where each colliery placed their banner in a selected spot. Picnic rugs and baskets were placed near the flags as families made their bases for the day ahead. Guest speakers addressed the crowd. This year John Burns MP., J. H. Wills, L. A. Atherley Jones, MP. and W. H. Thompson, Editor of Reynolds, took to the podium; the men delivered stirring speeches, which pleased the attentive crowd. Following this a number of people attended a service in the cathedral, where all those killed in mines through the years were remembered. Now the formalities were over, Micky looked around to see if he could spot the Kimblesworth banner where he knew Meg would be with the rest of the Coatmans. The banner was not too far from their own, and he soon spotted Meg, dishing out pie to her younger siblings. Bill saw Micky and called him over, and they all sat chatting and talking about the speeches, but then drifted off to enjoy the events going on around them. Meg helped her mother clear away the picnic.

'Mum, can I go and play now?' said Teenie — Meg's youngest sister.

'You canna go on your own, and I've got to stay and mind the things,' said Mrs. Coatman.

'I can take her, Mam,' said Meg. 'Howay, Teenie.'

Meg took Teenie by the hand.

'Do you mind if I join you?' Micky asked. 'I'll see if I can find you some cinder toffee.'

Micky, Meg and Teenie headed to the part of the field where there was a travelling fair. The sights and sounds were amazing. This was the highlight of the year for the local miners and their families, who were accustomed to the grey villages with dull noises coming from the collieries. Today was full of colour and life. They found a stall selling sweet treats, and Micky bought a bag of cinder toffee. He held the bag open for Meg and Teenie to take a piece.

'Eeh! That's lovely. Sticks to your teeth, mind,' laughed Meg.

Vendors shouted to the crowd, enticing them to spend their hard-earned cash. A coconut shy caught Teenie's eye.

'Can I have a go at that?' asked Teenie.

'You're too small to do that, Teenie,' said Meg.

'Howay. You can help me, Teenie,' said Micky, handing over his money and receiving three wooden balls in return. Teenie threw a ball as hard as she could, but it did not even reach the shy. Micky took the two other balls and had no problem dislodging a coconut from its stand and handed his prize over to Teenie.

'What is it?' she asked, gingerly taking the coconut.

'It's a type of nut. Shake it — you can hear the milk inside it,' said Micky. 'When we get back, I'll make some holes in it and get the milk out, then you can smash it open to get the coconut out.'

Teenie was delighted with her trophy.

'Come on. Let's see what else I can win you,' said Micky.

Meg and Micky each took one of Teenie's hands and lead her around the fair. Teenie went on rides, and Meg and Micky laughed and joked, relaxed in each other's company. It all came so naturally. Meg was as excited by the events as her little sister; Punch and Judy shows, dancers and musicians all entertained the enthusiastic crowds. The steam-driven merry-go-round was the favourite attraction, with all three of them enjoying the ride — laughing freely as the carousel horses carried them round and round. After a while, Teenie began to feel tired and thirsty.

'Best get you back to Mam,' said Meg, and they made their way back to Mrs. Coatman.

Teenie showed her mother her coconut, gibbering excitedly as she recalled what she had been up to. Micky looked at Meg and took her hand, leading her back to the hubbub of the fair. They had another ride on the carousel, watched side-shows and immersed themselves in the jollity of the big meeting. Time flew by. Meg noticed the sun was starting to sink in the sky.

'Micky, I'll have to get back home — it's getting late,' said Meg reluctantly. She didn't want the day to end.

'Aye, me too. Do you mind if I walk you back?' said Micky.

Micky and Meg walked hand in hand away from the crowds that still remained at the fair and headed through the fields to Kimblesworth. The chatter and laughter flowed naturally between them, and Micky realised that he would soon have to part from Meg as she returned home. He had to make sure they were going to see each other again. He stopped and turned to Meg, looking into her clear blue eyes.

'Will you see me again, Meg?'

Meg smiled and tightened her hold on his hand. 'Aye, I'd like that, Micky.'

Micky felt a surge pass through his body. He just wanted to hold Meg and never let her go. Micky pulled Meg closer to him and pressed his lips against hers. Meg didn't resist and their mouths melted into each other, passion flowing through their veins. This had been more than just a kiss. They looked into one another's eyes and both knew that their lives were now somehow permanently connected. Something had passed between them that neither of them understood. They had both kissed other people before, but not like this. It felt like a flame being ignited inside them — an eternal flame.

'I want to see you tomorrow, Meg. I'm on the early shift so I'll be around in the evening. Should I ask your Da if I can court you?'

'What if he says no? Then what? I don't think he would say no, but what if?'

'Well, I'll have to take that chance. It's only right that I ask your Da. Will he be home tomorrow teatime?'

'Aye. He's on earlies as well.'

'Champion. I'll see you tomorrow teatime,' Micky smiled. He had never asked permission to court a lass before, but he wanted to do things right with Meg. He knew this was special.

Micky and Meg went their separate ways as they neared Meg's home. They both had a skip in their step and smiles on their faces, excited by the day's events.

Chapter 9

Micky polished his shoes and brushed his cap before setting off to Meg's house. He had not wanted to tell Jacky about Meg in case Meg's father refused them permission to see each other, but Jacky had seen them together at the big meeting and pushed Micky to tell him. It also meant that Micky did not have to lie to Jacky about where he was going, although he made sure Jacky didn't tell anyone else; not yet, at least. As Micky approached the village he felt his stomach become knotted, and he felt slightly nauseous. How was he going to get the words out to ask Mr. Coatman's permission to court Meg? And what if he said no? Micky mentally prepared his speech and actions. He hoped that Bill and Tom would not be home. It was a nice evening, so they would probably be playing football in the field. The thought of Meg's beautiful face and the kiss they shared kept Micky focused. He strode up to the Coatman's house and knocked determinedly on the back door. Meg opened the door with a welcoming smile, which immediately soothed Micky's nerves.

'Hello, Meg. Is your father home?' Micky sounded serious. He wasn't sure who might be listening and wanted to appear courteous.

'Yes, come in, Micky. He's in the front kitchen.'

Mrs. Coatman was in the back kitchen, clearing dishes and cleaning up. Like most colliery houses, the downstairs consisted of two rooms known as the front and back kitchens, and upstairs there were three bedrooms; most colliery houses having just two..

'Hello, Mrs. Coatman,' said Micky.

'Hello, Micky. The lads are already out. They'll no doubt be up the field having a knock about.'

'I've come to see Mr. Coatman — if that's possible thank you, Mrs. Coatman,' said Micky sounding unusually formal.

Mrs. Coatman was intrigued. 'Yes, lad. Go through.'

Micky shot a glance at Meg and then, cap in hand, entered the room. Mr. Coatman was sat in his usual chair, pipe in hand. Meg's younger brothers and sisters were playing five stones on the floor by his side.

'Micky! Micky!' Teenie squealed excitedly. 'We got the milk out of the coconut and then smashed it to pieces in the back yard. It went everywhere, but we picked up the pieces and took the shell off and ate all the white bits. I've never eaten anything like it before; it was lovely,' Teenie chattered on.

'That's champion, Teenie. Did you save me a piece?'

'Yes, but our Tom ate it when I wasn't looking.'

'Never mind. I'll have to win another one, next year. Now, do you mind if I have a quick word with your Da?'

'Go and play in the yard a while pets,' said Mr. Coatman. He spoke gently to his children, but obediently they immediately took their five stones and went out of the room.

'What can I do for you, Micky?'

Micky shuffled from one foot to the other and fiddled with his cap. He was so nervous that it was an effort for him to look Mr. Coatman in the eye.

'I would like to court you Mr. Coatman, if Meg doesn't mind,' Micky blurted out. He didn't even realise he had said everything back to front.

Mr. Coatman smiled at Micky. 'I think Meg would be quite upset if you courted me, Micky, but I would be happy for you to court Meg if that's what she wants.'

Micky was relieved. The tension left him, and a huge grin spread across his face.

Micky and Meg were pleased they had received Mr. Coatman's permission to walk out together, but there were social graces that had to be met. A chaperone was expected when they were together and kissing in front of a chaperone, or anyone else, would not be acceptable. Being together and not being able to touch one another was painfully frustrating. Just a cuddle or a brush of lips would be something, but that was not possible. Tom and Bill found it amusing that Micky was courting their big sister. They liked Micky and were pleased, but they were protective towards Meg and made it clear to Micky that he was not to mess her about. Jacky was happy for Micky, but it meant he saw less of his brother. Micky continued to play handball and football with Jacky, but any other free time he had was spent with Meg. However, it was Micky's mother, Elizabeth, who put a spanner in the works.

'You are not courting a catholic girl, Michael,' Elizabeth said emphatically.

'But you don't mind me working down a pit with Catholics or playing football with them or drinking with them, so why not?' It was unusual for Micky to answer his mother back, but he felt she was being unfair and really could not see why there was a problem.

'You know it's wrong, Michael. Don't go near that girl again.'

'But mother…'

'I don't want to hear another word.' Elizabeth glared at Micky.

Micky gritted his teeth and clenched his fists to contain the anger and frustration he felt inside. He made a rapid exit, as he knew anything he might say would not help his cause. Micky knew it was pointless arguing with his mother. He knew she would not change her mind. Even though Catholics and Protestants worked together and drank together the older people, especially, felt it was not right that they should become involved with each other romantically. He loved his mother dearly, but his feelings for Meg were different. It was not a case of whether or not he was allowed to see Meg; he wanted his mother's approval, but he was going to continue to see Meg, whatever his mother said. He would just have to be more discreet. Micky knew he could trust Jacky to cover for him, although he would not want his brother to lie to their mother on his behalf.

Chapter 10

The following morning, just as the men were heading off to the colliery, ten-year-old May Collingwood ran to the door. She was red in the face and had tears in her eyes.

'Gran! Gran! It's me Mam; she's bad,' May managed to say, between breaths and sobs.

'Sit down and catch your breath,' said Elizabeth. 'Lizzie, get May some tea; she's parched. Now May, what's the matter with your Mam?' Elizabeth picked up her boots and sat down to put them on as she waited for May's reply.

'I can't. We've got to get back to Mam as quick as we can. Anna said so. She's looking after Mam on her own and doesn't know what to do.'

Just then Dan returned from his night shift.

'I'll get a cart and take you. I'll be as quick as I can,' he said, running out of the back door in search of an available ride. Ten minutes later, Elizabeth, May and Dan were heading down the track to Pelton Fell. When they arrived at Annie's home, they found Annie, unconscious in the bed she shared with her daughters. Elizabeth's heart skipped a beat as she thought her daughter was dead, but she kept a calm exterior and took a deep breath. She felt her daughter's forehead and felt for her breath. Annie's chest faintly rose and fell as she barely breathed.

'Fetch the doctor, Dan.'

Dan ran to the doctor's house and rapped on the door. The doctor's maid answered the door. It was still early, and the doctor had been called out in the middle of the night to attend to another patient, but without delay he was up and dressed and followed Dan to Annie's home. Dan and the girls waited outside as the doctor and Elizabeth attended Annie. Annie lay peacefully in her bed. There was nothing of her; she was skin and bones. Elizabeth was horrified to see how emaciated her daughter had become. On the few occasions they had seen each other, Annie had been mindful to wear plenty of clothes to disguise her gaunt body. Annie had been struggling to feed herself and her three daughters but had been too proud to ask for help. She had made sure that her daughters had the majority of the little food they had. Now Annie had developed an infection and had no strength left in her to fight it. Her body could no longer survive. There was nothing the doctor could do; it was too late. Annie's life slipped away.

Elizabeth stayed strong as she broke the news to her three granddaughters that their mother had passed away. It was only when she was alone that she let the tears flow. Dan returned to Sacriston with the horse and cart, while his mother stayed at Pelton Fell with the girls. Neighbours helped her prepare Annie's body, which was placed in a simple coffin. Elizabeth watched over the body for two days, until the funeral took place. Annie was placed in the grave already occupied by her late husband. Following the funeral, the girls packed the few belongings they had and moved to Sacriston with their grandmother and the rest of the household. Even though the home was already crowded, room would be found for three more children. Lizzie and Sarah had to share one bed while Anna, May and Catherine slept in the other bed. There were now thirteen people living in the two-bedroomed house: thirteen mouths to feed. It was challenging, but they would manage somehow.

Lizzie took the girls under her wing; she was happy to have younger girls to mother — especially the youngest, six-year-old Catherine. Sarah was not so enamoured; going from being the lady of the house to having a stepmother running the home, and now four younger girls sharing her bedroom. Sarah's romance was blossoming, and she was working long hours. She hoped she would soon be able to leave this overcrowded house and start a married life with her beau.

The lads all continued as before; having three girls in the house did not make much difference to them. They were the workers, and their mealtimes and bath times carried on as normal; the girls had to fit around them. Joseph welcomed the girls into the home; he agreed to any decision made by Elizabeth, and her family was his family. He continued to spend most of his free time sitting in his favourite chair, smoking his pipe and reading his bible, apparently oblivious to the increased commotion and activities going on around him.

Chapter 11

Jimmy and Betty's relationship blossomed. Jimmy had been able to return to work and was now a hewer, extracting coal from the coalface. His wages had increased slightly, although they were never assured, depending on the amount of coal he could extract. But this was the way things worked at the pit, and Jimmy was in the same situation as every other hewer. Betty agreed to Jimmy's marriage proposal, and her family suggested that once they were married they could move in with Betty's parents, until a colliery house came up.

The wedding was a small, but happy event. Micky was proud to be Jimmy's best man. There was love in the air, and Micky's thoughts turned to Meg. Micky wished Meg was there, but as far as his family knew they were not seeing each other. Their crime was to be in love. Micky wondered; if he had shown hate or discrimination to a Catholic girl would that have been acceptable? Whereas being in love with a Catholic girl and treating her without prejudice was considered wrong. The whole situation did not make sense to Micky. Did God condone segregation and bias? Or were things invented by man for his own means? In the past, and maybe still, it was convenient for Governments to drive wedges between religions and nationalities. It was easier to get men to do their dirty work when their hearts were full of hatred and ignorance. Micky missed Meg's presence and knew she would have loved the occasion. He wanted her to be there with him, showing her off to the rest of the family. Micky and Meg's relationship had to be kept a secret from his mother. It all felt decidedly wrong and unfair.

Elizabeth Mordue watched with pride as her son Jimmy married a decent protestant girl from their neighbourhood. It did mean that there would be one less pay packet coming into the home, but they would get by now Jacky was earning regular wages, and Joseph and his son Gilbert were both earning as hewers. She had heard rumours that Micky was still visiting the catholic girl in Kimblesworth, but tongues liked to wag and surely Micky wouldn't disobey his own mother? He was the most placid of her sons. Betty

44

had a younger sister who would be a good match for Micky. He would see sense.

Chapter 12

Micky and Jacky had another big handball match lined up and spent much of their free time practising. The evenings were still light, and they could spend hours on the court before daylight faded. Jacky became more mature as a player and a person. He did not try and make every shot the winning shot, but bade his time ensuring that when he did go for a point he won it. He was winning more shots and also tiring his opponents without them counteracting. Micky and Jacky were as one — knowing how and when they would play different shots and pre-empting one another's game. The only way they could practise together as a pair was to play against three lads or play with one hand tied behind their back, and still they would often win. They took on more formidable opponents and improved their standing in the handball rankings. There were not any football matches scheduled for the summer, but the lads regularly had a kick about, however it was at these times that Micky would slip away and meet up with Meg. At first their meetings continued to be chaperoned, but on one occasion Meg and Micky had managed to find a time when neither of them would be missed by their families and met on the path from Sacriston to Kimblesworth.

'Meg! At last. No beady eyes watching our every move,' said Micky taking hold of Meg's hands.

Micky tried to kiss Meg, but she backed away.

'Careful Micky. What if someone sees?'

'I don't care. I'm not worried if my mother finds out. I just want to be with you Meg.'

'What about me? Tongues will wag, and I'll show me Mam and Dad up.'

'Oh. Yes. Sorry, Meg. If you don't want me to kiss you then I won't.'

'I didn't say I didn't want you to kiss me — I just said I didn't want anybody to see you kissing me,' said Meg mischievously.

Micky smiled.

'Well, in that case…' Micky led Meg to a path she hadn't taken before. They left the path and waded through long grass. They walked for a few minutes before coming to an old stone wall. It was the remains of a long-forgotten dwelling.

'Me and Jimmy used to come here when we were lads. Look, that's where we scratched our names on the wall. I've never seen anyone else here,' said Micky.

'Eeh! Well I never! I've not been here before. It's so peaceful. I wonder who used to live here? Not that there's much left of it now,' said Meg.

'Whoever it was has been gone a long time; it's just us here now,' said Micky. 'So can I have that kiss?'

Micky and Meg carried on with their formal meetings when they had to act with restraint and formality, but they also continued to meet at their secret location as often as they could without arousing suspicion.

'Micky, I look forward to seeing you without anyone else around, but we can't just carry on like this. Your Mam doesn't even know we are courting; she'd go mad if she knew we were meeting up here. I don't like having to be kept hidden,' said Meg.

'Then I'll marry you Meg; if that is what you want. I just want to be with you,' said Micky.

'Is that a proposal, Micky? Are you asking me to marry you?'

'Aye. Yes. I mean it. Will you?'

Meg was flushed with emotion. She adored Micky and wanted nothing more than to be his wife.

'You know I would marry you tomorrow, Micky, but if your mother won't even let you court me, she's never going to let you marry me.'

'I'll talk to her again. She'll come round.'

Micky took Meg in his arms and held her close to his chest.

'I will marry you, Meg.'

Chapter 13

Micky wanted to find a time when his mother was alone, but that seemed impossible with a dozen people living in the house. Maybe it would be better to broach the subject when Dan or Jacky were around; surely they would back him up?

'Mother. There's something I'd like to ask you,' said Micky.

'What is it lad?' Elizabeth continued sewing a pair of trousers she was mending, without looking at Micky.

Micky looked at Dan who was reading a book of poetry; seemingly oblivious to their conversation.

'I'd like to marry Meg Coatman,' said Micky. He had decided it would be better just to come straight out with it.

Elizabeth pricked her finger on her sewing needle as she jumped to her feet. This added to her anger.

'You had better not have been near that girl. I told you you weren't to see her. We're not like those Catholics,' said his mother, her voice raised and nostrils flaring.

'They are no different to us. I love Meg and she loves me,' said Micky trying his best to stay calm.

'They spend all their money on drinking and gambling. I'll never let you marry a Catholic lass so you can just forget about it,' said Elizabeth falling back in her seat and sucking the blood from her finger. She took her handkerchief and mopped her brow, shaking her head.

'But mother…' Micky tried to continue his hopeless plea.

'Enough, Micky,' shouted Dan. 'You heard mother. Now I won't have another word on the subject. You're still only eighteen and you do as you are told.'

Micky held his tongue, turned and stormed out of the house. It was not as if he was committing a crime. His "crime" was to fall in love with a beautiful woman. He walked through the streets with purpose, but without direction. Before long his anger turned to despair, and he could feel the tears welling in his eyes. How could he expect Meg to wait over two years for him to reach twenty-one and be able to marry without his mother's permission? And how could he bear not being able to make love to her until they were married? Micky respected Meg, and he would do anything for her. If it meant waiting until he was twenty-one then he would wait, but would she wait for him? There were plenty of men in the villages who would jump at the chance of courting Meg — including Arthur Bateman. Micky could not imagine life without Meg.

Micky and Meg had arranged to meet the following day at the derelict building. Micky was always there before Meg, as it was easier for him to slip away. As he waited he felt his stomach churn, and he felt physically sick. The words that he would have to expel from his mouth were nauseating.

Meg appeared in the distance. As he watched her approach he was filled with love and despair. How could he expect this beacon of loveliness to hang around for a lad like him? Meg smiled and waved and hastened towards Micky, anticipating his warm embrace. She felt happiest of all when she was in Micky's arms. Micky enveloped Meg in his powerful embrace and kissed her hard; it felt as if she was breathing life into his soul and without Meg's kiss he would slowly die. As they withdrew from one another Micky looked lugubriously into Meg's eye.

'What's wrong, Micky?' Meg held Micky's hand in hers.

Micky found it hard to speak or even look at Meg. Meg was a woman; she was already twenty-one, and there he was three days before his nineteenth birthday and having to do as his mother commanded. Micky held Meg's hands but kept his head bowed and looked down.

'It's me mother. She won't allow me to marry you, Meg.' said Micky.

Meg felt her chest tighten and fought back the tell-tale tears. The flicker of hope she held had been extinguished.

'I see. We can't be married. So what now, Micky?'

'I still want to marry you Meg; I don't want anyone else. When I get to twenty-one me mother can't stop me, but that's two year off. I can't expect you to wait two years for me to wed you,' said Micky still unable to look Meg in the eye.

Meg followed Micky's gaze and silently pondered his words. They both stood in silence for some moments. Micky tried to imagine what Meg was thinking and realised that whatever happened he wanted Meg and would not just let her go. Why would she want a man who couldn't even look her in the eye? With a sudden burst of determination Micky cupped Meg's face in his hands and met her gaze. She was startled by his sudden change in mood.

'Meg I want you. If you can't wait two years then I'll have to live with that, but I love you and don't ever want anyone else to be my bride,' said Micky.

'Micky I'd wait forever for you. You know I would.'

They kissed passionately, sealing their relationship.

'I'll marry you Meg, as soon as I'm twenty-one, or before that if me mother agrees to it,' said Micky.

'Why don't we get married here and now,' said Meg. 'Our secret. Then when you're old enough we can do it by the law.'

'But I haven't got a ring to give you Meg.'

'We don't need rings. Let's just make a promise to each other.'

'Yes, Meg. I promise. I promise to be your man forever,' swore Micky.

'And I promise to be yours from this day on,' said Meg.

They kissed once more; the passion and excitement boiling over. Micky wanted to touch every part of Meg; to feel the woman who had sworn herself to him. And Meg wanted Micky to take possession of her. She was his, and she wanted him to have her. They belonged to each other now, and, as their passions raged, they soon became one.

Chapter 14

Micky and Jacky were having a kick around on the field.

'You seem chipper today, Micky. Funny, seeing as mother put paid to your romance,' said Jacky teasing his brother.

'Well, she can't stop me seeing Meg unless she locks me away and she's not going to do that, and what she doesn't know can't hurt her,' said Micky with a twinkle in his eye.

'I don't know why you want to be wasting your time seeing Meg when you could be playing football,' said Jacky innocently.

Micky smiled.

'Well, I'm playing football now aren't I? And lass or no lass I can still run rings around you, our Jacky,' said Micky, as he dribbled the ball around Jacky, leaving him kicking at thin air.

'As far as you are concerned I'm having nothing to do with Meg. That way you don't have to lie if mother or Dan ask questions,' said Micky. 'And you needn't say anything to Bill and Tom either.'

A few other lads joined the brothers, and they were soon immersed in their football training. Micky played exceptionally well that day. He had a spring in his step and nothing or no-one could stop him.

Micky and Meg continued their secret liaisons although the weather was deteriorating, and the ruins were not an ideal venue for their meetings. The first snow fell in December and there was a bitter chill in the air. Micky crouched behind the broken wall away from the biting wind. Meg was unusually late. He kept peering over the wall to see if she was approaching, but she was nowhere to be seen. He would wait forever for Meg, but if she was unable to get away he could be frozen solid by the time she arrived. Micky began to worry. Meg never let him down; supposing something was wrong? Micky decided to wait a few more minutes, and then he would have to go to the Coatman's home to make sure Meg was alright. He was still seeing Meg in the company of her family; they were just unaware of their clandestine meetings. It had not crossed his mind that Meg might just not want to see him; he unerringly trusted their relationship.

Micky was just about to head to The Coatman's home when he saw a huddled figure approaching. It was Meg. She looked as white as the snow and had dark shadows under her eyes. Micky ran up to Meg and enveloped her in his strong arms.

'Meg, you look frozen. Here shelter behind the wall,' said Micky. 'You shouldn't have come. It's too cold to be out.'

'I had to see you, Micky. I'm not cold, just a bit peaky,' said Meg.

'Even more reason to stay indoors. Let me walk you home; you shouldn't be out in this weather.'

'I have to tell you something, Micky. Before you hear rumours.'

'What is it Meg?' Micky was worried.

'Micky, I'm going to have a bairn,' said Meg, her face solemn.

Micky was stunned. His face went through a succession of emotions — from disbelief, to shock, to terror, to delight.

'Are you sure?'

'Aye. I've been sick every morning for the last two months, but I didn't want to tell you until I was sure. I'm sorry, Micky,' said Meg, head bowed.

'Sorry? It's me that should be sorry. But I'm not. I'm delighted. I'm going to be a dad,' said Micky, hugging Meg.

'Micky, we're not married, and we can't be married. The bairn will be born without a father.'

'But I'm his father. Me mother will have to let us get married now.'

'I wouldn't be so sure. She hates me. I'm a catholic.'

'Does your mother know? And your da?'

'No. Not really, but I'm sure they think something's up — what with me being sick. I tried to hide it, but I can't always.'

'Shall I come with you and tell them, Meg?' said Micky. He knew Mr. Coatman would be furious, but he could not let Meg take the blame. He had to accept the repercussions of his actions, although the thought of facing Meg's father terrified him. Mr. Coatman was a fair man, but Micky had had his way with Meg. It would not be Micky that was frowned upon — it would be Meg. She would be considered a disgrace and bring shame on the family.

'I'm not going to say anything yet, Micky. Not until I can't hide it anymore. Things can happen when it's so soon, so no point in saying anything just yet.'

'What are you saying, Meg? You wouldn't do anything dangerous or stupid would you?'

'I've already done something stupid, Micky. But that's not what I'm saying. I would never do anything to harm an unborn baby.'

'No. No. I didn't think you would. Sorry, Meg. I'm just confused.'

'I just want to keep it quiet as long as I can. Anyway, I'd best get home. I'm frozen.'

'I'll walk you home Meg,' said Micky wrapping his arm around Meg's shoulder and walking her towards the path. They walked huddled together against the adverse weather.

As they entered the village Meg tried to put some distance between herself and Micky.

'Meg. Soon everyone will know we're more than just acquaintances. We can't keep hiding it,' said Micky.

'I know, but just not yet Micky. I'll be the one who's discredited and have tongues wagging and doors closed on me,' said Meg realistically.

Micky knew this was true. His emotions were all over the place. He felt thrilled that Meg was carrying his child, angry that his mother had forbidden them to marry, guilty that he was shaming Meg, sad that he couldn't be with Meg, and he was worried — worried for the welfare of Meg and their unborn child.

Chapter 15

It was a cold February evening. Micky and Jacky had finished the early shift and were at home, tucking into a bowl of hot broth and mopping up the juices with chunks of stotty. Outside there was thick snow on the ground, so there was no chance of a game of football or handball. They were surprised to hear the voices of Bill and Tom Coatman outside their door. There was a loud rap on the back door before it was slung open and Adam Coatman, the eldest brother, burst into the house followed by his younger brothers. Micky leapt to his feet, spilling the broth, as Adam headed straight towards him and grabbed him by his collar.

'Micky Mordue! By the time I've finished with you you're going to wish you never came near my sister,' said Adam through gritted teeth.

Adam tried to pull Micky from the bench; bowls flying and smashing on the stone floor.

Bill and Tom ran after him.

'Leave him, Adam. It's not going to help,' pleaded Bill trying to step between Adam and Micky.

Jacky also came to Micky's defence and tried to get Adam off, but as Adam swung a punch at Micky it caught Jacky on the side of his lip. Blood began to trickle down Jacky's face. On hearing the furore Elizabeth stormed into the kitchen.

'Get out of my house! How dare you come into my house and act like animals?' she screeched ,brandishing her feather duster. She started to hit Bill and Tom over the head with her ineffectual weapon and they cowered, backing away from her.

Adam threw Micky back into his seat.

'Your son has got something to tell you, Mrs. Crossley,' said Adam. He turned and walked towards the back door. 'I'll see you some other time Micky — don't you worry.'

Bill and Tom scurried off behind him. Micky sat looking at the spilt broth; the piece of stotty in his hand squeezed to a pulp. Elizabeth dropped her duster and ran to Jacky's side; spitting on her handkerchief and wiping the blood from his face.

'What the devil was that all about?' she growled, looking at Micky.

Micky correctly assumed that Meg's pregnancy was no longer a secret. His mother would find out one way or another.

'Meg Coatman is… is… in the family way,' Micky spluttered.

'Well, what's that got to do with you, Michael? I told you months ago you weren't to see her anymore,' Elizabeth did not want to believe that Micky had anything to do with it.

'It's mine, Mam,' said Micky trying to be resolute.

'Don't you let that mucky hoit put the blame on you, our Micky. She'll have been with half of the village — knowing what Catholics are like.'

Micky felt the anger rise within him; not only had his mother stopped Micky and Meg from marrying, but she was also now unjustifiably maligning Meg.

'Meg Coatman is not like that mother. We love each other and whatever you say you can't change that,' Micky tried to stay calm.

'She's deliberately tricked you so she can get you to marry her. Well, she's got another think coming. There is no way you are going near that lass again — never mind marrying her.'

Elizabeth was in denial of the fact that Meg was expecting Micky's baby. Whatever he said to her, she was not having any of it. Micky knew he had to see Meg. He knew Adam would still be ready to give him a pounding, but he wanted to be by Meg's side and let her family know that he would never dessert her. Micky put on his boots, coat, and cap and despite his mother's protestations, left the house and made his way to Kimblesworth. When he arrived at Meg's home, he felt sick to the stomach. He knocked on the back door, not daring to enter without permission. It was Tom who answered the door.

'Your name is mud around here, Micky. I'd keep clear if I was you,' said Tom, trying to protect his friend.

'I'd like to see your father, if he's home, Tom,' said Micky, standing his ground.

Tom let Micky into the back kitchen. The family was seated round the kitchen table. At seeing Micky, Adam jumped to his feet, but fortunately, he was seated at the back and could not get to Micky.

'Sit down Adam,' said Mrs. Coatman to her son, holding up her hand. 'Let's hear what the lad has to say.'

Meg was sat next to Mrs. Coatman. Her eyes were bloodshot.

'Good evening, Mrs. Coatman, Mr. Coatman,' said Micky, holding his cap and nodding at the family gathered round the table.

Micky felt as if the many pairs of eyes that were focussing on him were penetrating his skin and burning his soul.

'I love Meg, and with your permission, I'd like to marry her,' said Micky, looking at Mr. Coatman.

'You'd better bloody marry her, you filthy bugger,' shouted Adam, rising to his feet once more.

'Adam, sit down and hold your tongue,' scorned Mrs. Coatman.

'I would have married Meg before… before… already, but I couldn't,' stammered Micky. 'My mother would not give me permission.'

Micky bowed his head.

'We not good enough for her? Your mother whose daughters have had bastard children and whose husband died from the drink,' hissed Adam.

Micky gritted his teeth and clenched his fists. It took every ounce of self-control he possessed to stop himself lunging at Adam. The death of his father and elder sisters still grieved him deeply. Although Elizabeth reprimanded her family when they sinned and clearly made her feelings of outrage known to them, if they ever brought shame on the family, she was always there for them in their time of need.

'Enough Adam!' Meg cried. 'I know Micky will stand by me. It's not his fault his mother won't let us wed.'

Micky was grateful to Meg that she had defended him, but he did not like to see her getting upset in her present condition.

'Sit yourself down, lad,' said Mr. Coatman. He did not say much, but when he spoke everyone listened.

Micky sat on a stool near the back door, the only place left to sit. The Coatman's were not going to make room for him around the table.

'So, what do you intend to do about the situation, Micky?' Mr. Coatman asked.

'Well, Mr. Coatman. If I could, I would marry Meg, but as you know my mother will not allow me to do so. But, I will marry Meg as soon as I can, and in the meantime, I will do all I can to help. It grieves me to be unable to do more. I am truly sorry.'

'Well, you're fortunate that our Bill and our Tom say you are a good lad. I believe that you will stand by our Meg,' said Mr. Coatman.

'God help him if he doesn't,' hissed Adam.

'Adam! Not another word,' said Mr. Coatman. 'Now Micky, you can continue to see Meg but only in this house. And when the bairn arrives you can chip in all you can to help out.'

'Yes, Mr. Coatman, thank you.' said Micky, truly grateful to the Coatmans for being so reasonable.

'And keep this quiet – and tell your family to do the same. We don't want folk knowing our business. Now, get yourself away.' Mr. Coatman, although sympathetic to Micky and Meg's plight, was unhappy with the situation and the shame Micky's actions had brought on their family. But he was a peaceable man and did not want to add fuel to the fire. There was nothing anyone could do to change what had happened.

When he returned home Micky's mother was sitting waiting for him.

'Are they trying to put the blame on you, Michael?' she asked.

'Well, it is my responsibility Mother,' said Micky.

'I'm not having it. That girl could have been with anyone.'

'Mother, I know Meg and I know she would not do that.'

'Well, if she goes with one lad when she isn't married, who's to say she won't go with others?'

'Mother, I'd like your permission to marry Meg, please.' Micky pleaded.

'You stay away from that girl and that family. I'll hear no more about it,' said Elizabeth, turning away from Micky and sweeping from the room.

Micky slowly climbed the stairs and climbed into the double bed he shared with his brother Jacky.

'You alright, Micky?' whispered Jacky.

'I'm going to be a dad, Jacky,' said Micky cheerily, typically focussing on the positive.

'Is that good?' asked Jacky, somewhat bemused.

'It will be. But as it stands Mother has forbidden me to go anywhere near Meg, and the Coatmans have made it clear that if I abandon Meg there'll be trouble. So, whatever I do I'm going to upset someone.'

'So, what are you going to do?'

'Meg is the person I care about most in the world, and I'm going to do everything I can to help her. I will marry her. Maybe not just yet, but one day I will.'

Chapter 16

The weather improved, and Jacky and Micky were able to kick the ball around once again. It was a relief to get outside and run. From the confines of the pit and their overcrowded home it gave them a freedom that energised their souls. When the snow clouds lifted, and the sun returned to the sky, the mood of the village also lifted. Daffodils emerged from the grass banks, and songbirds found their voices. The ice melted from the handball courts, and the brothers were able to whack the ball around once more; releasing pent-up energy and honing their skills.

Sarah Crossley married a local man who worked at the colliery and moved a few streets away. She was happy to leave the overcrowded bedroom she shared with her stepsisters and start a new life with her husband. The home they moved into was small, but it felt a lot more spacious to Sarah after having so many people living in the Crossley household. Joseph was sad to see his daughter leave the home but happy that she had found a husband and was making a life of her own. Sarah visited her father and Elizabeth regularly.

Micky visited Meg in her home. She could not conceal her pregnancy any longer, and her family had insisted she remain in the house — away from public view. If she were to venture out tongues would wag, and some folk could be hateful towards an unmarried mother. Meg's youngest sister, Teenie, was still only five years old, but Mrs. Coatman had been forty-one when she had had her. Now she was forty-six and the reality of her being able to have more children was diminishing, but everyone agreed that it would be best for the whole family to let the neighbours believe it was Mrs. Coatman who was going to have a baby. Her daughter, Martha, was fifteen and old enough to carry out all the duties that had to be done outside the home. She shopped and hung washing across the street. She brought in the coals, paid the tradesmen, fetched water and all the other chores that might be spotted by prying eyes. When asked, she told neighbours that her mother was in the family way once more and that Meg was caring for her as she was in bed unwell. The atmosphere was fractious between Meg and her mother, but Meg knew that her mother would not be enjoying being stuck indoors as the weather was improving; she was doing it to save Meg's honour. The two of them cleaned and sewed and polished and did anything and everything to keep themselves busy. Meg became frustrated — feeling like a caged animal. She looked forward to Micky's visits, but that added a different kind of frustration. Holding hands and a peck on the cheek were all that was allowed. They longed to embrace one another; to express the love they felt.

The weeks passed slowly until Meg woke in the early hours one morning in June — bedsheets sodden. She sat up and tried to get out of bed without waking her sisters, but they stirred.

'Meg! You've wet the bed! screeched Martha, who had put her hand on the wet sheets.

'Shush, Martha. Go and get Mam,' Meg said as a wave of pain went through her.

Meg doubled up in agony — gripping the bedpost. Teenie was woken by the noise and inadvertently rolled onto the wet patch of bed. Mrs. Coatman hurried into the room and sent the younger girl downstairs.

'Martha, go and put the kettle on the stove and bring up a bowl of hot water and bring a few clean towels please lass,' she said calmly, stripping the wet bedclothes from the bed. She pulled the potty out from under the bed and told Meg to try and use it. Mrs. Coatman soon re-made the bed and covered it with clean towels. Meg sat on the bed, waiting for the next wave of pain to pass through her.

'The pain's stopped Mam. I just feel so stupid for wetting the bed,' said Meg.

'That was your waters breaking; it means the baby will be on its way before too long. But don't expect anything to happen in a hurry. I was on all day and all night with our Anne — being the first bairn,' said Mrs. Coatman. 'I'll go and fetch you a cuppa and some breakfast. You're going to need something to give you some strength.'

Meg sat on the bed, alone in the room. She was frightened. She thought about Micky's sister Hannah who had died following the birth of twins. Hannah had been a strong young woman — a football player like her brothers, but then she had been forced upon by her employer, and following the consequences of that violation, was dead within a year —— her life so cruelly cut short. Meg wondered if Hannah had known she was having twins. What if Meg herself was carrying twins? It was always more dangerous to have a multiple birth. Mrs. Coatman returned with Meg's breakfast and noticed Meg was getting quite distressed.

'Howay, lass. No use getting yourself twisty. Like it or not, it's time for that bairn to come out, and there's only one way about it.'

'But Mam, I don't know if I can. What if there's twins or it's upside down or something?' Meg sobbed.

'I'm not going to tell you it's going to be easy, but if you get yourself in a state that's going to make things worse. Now get that tea drunk and have a bite to eat.'

Mrs. Coatman's brusque attitude hid the angst she herself was feeling. She would prefer to be giving birth herself, rather than watching her beloved Meg having to go through it. And with the future of Meg's relationship being uncertain, it felt that there was a cloud hovering above them rather than the excitement she had felt when she gave birth to her first child. Martha and Mrs. Coatman took turns staying with Meg in the bedroom. Meg's contractions became more intense and more frequent. The hours passed, and the light started to fade but Mrs. Coatman knew Meg still had some time to go before the actual birth.

'Martha, you and Teenie go in me and your Da's bed. Your Da will have to sleep in the chair or in with the lads tonight.'

The night was long, as Meg endured hours of ever-increasing contractions. At five in the morning Mrs. Coatman woke her husband and sent him out to fetch Mrs. Robinson. Mrs. Robinson had helped at the births of most of the Coatman children. As she entered the room, Mrs. Robinson was not surprised to see it was Meg she would be assisting rather than Mrs. Coatman. She had heard rumours that it was Mrs. Coatman who was confined with a child on the way, but this was a situation she had encountered on a few previous occasions; the mother's identity being kept hidden. People in the village would have their suspicions, but without real evidence the truth could be concealed.

Mrs. Robinson went about her business in her usual efficient manner. She took control of the situation and made Meg feel she was in capable hands. Although the pain was excruciating, Meg remained strong and resolute, and within an hour of Mrs. Robinson's arrival, Meg gave birth to a healthy baby.

'It's a lad,' Mrs. Robinson announced.

It was now six o'clock in the morning. Meg was exhausted but looked lovingly into the baby's face. He had Micky's eyes. Meg was eager for Micky to see his son but knew he would just be starting his shift at the colliery. Meg cuddled her son, who latched on to her breast without any difficulty. As the baby suckled, Meg could not stop looking at him — his perfect features. This tiny mite was a part of her and Micky. Meg felt a bond with her child she had never felt before, and in a way it scared her. She knew that a lifetime of responsibility and worry lay ahead, but it was a responsibility she cherished.

When it was time for Micky to finish his shift, Bill went to find him and discreetly tell him the news. Micky was black with coal dust, so hurried home for a bath and change of clothes before running to Kimblesworth to see Meg and their new arrival.

'They're upstairs lad. Wait here,' said Mr. Coatman. 'Martha, Micky's here to see the bairn.'

Meg was confined to bed, and Micky was not allowed to see her as such, so Mrs. Coatman brought the baby downstairs to show the new father.

'Say hello to your son,' she said, moving the sheet from around the baby's perfect face.

Micky looked at the baby who was sleeping in his grandmother's arms. A sudden wave of emotion rushed over him. The love he felt for this tiny bundle was overwhelming. He never thought he could have such strong feelings for a baby. But the love he felt for Meg was even stronger. He thought he loved her completely, but now he felt as if he was going to burst with the love he felt for this woman. He desperately wanted to see Meg but knew that was out of the question while she was lying-in.

As soon as Meg was allowed out of bed, Micky returned to the house. Meg sat in the front kitchen with their baby in her arms. The rest of the household was otherwise occupied, and Micky had some time alone with Meg and the baby.

'He's perfect,' said Micky, 'and you're the best lass a man could ever have.'

Micky gently kissed the baby's forehead and then softly kissed Meg on her lips. He knelt on the floor next to Meg's chair.

'So what's his name going to be?' he asked.

'I was thinking of naming him after our Bill. He's been a good friend to you and a good brother to me. So how about William?' said Meg.

'William; that's champion,' smiled Micky stroking his son's cheek.

It was torturous to Micky when it was time to leave. He wanted to stay with Meg and their child. That was where he belonged. Meg suggested to Micky that he did not visit too often — to prevent tongues wagging, but Micky found it hard to stay away. The neighbours knew Micky had been courting Meg; seeing him going in and out of the house following the birth of the baby made them speculate as to what was really going on in the Coatman household. There had been scornful gossip before the baby was born, and now the blether had increased. Micky strode up the road to visit Meg. Arthur Bateman spotted him and shouted out to him.

'How's Meg and your bairn?'

'Champion, thank you.' Arthur had caught Micky off guard. The words had left his lips before he could stop them. He wanted the world to know he was a father, but he knew it was in Meg and the baby's interest to keep it a secret. Arthur Bateman — of all people. Why had he opened his mouth?

'Ah, you let that slip easily enough — just like her drawers. She'd drop them for anyone, that whore Meg Coatman. Now you've got what you both deserve; a bastard.'

Arthur shouted, in order to allow anyone in the vacinity to hear. Micky could turn the other cheek if it was his reputation that was at stake, but when Meg and the baby were slighted, Micky had to retaliate. In the blink of an eye he laid into Arthur. Micky was a lot shorter than Arthur, but he was stronger and faster. He threw a punch at Arthur which caught the spot. Arthur was on the ground before he had a chance to raise his fists. But Micky was so incensed that he could not leave it at that. He pulled Arthur by his collar and landed another punch on his already bloody lip. Hearing the noise, Adam ran out of the house and managed to pull Micky off Arthur and restrain him.

'Get in the house, man,' ordered Adam.

Micky reluctantly let Arthur be and went indoors.

'Bloody animal. You proud of your sister getting knocked up by a proddy dog?' yelled Arthur.

Adam grabbed him by the throat.

'Shut your gob, or I'll finish off what he started. Now get lost, yer no-good bugger.'

Adam dropped Arthur to the ground, turned and went back in the house. By this time curtains were pulled back, and the whole street had witnessed the scene. Micky was sitting at the kitchen table. He knew he had to calm down before he saw Meg, and he had to face Adam who would not be pleased. Adam strode into the kitchen, but walked straight over to the pot of tea, brewing by the range, and poured them both a mug of tea and sat at the table with Micky.

'Get that down you,' he said handing the tea to Micky.

'Sorry, Adam. After all you've done for me, I've let you all down. I just couldn't stop myself,' said Micky.

'The nasty bugger had it coming. Folk had guessed what was going on, so it's just got it out in the open,' said Adam.

Micky couldn't believe his ears. He thought he would feel Adam's wrath, but Adam seemed quite pleased that Micky had taught Arthur a lesson.

'You're part of this family now, Micky, and in this family we stick together. I'd do anything for our Meg, and I know you would too.'

Elizabeth Mordue refused to have anything to do with baby William, she was still in denial that the baby belonged to Micky. However, Micky spent as much time as he could with Meg and their son, but he also had to fit in working at the pit and training for football and handball. Micky and Meg enjoyed the time they spent together, but they longed for the intimacy and privacy they had shared at the wall. Micky could not even give Meg a kiss when the family were there. And there was always a houseful at the Coatman home. If it was not the family themselves, there would often be friends or relations popping in. After a few weeks the focus of the household and the village went away from Meg and the baby, so

Meg felt she could go about her business as she used to. They planned a time when they could meet once more.

Micky waited by the derelict house, breathing in the fresh, clean air. The sun filtered through the trees and radiated onto his face. Micky basked against the wall; a warmth also coming from within at the prospect of spending time alone with Meg once more. In his dreamy state, he did not hear Meg approaching but was roused by her voice calling his name.

'Micky...Micky.' It was a hushed call.

Micky jumped and looked around him. Meg was struggling with the pram — trying to reach their meeting place. He ran over to her.

'I canna get the pram through,' she said.

Broken pieces of the wall and fallen tree branches made it impossible.

'I'll clear it, Meg. I should have thought to do it before you got here,' said Micky.

'Well, I haven't got long and that will take forever. Here, I'll take William out of the pram. You can lift it over.'

Micky hauled the pram over the obstacles, and Meg lay William back down. He stirred and snuffled. Micky and Meg tried to ignore him. It was a long while since they had been able to hold one another. Micky put his lips on Meg's. He felt as if his thirst was being quenched. He had missed the taste and feel of Meg. He wrapped his arms around her. Their relationship had reached a new level. They were bound by the baby that lay there next to them. William yelled. He had not appreciated being woken and then left to lie in the pram without attention.

Micky felt an overwhelming feeling of love, but also a painful feeling of physical and emotional frustration. Meg tried to rock the pram whilst they embraced, but William could not be hushed. Neither of them wanted to hear their son cry, and his yells were intensifying. They did not want to see William upset, but that was not their only concern. The noise might alert anyone that was walking along the path and reveal their meeting place. Meg lifted William out of the pram, and he soon calmed down and his eyelids began to close.

'I'm sorry, Micky. He'd have been alright if I hadn't lifted him out.'

'It's not your fault. Things are different now Meg. Can I hold him?' Micky wanted to envelop his son. He looked at the perfect features on his face. His pert pink lips that were like Meg's — his button nose and tiny ears. He was a bonny baby.

'I best get going, Micky. I'm walking to Sacriston to get some wool,' said Meg.

Micky handed William back to Meg and lifted the pram back onto the path, making sure there was nobody around. They walked together — Meg pushing the pram along the stony path through the woods.

'This is how it should be. Walking together as a family,' said Micky, ruefully.

'And it will be. When you're twenty-one,' said Meg remaining positive.

Chapter 17

November 1903

On a wet November morning, Micky was on duty at the colliery along with his brother Jimmy. Jacky was working on the surface sorting stones. Jimmy, being a hewer, was at the coalface, stripped to his waist, hacking away at the solid black wall in front of him. Micky was pushing the tubs that had been filled with coal. He battled with the unwieldy loaded tub, slowly edging it away from the coal face to the base of the shaft. As he heaved it around another bend, he heard an almighty crash from where he had come. Frantic shouts were coming from the face. Then Micky heard the sound of running water. Men were hurtling towards him escaping the gushing inflow. Micky knew there was just enough room to squeeze past the coal tub. It would take time to move it to a clearing — time which Micky realised they did not have. He was unable to let go of the tub, as it was not secure and would roll back. A fully loaded tub could easily crush anyone in its path. Micky grabbed a metal rod and wedged it under the wheel to stop it rolling.

'Get out! Get out!' Shouts came from men running towards the exit. They were deep in the belly of the mine.

'Jimmy! Where is Jimmy?' Micky's thoughts were not about his own safety, but that of his brother. He tried to head back down the mine, but men were running towards him making his progress impossible in the confined tunnel.

'You can't go back that way, lad. Get out of the way and get on back out,' screamed a miner. Micky did not know who it was; he could just see the whites of his eyes and teeth, as the coal-covered hewer pushed past him.

Micky could not go without Jimmy, but he was unable to get back to where Jimmy had been working.

It took some minutes for the realisation that there had been an incident below ground to reach the workers at the surface. Jacky became frantic, as men streamed out of the pit. Micky and Jimmy were down there. He ran to the mine shaft. He had to get down there and help. But men were escaping. Nobody was allowed down; it was a case of getting everyone out.

News soon spread around Sacriston village and then to the neighbouring village of Kimblesworth. As soon as Meg heard there had been an accident, she bundled William into his pram and raced up the path to Sacriston colliery. A crowd had gathered outside the pit, waiting for news of loved ones. The atmosphere was tense. There were hundreds of men below ground working their shift. As men reached the surface, they let their loved ones know they were safe, but families and friends of those who were safe stayed to support people still awaiting news. As time went by, those that had not heard anything became increasingly worried. Jimmy's wife, Betty, was there with Elizabeth. Meg decided it was best to keep her distance from the two of them. With two sons still unaccounted for, the last thing Elizabeth needed was to come face to face with Meg. Meg still respected Elizabeth's feelings — even though she had prevented William from being born within wedlock.

Neighbours brought cups of tea to the waiting crowd, as painfully slow hours passed by. William was becoming grizzly. He was ready for a feed, but Meg could not feed him in public. She had no choice but to leave the scene and head to her elder sister Anne's house nearby, where she could let William suckle. As soon as the baby was satisfied, Meg headed back to the colliery gates. She could not get close but could see a small group of men approaching the gate. Although she could not see him clearly, she recognised Micky's gait. He was walking with two other lads. Yes, it was definitely Micky, with Jimmy and Jacky by his side. Meg's heart leapt, and tears of joy welled in her eyes. She heard Betty call to Jimmy, and the three men spotted their mother. But Micky's eyes were scanning the crowd. Meg did her best to be seen, and Micky picked her out — his eyes drawn to her beautiful, smiling face. Meg braced herself — expecting Micky to go to his mother, but he did not. He said something to his brothers and left them. Micky headed towards Meg. Down in the cold, wet darkness of the pit, not knowing if he would get out alive, all Micky had thought about was Meg and William. The thought of his beloved Meg and his son had given him strength and resolution that he did not know he possessed. He had to be there for them — to provide for them and care for them. They were his world. Meg wrapped her arms around

Micky, and they kissed. They did not care who was watching. Elizabeth was overjoyed to see her sons safe and well, but when she realised where Micky was heading and witnessed the brazen embrace of the pair, she was seething.

'You best go and see your Mam,' said Meg.

'Aye, and wait for news of those still unaccounted for. Bye Meg. I wish I could stay with you.'

After their emotional encounter, Micky and Meg did not want to part, so they arranged to meet at the wall that afternoon. In the meantime, Micky went to see his mother, and Meg headed back along the path to Kimblesworth, full of relief.

The rescue operation continued throughout the day. Three miners were still unaccounted for. With a chance of further flooding, explosions or collapse, the rescue workers persisted in their efforts, putting themselves in great danger. A small electric pump was used, but it proved ineffective due to the amount of water in the mine. It took a further two days before an adequate pump could be brought from Newcastle. The water was slowly pumped out, as all hope of finding anyone alive faded.

The accident had occurred on Monday morning, and it took until Friday morning for the rescuers to be able to retrieve the bodies. Miraculously one of the miners, Richardson, was found alive. He had been entombed in an air pocket above the water level and was found standing on his coal tub. He was physically none the worse for his experience although very hungry, thirsty and tired; he went on to make a full recovery. The other two miners were less fortunate. Thirty-year-old John Whittaker and fifty-two year old Thomas McCormick had both drowned. John Whittaker's brother had worked the fore shift before his brother and had pricked the leader of the fault. He had reported it to the deputy and after inspection, as no water had appeared, there was no danger anticipated. However, as Whittaker had continued to hew coal from the vicinity, the barrier had been weakened, and the water broke through with immense pressure — forcing out coal and leaving a large hole.

Micky and Meg met as planned on the afternoon of the accident. Micky had cleared a path to the wall to enable Meg to push the pram through. William usually remained asleep. If he began to stir, a slight rocking of the pram was enough to placate him.

'I was scared stiff when you didn't come out of the pit, Micky. I don't know what I'd do without you,' said Meg, hugging tightly onto Micky. 'You must've been scared witless.'

'Well, I did come out so you've no reason to fret. I'll always be here for you, Meg.'

Micky did not want to talk about the accident. Being a miner was a hazardous job and there was always the risk of death or severe injury whenever a man did his shift down the pit. It was something that they could not dwell upon, or the job would be impossible.

Micky put an arm around Meg, kissing her, edging her towards the wall, slipping his other hand beneath her petticoat…

Chapter 18

March 1904

'For God's sake, Micky! Once is a mistake, twice is a bloody disgrace. Especially when you know you canna wed the lass. Haven't you heard of getting the train to Sunderland and getting off at Shotton? Mother is going to brain you when she finds out. That's if she believes it's yours and not Meg putting it around and blaming it on you. You're a bloody idiot, man. I'm surprised old man Coatman doesn't kick you from here to Hartlepool.' said Jimmy.

Micky had confided in him that Meg was going to have another baby. She had told him to be careful, and he usually was, but on one occasion he just lost control, and now Meg was expecting their second child.

'That's not much help, Jimmy. If you react like that, what's mother going to do? Maybe I should just pack my bags now.'

'Where would you go? You can't put your name down for a colliery house unless you're married; Me and Betty are still on the waiting list, even though we've been wed over a year. And you can't move in with us. Betty's family already have two lodgers, as well as me and the rest of Betty's family.'

'Mr. Coatman won't have me there without marrying Meg. I'll be surprised if he even lets her out of the house anymore, or me in it. I just want to do what's right for Meg.'

'Keeping your trousers up would have been a start,' said Jimmy.

'Come on, Jimmy. You know what it's like. Anyway, it's too late for that now. What am I going to do?'

'You'll just have to face the music and tell mother,' said Jimmy.

'Tell mother what?' said Elizabeth.

The brothers were startled to see their mother entering the back door, laden with shopping. Her face was solemn. They looked at one another. It was no use trying to deceive her. She would know they were hiding the truth. Micky walked over to his mother and took her bags from her and placed them on the floor.

'Sit down, mother, I've got something to tell you,' he said.

Jimmy decided it was best to make himself scarce and waited in the other room, his ear to the door.

'Meg is going to have another bairn,' said Micky.

Elizabeth became instantly flustered but did her best to dismiss what Micky was saying. She jumped to her feet and started to take the shopping out of the bags.

'Oh yes, and she's trying to put the blame on you again, is she? The scheming hussy. Well, don't you let her take you in, Michael. There could be any amount of men who could be the father of that hacky's bairn. The way she…'

'Mother! Enough!' Micky yelled. His patience had run thin, and as much as he loved and respected his mother, he could no longer listen to her saying such hideous lies about Meg, when it was him who was responsible for the current situation.

Elizabeth was taken aback. Micky never raised his voice to her; he was the quietest of her sons. She fumbled for the edge of the table and slowly lowered herself onto the bench.

'William is my bairn, and now Meg is going to have another baby, which is also my bairn,' said Micky, lowering his voice but remaining resolute.

'Her belly is beginning to swell, and soon it will be obvious that she has another bairn on the way. Folk will know it's mine. What will our family look like when they see that we shirk our responsibilities? You have to allow me to marry Meg, mother; I implore you.'

Elizabeth knew Micky was right. She had not wanted to believe that he would father the child of a catholic lass. Even if it was Micky's, lads make mistakes. But now that she was carrying a second baby, it would be the father's family that was put under scrutiny. To give a lass two bairns and not marry her would look bad on Micky and the family.

'Are you sure, Michael?' said Elizabeth, her face etched with sadness and despair.

'Yes, mother.'

Tears welled in Elizabeth's eyes, and she looked away and into the fireplace. Elizabeth sat in silence staring at the flickering flames.

The situation was not going to go away, and as much as she resented Meg and did not want Micky to marry into a catholic family, it appeared there was no option. Micky had always been

72

such an easy lad to raise — never getting into fights, always being helpful and thoughtful. She would not have known he was there for much of his life; he just slipped quietly into the background and got on with things as the rest of the family went through their ups and downs. And he looked so much like her own beloved father, God rest his soul, especially around the eyes.

Elizabeth's thoughts went back to when Micky was a baby. Even though he was her eighth child, she still remembered the emotion she felt when he was placed in her arms. Some of her children had looked like strangers, taking after their father's side of the family or some distant aunt, but not Micky. He had always looked like part of her family; it was as if she had known him before, as she looked into his new-born eyes. And now she wondered if she knew him at all. He was keeping secrets from her, disobeying her. This woman had come between them, and she wasn't going to go away.

Micky sat in silence, waiting for what seemed an eternity, waiting for his mother to say something.

'Well, you'd better marry her then,' she said, biting her lip. She got up from her seat and started poking the coals in the fire, her shoulders silently shuddering, holding back her sobs.

Micky felt as if a weight had been lifted from his shoulders, and that if he made a little effort, he could take off and fly straight out of the door to Meg's house. He was relieved and overjoyed, but knew he had to keep his happiness in check as his mother stood distraught next to him.

Solemnly he replied, 'Thank you, Mother… If we have a lass, we'll call her Elizabeth, after you.'

Micky turned and slowly walked outside, but as soon as his feet touched the pavement, he ran like the wind to tell Meg the good news.

Micky and Meg were married on the ninth of April 1904 at the Durham registry office. Bill and Jimmy were the only ones in attendance. There were no celebrations. With the money he had put away, Micky bought Meg a rose gold ring to wear, knowing that this day would come. Once they were married, the Coatmans allowed Micky to move into their home. It was another wage coming in; however, Elizabeth would struggle financially, having lost Micky's income. There had to be some rearranging of the sleeping arrangements to allow Micky and Meg their own room. The Coatman's were lucky enough to have three bedrooms. The girls slept in one room, the boys in another, and Mr. and Mrs. Coatman slept in the tiny box room. They gave this up for Micky, Meg, and William, and they slept downstairs on a put-you-up. They were hoping it would not be for long, as Micky had put his name down on the housing list, in the hope that a home might come up for his new family, but there was a shortage of homes in Sacriston and Kimblesworth. The only ones that might become available were too squalid for young children. The Coatmans would prefer to live in cramped conditions in their clean, well-built home for the time being, rather than having the newlyweds and their young family live somewhere damp and dirty.

'Are you sure you're alright down here, Mam?' asked Meg. 'I feel wrong turfing you two out of your bed, what with Dad's back and all.'

'You and Micky need your own room; you've waited long enough. And besides, that bed up there isn't the most comfortable, so it won't make a difference to your Da,' said Mrs. Coatman.

'Thanks, Mam. For everything,' said Meg, kissing her mother.

Meg went to the bedroom, where William was asleep in the cot, which had been squeezed into the room at the end of the bed. Micky was there, looking at his sleeping son. Meg gently closed the door and sat on the bed next to Micky.

'I canna believe we're actually married, Micky. I feel like me Da will come in any minute and hoik you out of here and brain you for being with his daughter.'

'Well, we are married, Mrs. Mordue. And I'm a very lucky man.'

'Mrs. Mordue! Eeh, that doesn't sound real,' said Meg. 'I am, aren't I? Mrs. Mordue.'

Micky kissed Meg. They could finally demonstrate their love for each other without guilt or fear, and in the luxury of a warm bed with a roof over their heads. Micky slowly undressed Meg. The hurried, veiled passion of their meetings at the wall was a thing of the past.

Chapter 19

The weeks passed, and Micky became one of the family. He was happier than he could remember. He had his new wife and his little lad; he shared a home with his friend Bill, and he saw his brother Jacky regularly — playing football and handball whenever he could. Jacky also spent a lot of time at the Coatman's home, as that was where his brother and friends resided. Work at the colliery continued as it always did. The conditions in the mine were treacherous, but the camaraderie amongst the miners and the pay packet at the end of each week made it bearable.

William's first birthday was not celebrated; birthdays were not something anyone worried about. He was growing into a fine, boisterous little lad, tottering around the kitchen, and being spoilt by his uncles and aunts. He was into everything and had to be watched all the time. His happy disposition was a ray of sunshine in the grey, coal-fuelled world of Kimblesworth village. Meg noticed that the baby she was carrying did not kick or move as much as William had done, and her belly was not getting as big as it had in her first pregnancy. Maybe she had got her dates wrong? Or maybe this one was a girl; she had heard that girls carried differently to boys.

It was a hot and humid June morning when Meg felt a few twinges, and her back felt as if it was going to break. She said nothing to Micky as he went off to work the early shift. Meg tried to make herself comfortable, sitting on the kitchen bench, stretching, bending.

'Mam, I think the bairns on its way,' said Meg, 'but it can't be — it's too soon.'

'Are you sure you have your dates right, Meg?'

'Aye. It shouldn't be coming for a couple of months yet.

Meg doubled up in pain.

'I need to go to the netty.'

'You stay in here lass. I don't want you going out to the privy. I'll bring you the pot. Go upstairs and lie down,' said Mrs. Coatman.

Meg gingerly made her way up the stairs to her room. When she used the pot, there was a large amount of blood. Mrs. Coatman attended to Meg and sent Martha to fetch Mrs. Robinson. Meg went through the labours of childbirth, but it all happened much quicker than it had when she gave birth to William. The baby arrived that afternoon. Its tiny lungs were not strong enough to support it, and it died within seconds of being born. Meg had been correct with her dates. Mrs. Robinson wrapped up the tiny body in a white cloth and took it away with her. Meg felt exhausted and heartbroken. Meg had prepared herself for the arrival of her second child — imagining the baby's tiny features; its soft skin and unique smell. She had pictured William with the baby — proud to be a big brother. She had knitted a small, pink bonnet as she secretly thought she was carrying a girl. Meg felt guilty as if the baby had been born early due to something she had done wrong. Had she lifted something too heavy? Had she walked too far? Had she squashed it when she lay in bed? She was dreading Micky's return from work; she felt a failure.

Micky was oblivious to the day's events when he returned to the house after his shift. As soon as he entered the house, Mrs. Coatman explained the situation. He wanted to run up the stairs and comfort Meg, but he had to remove his coal-covered clothes and hurriedly take a dip in the bathtub to remove the worst of the muck and filth, which coated his skin and hair.

Meg lay in bed — her face pale, and her eyes red and puffy. Micky sat on the bed by her side and held Meg in a warm embrace.

'I'm so sorry, Micky. I don't know what I did wrong,' sobbed Meg.

'You did nothing wrong; don't blame yourself. There must have been something wrong with the baby; if it had survived it would probably have been sick or not right and suffered its whole life.'

Meg was reassured by Micky's words; he was probably right. The baby was never mentioned again. Like many things, it was something that wasn't discussed. Meg was expected to put her grief and pain to the back of her mind. Meg had to stay in bed for ten days, as she would have done if the baby had survived. Without a baby by her side to watch over and nurse, this was torturous for Meg. Her thoughts were consumed by the loss of her baby. She did not know if the baby was a boy or a girl; at the time she was too stunned to even think about it; now, she could not bring herself to ask her mother. It did not really matter anyway. Meg imagined the baby as a cherub; praying that Susannah and the baby would be together in heaven. Meg withdrew into herself. She hardly touched the food her mother brought to her. She either lay in fitful sleeps or stared blankly at the walls. The ten days passed slowly and painfully.

On the day Meg was allowed to leave her bed she wanted nothing more than to pull the covers over her head and go back to sleep. Mrs. Coatman had other ideas.

'Howay, Meg. William wants his breakfast, and I've got work to do; it's washing day. The lads are at work, and the bairns are at school. Here's a bowl of warm water; get up and give yourself a good wash and get some clothes on, Pet. I need to wash your sheets.'

Mrs. Coatman placed the bowl of warm water on top of Meg's chest of drawers.

Meg said nothing, but after her mother left the room, she knew she had to face the world — even though it was the last thing she wanted to do at that moment. William was her responsibility — not her mother's. Very slowly, she hauled herself out of bed. Her legs felt weak and shaky. Meg sat back down on the edge of the bed. She reached for the cloth in the bowl, squeezing out the excess water and placing the warm damp cloth on her skin. She vigorously rubbed her face, trying to revive herself. Meg then stripped off her nightclothes and washed herself all over, before putting on clean clothes. The dress felt heavy and stiff. Meg leaned against the wall and made her way to the door, gingerly descending the wooden stairs. Her mother was in the back kitchen with William.

'Ah, William. Here's your Mam. Sit at the table with her, and I'll fetch you both some porridge. There's a cup of tea for you, Meg,' said Mrs. Coatman, placing the warm, sweet tea on the kitchen table.

Meg sat down; she felt exhausted. She took a sip of tea. Meg did not have any appetite for the porridge her mother placed in front of her but forced a small spoonful into her mouth. The porridge tasted good. Meg had not realised how hungry she was. She helped William with his porridge. William looked up at her with his big blue eyes. He pointed at Meg and with a big smile on his face said, 'Mama.'

This melted Meg's heart. Tears flooded from her eyes — pent-up tears of sadness for the baby she had lost, mingled with tears of joy and love for her young son. Meg wrapped her arms around William and held him close to her chest as she sobbed. Her mother pretended not to notice and discreetly left the room, leaving her daughter to vent her grief.

Chapter 20

The summer was wet and windy, with few days of sunshine. Micky and Jacky played handball come rain or shine – making the most of the light evenings. They continued to work hard and play hard. Towards the end of the summer, the football season was due to resume. Micky took a trip to Spennymoor to check fixtures and have a pre-season meeting with the team. Spennymoor United AFC had been accepted into the Northern League, so this season's games would be much more competitive and of a higher standard than before.

'Is your brother still available to play for us, Micky?' asked the manager.

'Aye. He's keen to play if there's room in the team,' said Micky.

'Make sure he's here next Saturday, and he should get a game.'

Micky could not wait to get back to Sacriston and let Jacky know that he was to be part of the team. It would be a big step up for Jacky, but Micky was confident he would be able to cope. Jacky was thrilled to be given the chance to play for Spennymoor. Not only would he be playing for a much higher standard team, but he would also be playing alongside his brother. Now that Micky lived with the Coatmans, Jacky did not see him anywhere near as often as he used to.

'You're going to notice a difference in the opponents, Jacky. You'll not be able to skip round these lads so easily,' said Micky as they sat on the cart, on their way to Spennymoor.

There were no pre-match talks or training; the players were just informed who would be playing and left to get on with it — with exception of the goalkeeper.

'If you get the ball, try and run away from the defence, up the wing. Then when you've drawn them out, cross the ball in ,but mind you don't pass it to a player who is offside,' said Micky.

'Why! I know I wouldn't give it to a lad who's offside, but I don't usually pass it. I usually run at the defenders,' said Jacky, having confidence in his own game and not convinced that he needed to pass the ball to anyone.

'We'll see,' said Micky.

As the match against Darlington kicked off, it was soon evident to Jacky that the speed and skill of the opponents were better than he had experienced. He tried using his speed to dribble past defenders but was crowded off the ball. The opponents worked as a team in a way that he had not experienced before. Although they were not professionals, and hadn't been coached, they knew each other's strengths and had a structure to their game. Jacky became frustrated. Time and time again, he chased players and when he had them in his sights, they would send the ball across the pitch to a waiting player. He was running all over the pitch and hardly touching the ball. Micky could see that his brother's frustration was getting the better of him and hoped Jacky would not do anything rash before the halftime break — which could not come soon enough. Spennymoor were two goals down and did not look like scoring; they had not had a shot on goal.

'Jacky you're doing fine, but remember to let the ball do the work. You can't catch these lads on the ball. You have to think ahead — think where the ball's going to go, and look to see if any of our players are already there. At Sacriston, you knew you were the best player on the pitch, but here it's a different story. You're part of a team that can all do their job. You've got to work out your place in the team and not try and get involved in every move,' said Micky. 'If you're standing in space and you're not offside, we'll get the ball to you.'

'Aye, I know you're right, Micky. It's just not how I've played before. I don't want the others to think I'm no good,' said Jacky.

'Well, stop trying so hard and just think about what you are doing. I know you can play, and if it was one against one you'd be hard to beat. But this is a team game, and you're part of the team.'

Jacky thought about Micky's words and knew he was right. It was hard for Jacky to adapt his game, as he was the key player at Sacriston. He knew he needed to use his head just as much as his feet, but instinct had his feet flying towards the ball.

During the second half, Jacky stopped chasing the ball quite as much. Partly because of what Micky had said and partly because he was simply getting too tired to keep running non-stop. He had to think about when to make a run and when to save his energy. He was quite surprised that the game carried on without his permanent involvement in every move. His team were good. Spennymoor were getting into their stride, and Micky made a brilliant run up the right wing and crossed the ball to a teammate, who fired the ball into the back of the net. It was two goals to one, and Spennymoor were becoming the dominant side. The players from both teams were tired, as this was the first game they had played for a while, but they kept battling hard. The final whistle went. It was a victory to Darlington. The home supporters were disappointed, but they had seen their team improve in the second half and had reason to be optimistic about the season ahead.

'Well done, lad,' said the Spennymoor manager patting Jacky on the back. 'You've worked hard, and you'll soon get used to the other players.'

Jacky had not expected any praise from the manager; their side had lost, and he had failed to score. But the words had lifted him, and he now felt he had not let the side down.

'We'll go over the field tomorrow and practise some crosses,' said Micky.

'Aye, that would be champion,' said Jacky.

Chapter 21

Micky and Jacky struck up a great relationship on the field for Spennymoor. They instinctively knew each other's movements, on and off the ball, invariably being one step ahead of the opposing defence. Jimmy had managed to recover to the extent that he could also return to the pitch, but he took up a defensive role for Spennymoor. He was a clever player and used his strength and experience to compensate for the speed and agility he had lost since his injury. The three brothers were key players for Spennymoor and gained a good reputation around the area. They played throughout the winter months, helping their team gain promotion to the Northern League — the principal amateur football league in the country. When the football season was over, their spare time was spent playing handball. Although Jimmy was, once again, playing football, he did not return to playing handball. This required much more stamina, as games would last for hours on end, and his foot could not endure the constant twisting, darting runs required from playing the game. Micky was relieved. He had loved partnering Jimmy on the handball court but knew their games were too similar to complement each other. Jacky was a different player to Micky, and when they played together, there was no part of the game they could not master. Games were organised in Sacriston and the surrounding villages, and large sums of money exchanged hands. To make the games more interesting, and to even things up, Micky and Jacky would play with a hand tied behind their back. There was just one duo that the Mordues had failed to beat — Ralph Roberts and Alfie Shaw. They were world handball champions, but Jacky and Micky were ready to make a challenge for the title.

The game was organised and set to take place in Newcastle — Shaw and Roberts hometown. Micky and Jacky practised for weeks — knocking balls around the court, toughening the skin on their hands, and developing their game. There was the added incentive of the prize money at stake; £20 to the winning pair. A huge crowd gathered to watch the match.

The game started slowly, with both pairs playing cautiously. Jacky was nervous. He was thinking of what was at stake. This was the biggest match of his life, and he did not want to mess it up, but that was exactly what he was doing. He was putting too much pressure on himself and dwelling on the consequences of losing, rather than focussing on the match. The Mordues started to trail, and their supporters were becoming agitated. Some of them had foolishly gambled more than they could afford on the match. They knew Jacky was not playing anywhere near as well as he could. Micky knew he needed to shake his brother out of his current negative mental state. Micky looked Jacky straight in the eye.

'One point at a time, Jacky. Just think about the point we're playing — nothing else.'

The sincerity that shone from Micky's eyes, as he spoke those simple words to his brother, brought Jacky to his senses. What had he been thinking? The money and the glory were nothing compared to Jacky's desire to please his brother. Micky had stood by him and encouraged him. They were a team, and Jacky was not going to let Micky down. Yes, he would fight for every point. He would run like he had never run in his life and keep every point alive. The colour returned to Jacky's face and the spring returned to his step. The match was not easy — especially as Micky and Jacky had to come from behind, but they clawed their way back into the match. Their supporters were buoyed by Jacky's sudden return to form and added their voices to the momentum. Jacky's legs moved like pistons around the court, and Micky was charged by his brother's energy. The match went on for five hours; sweat poured off the men's brows. Their clothes were stuck to their bodies. Blood oozed from cracks in their hands, but they continued to battle. Shaw was the first to show significant signs of fatigue, and this was noticed by the Mordues. Whenever they were able, they played the ball away from Roberts — asking more and more of Shaw. His legs were buckling and his hands bleeding. He was the hare at the mercy of the whippets. In one last act of desperation, Shaw threw himself at the ball. He missed and went crashing to the ground. The point and match were lost. Micky and Jacky Mordue were crowned world handball champions.

Micky and Jacky returned with the crowd of supporters back to Sacriston and Kimblesworth. Their bodies ached and their hands throbbed, but they were elated. They were now local heroes. The press had been at the match, and it was reported in the newspapers the following day. Everyone in the villages knew the brothers and were proud to have such great athletes amongst their people.

Meg was proud of Micky. He spent a great deal of his free time playing sports with his brothers, but there were a lot of worse things he could be doing. Micky always went home to Meg and made her feel special when he was with her. He adored his wife and young son, and they adored Micky in return.

Chapter 22

The following week, Jacky was knocking a ball around the handball court when he felt as if he was being watched. Sure enough when he looked round Mabel Turner — a girl from the village, whose parents owned the village newsagents, and who Jacky had known for some time, was watching him. It made Jacky feel uncomfortable so he stopped playing and started to walk away, but Mabel approached him.

'Going already, Jacky?' she asked.

Jacky was not confident with girls and looked at his feet — mumbling and nodding his head.

'Would you like a cigarette?' she asked.

Now Jacky was completely perplexed. What was she playing at?

'No,' he said brusquely.

'Alright, I was only asking. That's no way to talk,' said Mabel.

Jacky felt embarrassed.

'I don't want one, thank you,' he said.

Mabel was not easily deterred. She walked with Jacky along the street — which made it awkward for Jacky, as he was simply walking to get away from her.

'It must be great being able to play handball as well as you do. Not that I've ever played handball. I don't see much point in hitting a ball at a wall for hours on end.'

If she was not a girl Jacky would have laid into her there and then. She seemed to be deliberately antagonising him. What was she playing at?

'Well, I'm going to find a different wall to hit it against. One where you can't find me,'

'Don't do that on my account. If you don't want me to watch you I won't look. Which is a shame as I like watching you, Jacky.'

'Well, you put me off,' said Jacky.

'But you have hundreds of people watching you when you play a match.'

'Aye, but they're watching the game — not me.'

'If I went to a game, I'd be watching you.'

Jacky was simultaneously angry and flattered.

'Well, watch my next match and then you can look at me without me knowing so we'll both be happy,' he snapped and ran off before Mabel could reply.

As soon as he turned the corner he slowed down. What was that all about? Mabel Turner. She'd always been a bit of a loudmouth and had upset a few people with her sharp tongue, but Jacky had noticed for the first time that she was very pretty and quite shapely. He shouldn't have been so abrupt with her. But then what did she expect? Watching him like that. And offering him a cigarette. Her — a lass.

Jacky played a singles match the following Saturday. It was only a local match. Jacky was playing a man about ten years his senior, but an experienced player who could hit the ball as hard as any man. Quite a few spectators turned up to watch the game, and as usual money was changing hands. Jacky was winning quite easily and enjoying the game when he noticed Mabel in the crowd. She smiled at him in a way that made him uncomfortable. He lost the next few points, as his mind strayed from the game. On hearing the crowd getting behind his opponent, Jacky was roused back to the moment. This helped Jacky to refocus his mind on the game and put all thoughts of Mabel to one side. He concentrated on every rally and won point after point. To the delight of his supporters, Jacky won the game. Jacky and his opponent were fatigued and sat chatting to each other — discussing the game while drinking the large mugs of tea they had been handed. The crowd dispersed, and Jacky was ready to leave, when he saw Mabel. She appeared to be waiting for him. Jacky felt tired and did not want to have to talk to Mabel, but she intrigued him, and she did look nice in the blue frock she was wearing. As she approached Jacky, he looked away — pretending to tie his laces.

'Hello, Jacky. Well done for winning the game,' she said.

'You put me off, looking at me,' said Jacky.

'You said to come and watch you playing a match, Jacky. What's a lass supposed to do?'

Jacky could see that he was being unfair, but he knew Mabel was being deliberately brazen.

'You played so well, Jacky. Your hands must be very strong,' she said, taking Jacky's hand in hers.

Jacky could feel the colour rush to his already flushed face. Mabel's flattering words and seductive actions, as well as her voluptuous physique and pretty face, made it impossible for Jacky to snub her. He liked the attention he was receiving — although it made him feel uncomfortable.

'Did you like watching the match?' Jacky asked, his voice stilted.

'Oh, no. The game was boring. But I liked watching you, Jacky. You're so fast.'

Jacky was flattered and wanted the conversation with Mabel to flow, but it was difficult for him to know what to say. It wasn't the nervous butterflies of initial attraction that Jacky felt. He didn't feel like that. No, it was that Mabel intimidated Jacky. She was too self-assured.

'I'll let you walk me home, Jacky,' said Mabel.

Mabel's home was somewhat out of the way, and it would have been much quicker for Jacky to head straight home. He was tired, but he did not feel he had an option; it was more of a command than a request. Mabel continued to compliment Jacky, and he tried to respond with the replies he thought she would want to hear. A couple of streets away from Mabel's home, she insisted she could walk the rest of the way alone. And then Jacky realised why she chose this place to say goodbye to Jacky. It was away from the prying eyes of the neighbours. Mabel took hold of Jacky's hands and pecked him lightly on the cheek, and without another word ran off home, leaving Jacky feeling shell-shocked and wanting more. Mabel had him hooked.

Jacky could not get thoughts of Mabel out of his head as he lay in his bed that night. Part of him hoped he never saw Mabel again. He was not used to girls being so forward and had a feeling that things would only lead to trouble. Another part of him longed to see her again, and as soon as possible. She was a very attractive young woman, and Jacky felt a physical desire towards her that he had never experienced before. The following day Jacky went to the newsagents, in the guise of buying a newspaper. To Jacky's disappointment Mabel was not in the shop, but as he spoke to her mother as he was counting out his money, Mabel appeared from the back room.

'Hello, Jacky,' she smiled — all sweetness.

'Hello Mabel,' said Jacky, not knowing what to say to her with her mother present.

Jacky left the shop, paper in hand, and slowly walked back towards his home. It was not long before he heard footsteps hurrying behind him. When he turned he saw Mabel approaching.

'I was hoping you might come in the shop today,' said Mabel. Her manner had changed completely, now she was out of sight of her mother.

'Aye, I was wondering if you'd like to walk out with me sometime today? said Jacky, his loins, not his head, controlling his words.

Jacky started seeing Mabel on a regular basis. Mabel was very demanding of Jacky's attention and yet seemed slightly irritated by him. One minute she would be praising him and boosting his ego, the next she would be belittling him and making him feel a fool. She would talk him into buying things for her, and Jacky found his money never lasted very long if Mabel had anything to do with it. But he liked buying her things. He did not have much regular money as he had to give the little he earned straight to his mother, and she would give him a pittance in pocket money. And that was something else Mabel was not happy with; Jacky was still working on the surface of the pit and was in no hurry to go below underground, but Mabel made him feel unambitious and cowardly. According to Mabel, real men went down the pit and worked at the coal face. And Mabel was a tease. She would reveal her cleavage and give Jacky a glimpse of her stockinged legs, but they were strictly out of bounds. Jacky was not in love with Mabel; he was not even sure if he liked her, but she had a hold over him. The one thing Mabel did not try to control was the amount of time Jacky spent playing sport. He played handball in the summer and football for the rest of the year. Mabel knew that to try and put a stop to that would be foolish. And besides — the money he made in winnings meant he could buy her things her friends did not have.

Mabel continued to tease Jacky about working on the surface of the pit rather than underground, and so when the opportunity arose for Jacky to become a putter, he took it. He would now be going back to the depths of the mine moving coal tubs. He was reluctant to go back underground, but the pay was better, and he did not want to appear cowardly. Jacky sometimes worked in the same part of the pit as Micky. Micky and his workmates were hewers who extracted the coal from the coal face. Jacky and the other putters shovelled it into tubs and moved the tubs to the bottom of the shaft. It was hard work, and Jacky hated the stench and darkness that surrounded him all day, every day. Jacky and the other miners passed the time talking about football or handball, but always keeping one ear open to the slight creeks and groans of the pit. It was like a sleeping monster. The sounds emitting from the belly of the earth were generally familiar and constant, but if an unusual noise resonated from the dark depths of the mine, the workers would be on full alert. Rock falls, gases and water could engulf them at any time. Hewers were paid by the amount of coal they produced. On occasions the seam was more copious than expected, and the amount of coal extracted would exceed expectations, but at other times the walls would suddenly become thin or barren, and the miners knew their wages would be low. It was difficult having to depend on an unknown quantity, over which they had no control.

Jacky and Micky were fortunate that their wages were often subsidised by the money they made playing handball. This was only during the summer months, as they concentrated on football the rest of the year, but Micky was canny enough to put his away for harder times. The only time he had been reckless with his money was the time he bought Meg the ornate rose gold ring he had given her on their wedding day. Jacky, however, was not as shrewd. If he had money, it would burn a hole in his pocket. He spent money on Mabel to keep her sweet, but he also liked to go the rabbit stakes on a Sunday and bet on the dogs. If Mabel knew he was gambling she would be furious, but she was always happy when Jacky bought her nice things when he'd had a win.

Chapter 23

Soon, Meg was expecting another baby. She was fraught with worry following her last pregnancy. Her belly soon swelled, and she felt the baby kicking inside her.

'Mam, what if this one comes early as well? What if I've got something wrong with me that I can't carry a bairn?' said Meg.

'I'm sure everything will be fine, Pet. Like I've said to you before, hope for the best but prepare for the worst. We never know what life will throw at us, so we have to be ready to face anything, but we can't live our lives continually thinking bad things are going to happen; we have to hope and pray that everything will work out for the best.'

In June, Meg gave birth to another healthy son who they named Tucker. When he was a couple of months old, Micky wanted to take him to see his mother.

'Come with us, Meg. She's come around to the idea, by now,' said Micky.

'I'm not setting foot in her house unless I'm invited, Micky. I want to know I'm welcome.'

Micky took William to his mother's house. He had started taking the boy on a regular basis.

'I'd like you to meet your other grandson, Mam; our Tucker.'

'Well, you can bring him here by all means,' said Elizabeth.

'He's a baby and I'm not pushing a pram like a woman.'

'Why can't his mother bring him round?' said Elizabeth.

Micky was unsure whether or not she had realised what she had implied.

'Meg would have to come in the house if she brought the baby, Mam. Would you be happy with that?'

'Well, I don't know about happy,' she said.

'But you would let her in?' said Micky.

'Aye, I'd let her in,' said Elizabeth.

This was a huge leap forward for Micky. He was inwardly delighted. He knew that if he brought Meg to the house, his mother would make her welcome. She was a proud woman and good manners were important to her.

'We'll bring the baby next Sunday, Mam.'

Meg had butterflies in her stomach, as she pushed the pram to Sacriston — her husband at her side.

'Are you sure she doesn't mind me coming, Micky?' she said.

'How many times do I have to tell you, flower? You've got nothing to worry about. And besides — if she starts, we'll be straight out the door.'

'So there's a chance she might start? Oh, Micky. Do we have to go?'

'She won't start. Howay, stop fretting.'

Micky put his arm round Meg's shoulders in a reassuring hug. William ran ahead — his tiny feet kicking at anything that lay on the path.

'Mind you don't scuff your shoes, young man,' called Meg, glad of the distraction.

When they arrived at Elizabeth's home they left the pram in the back yard and knocked and entered through the back door.

'Mam, hello,' called Micky.

Elizabeth was in her Sunday best. Her face was stern, but her voice was pleasant.

'Hello, Micky, Meg. Come on in,' she said. 'I'll make some tea.'

'This is our Tucker,' said Micky, pulling down the blanket from the baby's face.

Meg held Tucker so that Elizabeth could see him.

'He's a lovely baby. A proper Mordue,' said Elizabeth, stroking his cheek with her finger.

She went to her purse and pulled out a coin which she placed in Tucker's tiny hand.

'Come and sit down,' said Elizabeth.

Jacky, Dan and Joseph were in the front kitchen, looking at a newspaper and discussing football. Meg had never met Dan before but knew Jacky very well. Dan stood and offered Meg his chair; a rather worn and well-used wooden armchair. They tried to make her feel welcome, as they knew how much it meant to Micky. Jacky was very fond of Meg and had beseeched Dan to welcome her into the home — not just for Micky's sake. Meg perched on the edge of the seat holding Tucker. She could not stop herself from looking around the room, taking in the décor and ornaments. The room was immaculate. Although the furniture was old, it was of good quality and fitted well in the room. In the corner stood a large grandfather clock marking time. There was a glass cabinet containing a collection of crockery and ornaments at one side of the room, and on one of the shelves were a couple of books. Meg had never seen books in a home before. She tried to read the titles, but they were out of view, but one looked like a bible. There was not a thing out of place; no toys or playing cards piled in a corner, or clippy mats on the go.

Elizabeth entered the room, carrying a tray with a china teapot and six cups and saucers. She poured the tea and handed a cup and saucer to Meg. Meg's hands were trembling, and the cup rattled in the saucer as she took hold of it.

'Thank you, Mrs. Crossley,' she said, her voice barely audible.

The men chatted, and William tottered around the room. Meg was terrified that he would touch something he should not and was pre-occupied with trying to control him. She quickly drank her tea and made motions to Micky that it might be time for them to leave. Micky was too busy talking to Joseph, Dan and Jacky, and Meg was forced into making polite conversation with Elizabeth. At first Elizabeth was short and reserved, but as Meg chatted and complimented her she began to warm to Meg.

'It is a lovely tea set you have, Mrs. Crossley, and that was a lovely cup of tea,' said Meg.

'It was my mother's. It's been in the family a long time,' said Elizabeth.

Just then William leapt up and knocked the cup and saucer Meg held.

'William!' she shrieked.

Elizabeth's face was a picture of horror. The noise woke baby Tucker, and he let out a yell. William started crying and ran to his father's side. The cup toppled off the saucer, but thankfully it was empty. Everyone stared as the cup fell through the air. Luckily it landed on the mat and remained in one piece. Jacky leapt to Meg's side and picked up the cup and took the saucer from Meg's hand.

'No harm done,' he said.

Meg was a bundle of nerves.

'I think we should be heading off now,' said Micky, trying to pacify William.

Meg could not get out quickly enough. Tucker and William were bawling. Meg felt that what had been a successful visit had turned into a disaster. She laid Tucker in the pram outside the back door and they hurried out of the back yard.

'Well that went well!' said Micky wryly.

'Oh, Micky. I knew I shouldn't have gone there,' said Meg.

'It wasn't your fault, Meg. Mam's got enough grandchildren to know what they're like.'

'She'll never let me back in the house,' said Meg.

'She will. The cup didn't break — and even if it had it's just a cup.'

At least the ice had been broken.

Chapter 24

At the start of the 1906/07 football season, Spennymoor United were up against Bishop Auckland. Spennymoor wanted a good start and to be part of the chase for the amateur Northern League title. The rain kept off, but the skies were threatening as the game kicked off. Jacky, Micky and Jimmy were all playing. They had travelled the nine miles to the ground and were looking forward to the challenging game ahead. Jacky and Micky always had a bet as to who would score most goals in a season, and Micky had always won. This season Jacky was determined to beat his brother, but both brothers were team players and would not try and increase their personal tallies to the detriment of the side.

Play started at a fast pace, but Bishop Auckland were away from home and played a cagey game; keeping their defence tight and difficult to penetrate. Jacky and Micky both made some blinding runs down the wings only to have their final crosses headed away by the Bishop Auckland defence, but the brothers outclassed the other players. Micky felt frustrated with the lack of shots on target and the inability of the Spennymoor middlemen to get their heads or feet to the end of the crosses he and Jacky continued to supply. Seeing an opening, he cut inside the Bishop Auckland defender — using his pace to find space. He continued his run — weaving through players before having a crack at the ball. He hit it low and hard past the remaining defender and to the far side of the goal — out of reach of their keeper. The ball ended up in the back of the net. 1 – 0. Jacky was the first to congratulate his brother. This changed the dimension of the game, as Bishop Auckland now needed to score. As they attempted to attack the Spennymoor goal, they left gaps in their defence which Micky and Jacky were able to exploit. The crosses kept coming in, and it was not long before United scored again. Jacky and Micky both found the back of the net with darting runs that left the defence lumbering in their wake. 4 – 0 the final score. A terrific win for Spennymoor, and the perfect start to the season. There had been talk of scouts being at the match, but that had not been on the brother's minds as they concentrated on the game, eager to add to their goal tally.

The Barnsley scout had been very impressed with the brothers — especially Micky, and was in conversation with his associate.

'What's their background? Miners? Families?'

'Aye. The elder one has a wife and two bairns. Works at Sacriston Colliery'.

'And the younger one?'

'Still lives at home in Sacriston. Also works at Sacriston pit.'

'We'll go for the younger one; shame about the older one — great player — even better than his brother, but we can't think of taking on a lad with that much encumbrance.'

Jacky and Micky were informed of the presence of the scout, but nobody said anything that day. The following week Spennymoor were away to Stockton, and the brothers travelled twenty-five miles to the match. The scout turned up at Stockton, accompanied by an official from Barnsley Football Club. They watched the Mordue brothers play with their usual skill — standing out from the rest of the players. Stockton was a good team, but Spennymoor managed a 2 – 2 draw, with Micky and Jacky putting in some great runs and crosses. Towards the end of the match, the two Barnsley men approached the Spennymoor manager and asked for a meeting with Jacky. After the final whistle they called Jacky over, and the four men chatted for some time. Micky and some of the other players waited patiently for Jacky, curious to know what was being said. After some handshakes and nodding heads, Jacky left the men, all smiles, and approached Micky and the other lads.

'What was that all about?' asked Micky.

'Micky, they want me to sign up with Barnsley.'

'What, playing professionally?'

'Aye ,playing in the second division.'

'Is that what you want to do?' asked Micky, already knowing the answer.

'Imagine that! Getting paid for playing football. I can't believe it. But why did they pick me and not you Micky?'

'You're a great player, Jacky.'

'You're better.'

'It's probably just that they see something in you that they don't in me Jacky,' said Micky, but he had an idea he knew the real reason he had not been selected.

'Well, I don't know about that. But Jacky, you will have to move to Barnsley, and they'll have to set you up with somewhere to live. They wouldn't want to be doing that for a man with a wife and family, unless he had already proved himself as a professional,' said Jimmy.

'Is that why? Oh, I'm sorry, Micky,' said Jacky, caught between elation and pity.

Jacky thought for a while. 'What about, Mam? She'll have to give her permission. She's never going to let me go to Barnsley.'

'You never know with Mam. But what about Mabel? She won't be happy to see you go.' said Micky, hoping that Jacky wouldn't base any life-changing decisions around Mabel. He could not understand what Jacky saw in her.

'Oh, Mabel. Well, she won't be able to stop me, and she won't be able to follow me there.'

'Sounds like you'd be glad to get away from her, Jacky.'

Jacky returned home, and although he had planned to choose his moment to mention the offer to his mother, he just blurted it out as soon as he saw her.

'Mam, I've had an offer from Barnsley Football Club; they want me to join the team,' said Jacky, hardly able to suppress his excitement. Jacky knew he would need his mother's permission before he could leave the family home, with his father dead, and Joseph getting older, and all but one of his brothers having left home — his mother relied on Jacky's income.

'That would mean you'd have to move wouldn't it, Jacky?'

'Aye, Mam. I'd be on a wage; not a lot, but enough to live on.'

'You'd have to give up your steady job at the pit to play football?'

'Mam, when I play football or handball I am the happiest man alive. I know I won't be on much of a wage, but I don't have a family to support, so I'll get by.'

'What about us, Jacky? Aren't we your family?'

'Why aye, you know what I mean, Mother.'

Elizabeth turned her back on Jacky and pottered around by the range — banging pots and pans. Just then Dan returned from the pub. News travelled fast around the villages.

'Jacky, man! What's this I hear about Barnsley being after you?'

Jacky threw a sideways glance at his mother before replying in an almost apologetic tone.

'Aye, they want me to start this season with them. I'd be on a wage and I'd have to move to Barnsley'.

'That's champion, lad. Eeh! Who'd have thought a man could make a living out of playing a game that he loves. So when are you going?

Their mother turned swiftly and spoke vehemently to Dan.

'That's right, you encourage the lad! Whoever heard of a man giving up a steady job and going off playing football? He's not a bairn any more. What about the time he gets too old to kick a ball about? What about the time he meets a lass and wants to have a family? How's his wife going to feel being married to a man that plays football for a living? Whoever heard of such nonsense?'

The anger was growing inside Dan. He bit his tongue, but he never raised his voice to his mother. Turning to Jacky, his voice was sombre and steady.

'There was another accident at the pit today; nobody was killed, but two men had a lucky escape. One of them was the Barton lad. That could have been any one of us down there. Every day we go down ,not knowing if we'll come out alive; come winter we never see the light of day from week to week; any amount of men have trouble with their chests after breathing in the coal dust, year after year. Now, Jacky, if you've got the chance of getting away from all that and get paid for doing something you love, well, I'll be buggered if I'm going to get in your way. How about you, Mother?'

Elizabeth glared at her son ,banged the kettle down on the range, and strode out of the room.

'Thanks, Dan,' Jacky whispered, not wanting their mother to hear.

'Mam's got to give you the nod Jacky, but don't you worry — you leave her to me.'

Dan never stood up to his mother; he was always there for his mother, and she knew that Dan would never leave her. But he also knew how much football meant to Jacky and felt excited for him at having the opportunity to move away from the dangers and hardship that epitomized a mining village. Even though Dan had decided to remain a bachelor and support his mother, he knew it was his mother who ultimately had the final word in any situation, and Dan was happy for that to be the case, but he did not want to see Jacky miss this incredible opportunity.

'It's not just Mam, Dan. What about Micky? It should have been him they took; he's a better player than me.'

'Our Micky has made his own choices, Jacky. He's got Meg and the bairns, and no football club would want to take on a lad with a family in tow. They chose you Jacky — not our Micky. They must have seen what a good player you are, and you'll get better, man. Micky will want what's best for you; you know that.

'Do you think I should go to Barnsley, Dan?'

'It's your decision Jacky, but I think you know what you want to do.'

'I know what I want to do, but I don't know what I should do.'

'You are young; you haven't got a wife and children to worry about, and mother is not your responsibility.'

'I've dreamt of this moment for a long time — especially since my first day working at the pit.'

'Well, your dream is about to come true, Jacky, and anyone who knows you will be pleased for you and not resent you for it.'

'But I feel so bad about Micky.'

'Have you had a word with him?'

'Aye, he knows I've had the offer, but he doesn't know I'm going to take it. What shall I say to him?'

'You'll know what to say when you see him. He'd rather you said something than avoided him and said nout.'

'Aye, Dan, you're right. I'll go and see him now.'

And with that Jacky left the house and made his way along the track towards Kimblesworth. Jacky found Micky at the wall — hitting a ball. It was not often that Jacky saw Micky strike the ball with such vehemence.

'Hey, Micky!' Jacky called, but Micky was oblivious to anything around him.

Jacky walked over and jumping, caught the ball. Micky had not seen him and was taken by surprise.

'Jacky! Just thinking about you. Have you had a word with Mam about the Barnsley move?' Micky did not look Jacky in the eye. He was pleased for his brother but found it hard to hide his disappointment.

'Mam's not happy about it, but Dan's behind me and is working on Mother. What about you Micky? How do you feel about it?'

'I'm pleased for you, Jacky. I really am.'

'But, Micky, they should have taken you. You know you're better than I am.'

'We both know why they didn't take me. I've got Meg and the bairns. They mean more to me than the football. I couldn't afford to keep them on a footballer's wage. You're a good player, Jacky, and you'll get better. Now don't worry about me. Get away from the pit and get paid for doing something you love.'

'We'll still be the best handball pair in the world, won't we Micky?'

'Aye. No one's going to be beating us for a while yet,' Micky said, taking the ball from Jacky and hitting it against the wall. 'Come on then — let's knock around while we can.'

Jacky smiled at his brother, but his happiness and excitement at the prospect of playing football full time were marred by the sadness he felt at having to leave Micky. And knowing that his brother could outplay him made him feel he was undeserving of the opportunity he had been given. They were soon lost in their game of handball — both trying to enjoy the time they were spending with each other, without thinking of their imminent parting.

'Have you told, Mabel?' Micky asked. 'You'll have to tell her yourself.'

Jacky was dreading telling Mabel. He hoped he could just slip away to Barnsley without her knowing but knew that wasn't going to happen.

'Well, I'm off home, Jacky. I'm pleased for you — really pleased. '

Jacky continued to hit the ball around the court, a spring in his step, as Micky trudged away.

Micky walked into the backyard and found Meg taking nappies off the washing line. Without a word he walked over to her and held her in his arms in a long embrace.

'What's that for?' said Meg softly.

'You mean more to me than anything. And never forget that,' said Micky burying his face in Meg's neck.

When Jacky returned home, his mother served up a bowl of broth to Jacky and Dan and they sat at the kitchen table, tearing pieces of bread from the loaf and dipping it into the hot liquid. Jacky was anxious to know if his mother had thought any more about his impending career move but did not want to rile her by appearing impatient. Thankfully, it was Dan who brought up the subject.

'Mother and I have been talking about your offer, Jacky,' said Dan.

There was a long pause as Jacky waited anxiously for Dan to continue. Why couldn't he just come out with it instead of torturing Jacky like this? Dan slurped his broth and methodically stirred the contents of his bowl. The suspense was torturous.

'Mother has decided to give you her permission to accept Barnsley's offer,' said Dan solemnly.

Jacky looked at his mother and saw the pained expression on her face. Her lips were shut tight and she concentrated on busying herself in the kitchen. Jacky wanted to cheer and leap around the room, but he knew he must respect his mother's feelings.

'That's champion. Thank you, Mother,' said Jacky.

He looked at Dan and they smiled knowingly at each other — careful that their mother did not witness their delight.

Chapter 25

The following day, Jacky reluctantly decided to visit Mabel and break the news to her. He had not got far when he saw her approaching. He should have seen her as a vision of beauty; she was wearing a pretty dress and her soft, flowing hair was framing her beautiful face. But by now Jacky saw past the dazzling exterior, and the sight of Mabel made him despondent. His stomach clenched, and he forced a smile.

'You seem happy, Jacky. And I intend to make you even happier,' she said.

'Oh, Mabel. I was just on my way to see you,' said Jacky.

'Well, that's a bit of luck. Come on, let's go back to my house. There's something I want to show you.'

Mabel took Jacky by the hand and led him to her home. She lived in a flat above the shop with wooden stairs at the side of the building. Jacky had only been to her home on a few occasions, when her parents were home.

'Me father's gone to Durham to make a collection, and Mam's working in the shop,' she said, closing the door behind them. Sit down. Would you like a drink?'

Jacky was shaking. 'A cup of tea would be nice.'

But Mabel ignored him and headed for the sideboard and brought out a bottle of whisky.

'A proper drink, Jacky,' she said, pouring the amber liquid into two glasses. She handed one to Jacky.

'Cheers!' she said, clinking her glass against his before tipping its contents down her throat in one go.

'Your go,' she said, wiping her lips.

Jacky was not a whisky drinker but did as she instructed. The liquid burnt his throat, and he coughed violently. Mabel laughed. She sat on the settee next to Jacky and exposed even more of her stockings than usual. She took Jacky's hand and placed it on her thigh. Jacky, having just recovered from his coughing fit, felt completely uncomfortable. His mouth was dry, and he was coming out in a cold sweat. He knew his hand was clammy against Mabel's leg. Mabel put her hand on his chest and started unbuttoning his shirt. Jacky flinched.

'What's the matter, Jacky? You've waited a long time for this,' Mabel whispered, putting her lips on Jacky's mouth.

Jacky was in a panic. He should be feeling happy and aroused, caught up in the moment of passion and love, but he felt tense. He did not want to move his hand up Mabel's thigh; he wanted to take his hand off her leg and put it in his pocket. He did not want his lips to melt onto hers; he wanted to shut them tight. He did not want Mabel to touch his chest with her silky soft hands; he wanted to do up his jacket. What was wrong with him? He did not want to offend Mabel. She was a very attractive lass, but this did not feel right. Mabel had him wrapped around her little finger for months now, and he had gone along with it, but this was different. He was a man. Would it make him more or less of a man if he stopped her advances and walked away? Or would it make him more or less of a man if he succumbed to her and had it away with her? Jacky's head was spinning, and it was not just the whisky. He pushed her hand away and stood up.

'I'm sorry, Mabel, but this isn't right. You're a bonny lass, but I've got to go,' said Jacky.

'But, Jacky. I thought you loved me,' said Mabel, appealingly.

'I'm going to Barnsley, Mabel. I'm leaving Sacriston.'

'But you can't, Jacky. You can't just go. What about me, Jacky?'

Jacky could suddenly see that that was what it had always been about; about Mabel. She had used Jacky and he had let her. He felt quite repulsed by her; exposing her body trying to catch her prey. She did not care about Jacky and he could see that now.

'I'm going, Mabel,' he said ,and buttoning up his shirt, he left. He shut the door and was walking down the stairs when Mabel opened the door — clutching the top of her dress and straightening her skirts.

'And don't you dare come near me again. You're disgusting. You filthy bugger,' she screamed after him, pretending to burst into tears.

There were plenty of people in the street who witnessed the event and jumped to the wrong conclusion — as Mabel had hoped they would. Tongues wagged and gossip spread; events being fabricated and exaggerated. Jacky kept his head down and walked home as quickly as he could. He was dazed from the experience and felt angry and confused. He did not care what people thought — he knew he had done nothing wrong. He was relieved that he had escaped the web Mabel had been weaving; he had good reason to have nothing more to do with her. Now he wanted to go home and forget the whole thing.

Jacky was on the early shift the next day and tried his best to concentrate on his work. A lapse in concentration when dealing with tonnes of coal could prove catastrophic, but all he kept thinking about was Mabel. Why had he been such a fool and let her into his life? How could she be so manipulative? Why didn't he just bed her? He may as well have done as everyone thought he had done a lot worse. His workmates knew something was wrong, but Jacky just made out that he was feeling unwell. He could not open up to anyone. Maybe he would find Micky and have a word with him when his shift finished? But Jacky hoped that by not saying anything the whole thing would go away. Speaking about things makes them real. When Jacky returned home from his shift that evening his mother welcomed him with a face like thunder.

'Have you got something to tell me, Jacky?' she said. Her calm, even tones belied her portentous appearance. Jacky was hoping his mother might be referring to something else. Maybe he had left dirty footprints on her clean step, or maybe she had found out he'd been betting on the dogs.

'No. What have I done?' said Jacky looking guilty.

'Mabel Turner. I hear you've… well…I can't say what I heard, but it's not something I would expect from any of my sons, or any decent man.'

Jacky had bottled up his emotions, and although he had not wanted his mother to know about the incident with Mabel, he could not accept any blame. He was being treated unfairly; how could his mother even give credence to such false claims? Jacky was angry with his mother now as well as with Mabel and all the other loose-tongued women who revelled in spreading lies. Jacky blurted everything out; anger and distress erupting from within him.

'She tricked me, Mam. I didn't lay a finger on her. She's lying. How could you believe it of me? What do you take me for? Mabel Turner is a witch. She's the one that took me up to her room and couldn't wait to get her drawers off. But she didn't, because I got out before she had the chance. She's not right in the head — she's crackers, and that's why I got out of there. But then she goes shouting after me — making out it was me. I didn't do anything, Mam. I promise.'

Jacky broke down in tears. His mother just looked at him. She had not seen him cry since he was a small boy. There was no conciliatory hug. But she believed Jacky. Mabel was known for being a bad lass. And her Jacky was a good lad.

'Get in the tub before the water gets cold,' she said and turned to stir the stew that was on the range.

The following day, unbeknown to Jacky, Elizabeth had gone to the sweet shop where Mabel and her mother were working. After that, Mabel changed her story. Who would have really believed Mabel Turner? Most people when there was a scurrilous story to pass on. Even when the source is unreliable, a scandal becomes fact as the wagging tongues and eager ears are desperate for a drama to break the monotony of their daily lives. There had been enough real drama in the Mordue family; Elizabeth ensured fictitious events were not added to this.

Jacky called in to see Micky and Meg.

'I hear you're not seeing Mabel anymore, Jacky,' said Meg.

'No,' said Jacky. 'Thank God. I don't know what she was playing at.'

'I can guess,' said Meg. 'If you give her a bairn then you'd have to marry her and take her with you to Barnsley.'

'They wouldn't take me if I had a wife and a bairn.'

'Then, you'd have had to stay here —with Mabel, and carry on down the pit.'

Jacky knew that Meg was right. Mabel would have ended Jacky's football career before it had even started. He despised her. He had had a lucky escape.

It was a few weeks before Jacky was to start at Barnsley, and in that time he played the biggest singles handball game of his life to date. He had to beat Mo Anderson, a Sunderland lad, to become

Champion Handball player. The crowd was huge. Bookies set themselves up in the local pub, employing runners to take bets on the outcome of the match. Public interest was high as this could be the first time a player was both singles and doubles champion concurrently. Micky stood at Jacky's side giving him support and helping him prepare for the game. Mo Anderson was a great player. He was older than Jacky and taller and stronger. He just seemed to stretch out an arm and a leg and he would cover the court easily.

Jacky was now nineteen and was as fast as any man — with seemingly endless endurance. He was not tall, and he was still not as strong as Micky (but then few men were), but he knew that he could run like the wind, and keep on running. Jacky's hands were hard from the years he had played the game; the skin on his palm thick and rough as if he were wearing a glove — as were Anderson's. Jacky knew that if he was to have a chance against Anderson, he needed to play the game at a fast pace and outrun his opponent. As soon as the game started Jacky was running around the court like a whippet — not allowing Anderson to slow the game down. Anderson's loyal supporters were encouraging him and trying to get behind their man, but from the start it looked as if there would only be one winner: Jacky. Jacky did not let up at all as he stretched his lead; he was single-mindedly determined to win this game, and that was all he was focussing on. He wanted to keep the momentum going and finish the job. The ball ricocheted around the court at such speed, it was difficult for the crowd to track it, but not for Jacky. There was hardly a shot that he did not reach — not only returning the ball, but also placing it; making it difficult for Anderson to return. Jacky's supporters were cheering every shot, which inspired Jacky all the more. He was brilliant. Jacky won the game easily, and the cheers reverberated around the wall and the town. Jacky Mordue was both singles and doubles handball champion.

Jacky continued to work at the pit until the week before his move to Barnsley. He gave his wages to his mother and promised to send her any money he could, but a footballer's wages were poor, and Jacky would have to pay board and lodgings in Barnsley. He had a single suitcase containing his belongings with his football boots carefully packed inside. Dan, Jimmy and Micky were going to accompany him to the railway station, but Elizabeth said her farewells at their home. She had always been overprotective of her youngest son and found it hard to accept that he was now moving away and would be all alone.

'Who would have thought you'd be going over a hundred miles away from us?' she cried.

'Mother, it's no time at all on the train. I'm sure I'll be back regularly,' said Jacky, trying to reassure her.

He did not share her melancholy and did his best at hiding his excitement at leaving and starting his new life. 'I'll write as soon as I can.'

Elizabeth wiped her eyes and hugged her son in an unusual show of affection.

'Gan canny, lad,' she said.

And with that Jacky left the home and neighbourhood he loved. It was unusual for a man to leave the village, other than to work in a pit in a different village, so as he left, suitcase in hand, neighbours stood on their doorsteps wishing him well, or peered from behind curtains.

Chapter 26

As the train approached, steam filling the air, Jacky said his goodbyes to his brothers. He got into the train carriage and placed his suitcase on the luggage rack. His head was swimming with emotions. He was sad to be leaving his family and friends and worried that he would not be good enough to fulfil the expectations of Barnsley football club, but more than that, as the train left the grey buildings and trundled off into the countryside, steam bellowing and whistle blowing, Jacky felt thrilled at the prospect of becoming a professional football player. It was beyond his wildest dreams, and he could or would not believe it until he had played his first match and had his pay packet in his hand.

Micky missed Jacky, but his life was so busy with work, football and his family that he did not have time to dwell on it. A colliery house came up for Micky and Meg in Sacriston, which they were eager to move into, as Meg was now expecting another child. Although there were already four of them sleeping in the tiny box room of the Coatman's home, it was not so much the overcrowding that made Micky and Meg want to leave, but the chance of having a place of their own — although they knew they would probably have to take in lodgers to make ends meet, as Meg had to stay at home and look after the children and run a household.

'You know you can stay here, Pet,' said Mrs. Coatman. She knew the house that Meg and Micky had been given was old. It should be demolished — not lived in.

'I know, Mam. But it's not fair on you and Da to sleep on that uncomfortable put-you-up; I know it's not helping Dad's bad back. Micky and me need to have a place of our own. And it's nearer Sacriston Colliery, so Micky won't have as far to go to work. We appreciate you having us here, Mam, but it's time for us to go.'

They piled the few belongings they had onto a cart and made the short trip from Kimblesworth to Sacriston. They knew the house they had been allocated was old and not in the best part of Sacriston, but they were not prepared for the living conditions in which they found themselves. The house was dark and dingy and smelt of damp. The first time it rained water poured through the upstairs ceiling. The windows rattled and were very small, making it feel as if it was permanently night-time. Micky and Meg tried to stay positive and did their best to smarten up the house. Micky attempted to fix the roof — he knew that trying to get the owners to do the job would be fruitless — but he could not afford the materials needed. Meg scrubbed every wall, ceiling and floor with the help of her younger sister, Martha. The range was inefficient, and the nearest water tap was a long walk down a muddy track. The communal middens were in disrepair and reeked. There were two bedrooms and one room downstairs, which functioned as the kitchen, dining room and living room. Once Micky and Meg had done all they could to make their house a home, they took in two lodgers who shared the tiny box room. They were an older man and his son who had recently moved to Sacriston looking for work; their wife/mother having died. The money they paid helped pay the bills, but Meg found it hard looking after three pitmen and her two young sons with another baby on the way. Such a situation was commonplace in the village. Meg did not look at her neighbours with envy or malice. Every family in the community lived in similar conditions, and there were a lot worse off than the Mordues. There was always the threat of the workhouse for those whose husbands could no longer work or had died. Everyone pulled together helping where they could. Micky's life was full; working, playing football and handball, trying to earn some extra money, and then spending the small amount of spare time he had with Meg and the boys. But Meg's time was spent cleaning, cooking, collecting water, shopping, feeding her youngsters and washing and drying the constant flow of coal-covered clothes and dirty nappies. She woke early and went to bed late. In the evenings she sat and darned socks or mended clothes or set to work on a clippy mat that would always be on the go. The times when she would escape to the outdoors and meet Micky for their secret rendezvous seemed an age away. Meg looked forward to night times with Micky; wrapped in his arms. With his warm breath on her face, her fatigued body relaxed into a much-needed slumber.

Chapter 27

Jacky was apprehensive as he alighted the train at Barnsley. He had directions to the house where he would be staying, which was not far from the railway station and even nearer to Oakwell — Barnsley's football ground. There were another couple of Barnsley players living at the house, and Jacky soon struck up a friendship with the other lads. The Barnsley manager, Arthur Fairclough, was a stern but fair man. He was good at his job and ensured he got the best out of his players.

Barnsley had been on a losing streak when Jacky joined the team. They had lost four consecutive games and were finding it difficult to score a goal. Jacky's debut was away at Lincoln. Jacky had never travelled as far south before. Prior to joining Barnsley, he had not been outside the north-eastern corner of England. He was filled with nervous excitement as he prepared to run onto the pitch, surrounded by a team of men he had only just met. As the game progressed, Jacky knew he was not making any impact on the game. He misread his teammates' play and squandered the chances that did come his way. At half time the manager said some encouraging words to Jacky, and he settled into the game. However the team failed to score and lost the match 1 – 0. Heads were down on the train journey back to Barnsley, but Fairclough was full of optimism and lifted his team's spirits, pointing out the positives from the game. The next game was at home to Burton United. Fairclough's positivity transferred to the players. Jacky felt confident as the game kicked off. The players pulled together and played as a team. Jacky scored his first goal for the club, and the game ended 6 – 1 to Barnsley. This was a turning point for the team, and Jacky's time at Barnsley was a successful one. He made twenty-five appearances for the club, scoring 12 times. Jacky absolutely loved his new job, playing football and getting paid for it. He would never complain about anything to do with his new life for it did not compare to life at the pit. It was a joy to be clean and not constantly coated with coal dust. The men he played with were good company. There had been a lot more banter and crack at the pit, but there had to be otherwise the miners would have been driven to despair working in a black hole day in, day out. Football was a joy in itself, and the jokes and chat between the players were just an added bonus.

Jacky travelled with Barnsley up and down the country. The furthest games were against Clapton Orient and Chelsea in London, but most of the teams were nearer — with Leeds nearby and many Midlands teams in the league. Jacky missed his family — especially his brother Micky, but he made many friends and kept in touch with his family, managing to get up to Sacriston occasionally, playing handball matches with Micky.

Early in 1907 Jacky was on one of his visits home.

'Mother, I've got some news,' he said, tentatively.

'What! What's happened?' asked Elizabeth, fearing the worst.

'I'm moving to London. Woolwich Arsenal want me.'

His mother sat down. 'London! You're moving down to London? There's all sorts live in London. You cannot be going there on your own, Jacky. Lord help you.'

'Mam, by all accounts London is a marvellous city, and Woolwich Arsenal are a fine team.'

'Aye, and they're in the first division. That will mean he'll be coming up to play Sunderland and Newcastle,' said Dan.

'And Middlesbrough. So you might even be able to get to see us play, Mam,' said Jacky, with a smile.

'You'll not get me inside a football ground,' said Elizabeth.

'So how come you're going to Woolwich Arsenal, Jacky?' asked Dan.

'Well, you'll never guess what they're paying for me. Four hundred and fifty pounds!'

'Never!' said Dan.

'Aye, four hundred and fifty pounds! They think I'm worth four hundred and fifty pounds. Not that I'll be seeing any of that.'

'Well, you're a great player, Jacky. And I expect Barnsley will be glad of the money.'

'Aye, I haven't got much of a choice, truth be told. Woolwich Arsenal want me, and Barnsley want the money.'

'Well, Jacky, you be careful. I'm not happy about you going to London, of all places,' said Elizabeth, still sitting, shaking her head.

Jacky called at Micky and Meg's home. He let himself in the back door. Meg looked very uncomfortable. She was seven months pregnant and trying to get the house ship-shape before the baby's arrival. Micky was reading his newspaper, and William and Tucker were play fighting.

'Reading about Barnsley's lightning-fast winger?' joked Jacky.

'Jacky!' Micky jumped up and shook his brother's hand, patting him on the back. The boys wrapped themselves around Jacky's legs.

'What are you doing home? I thought you weren't coming home until the end of the season?' said Micky.

Jacky told Micky of his imminent move to London.

'First division football! That's grand, Jacky.' Micky was genuinely pleased for Jacky. Despite his tough life, Micky would not have wanted to go all the way to London. He was happy being by Meg's side and with his sons.

'You'll have more travelling as well, Woolwich Arsenal being the only London team in the league.'

'Aye, I'll be up here a few times. You will come to the games won't you, Micky?'

'If I'm not working, try stopping me. Although I won't be cheering on the southerners. I hope you lose those games,' Micky laughed. 'Howay, you can buy me a pint at The Robin Hood. Leave Uncle Jacky alone now lads — we're off out. Be good for your Mam.'

And with that, Jacky and Micky set off to the pub together. Micky was keen to hear all about Jacky's life as a footballer. They called on their brother Jimmy, and he joined them.

'Jacky! Good to see you. Before we go there's someone I'd like you to meet,' said Jimmy.

The lads went in the house. Betty sat cuddling their new baby.

'Meet Jack, our new addition,' said Jimmy. 'Named after you.'

'Well, I never. That's champion,' said Jacky. 'That deserves a celebratory drink.'

The brothers went to the Robin Hood and had their celebratory drink…and then a few more pints.

Chapter 28

Jacky moved into a room in a house in Plumstead, within walking distance of the football ground. Two of his teammates stayed in the same lodgings as Jacky; Jim Ashfield the goalkeeper and Tim Coleman: Woolwich Arsenal's leading scorer and something of a celebrity. Jacky soon struck up a friendship with the men. Tim had lived in the house for four years, and Jim had lived there for seven years. Jim's wife Bertha and child, Agnes, also lived in the house — along with Kate, Bertha's sister, and a young woman called Mary-Ann. The house belonged to Mrs. Shoebridge. She was a widow and a dressmaker. Kate and Mary-Ann worked for Mrs. Shoebridge. It was a houseful, but Mrs. Shoebridge needed the money since her husband had died. Jim had been a lodger for a few years, and when he married Bertha, Mrs. Shoebridge agreed to let him stay and bring his new wife to the house as long, as she was prepared to take over the domestic chores. That allowed Mrs. Shoebridge to concentrate her efforts on her dressmaking business. Kate and Bertha had lived in Liverpool with their widowed mother. They had had to find work as soon as they could, as their mother could not afford to keep them. They needed to be the breadwinners of the family. Bertha and Jim had been sweethearts since childhood, and once Jim had established himself in Plumstead, he was able to marry Bertha, and she moved down from Liverpool. When Mrs. Shoebridge was looking to employ another dressmaker, Bertha suggested Kate, so she too moved from Liverpool to the house where Bertha lived. Kate paid rent and sent the remainder of her modest wages back to her mother.

Jacky could feel himself blush and become hot under the collar as Kate and Mary-Ann entered the room and approached the dinner table. Jacky was not used to spending time in the company of young ladies who were single and independent. All the lasses in Sacriston lived with their families or in the staff quarters of the homes where they served. Kate in particular caught Jacky's eye. She had chestnut hair pulled on top of her head in a bun and a splattering of freckles on her cheeks. He found her green eyes bewitching. But Jacky

remembered falling under the spell of another enchantress —
Mabel, and that had been an experience he did not want to repeat.

'Jacky, I haven't introduced you to my sister-in-law, Kate,' said
Jim, standing as the girls took their seats.

'Kate, this is Jacky. Jacky, Kate.'

Jacky stood up.

'And this is Mary-Ann,' said Jim introducing the other young
lady.

Jacky waited for them both to be seated before sitting back
down. His face was flushed and his mouth dry. Jacky tried to appear
calm and relaxed, but it was obvious to everyone that he was
flustered and nervous. He just was not used to this kind of situation.
The conversation flowed amongst the others, but Jacky stayed
unusually quiet and concentrated on his decorum. He may have
been brought up in a working-class home, but his mother had taught
all her offspring good manners, and Jacky did not show himself up.
When the meal was finished, and the women had cleared the dishes
from the table, Kate and Mary-Ann made their excuses and retired
to the room they shared. At last Jacky felt he could breathe once
more.

Jim had noticed how uncomfortable Jacky had been around the
girls and teased Jacky. He saw his younger self in this
inexperienced youth and felt protective towards him. Tim, on the
other hand, was confident and chatty. He had had his fair share of
harsh treatment by fans and the press but had always strived to
entertain. As with many professional footballers, Tim was working
class. There seemed to be a disparity between the way they were
treated compared to their teammates from more privileged
backgrounds. This riled Tim, and he often caused ruffles by
speaking his mind. Tim was also a showman. He felt that spectators
came to matches to be entertained, not watch their team grind out a
dull 1 – 0 victory. He had a spark in his play that was unique.

Jim took Jacky under his wing. He showed him the places he
should and should not go to around Plumstead. He kept an eye on
Jacky and ensured some of the more 'difficult' members of the club
treated him fairly. Jim enjoyed having the younger lads around, and
the three men soon became great friends. They worked and played
together. Tim was a joker and entertained the other two with his
antics. He also made the girls laugh and put everyone at ease when

they were together. Jacky settled into life in the south easier than he had expected, but he missed his hometown and his family. The Woolwich Arsenal manager, Phil Kelso, was a man who took the game very seriously and did not accept any nonsense from his players. He expected high standards from his team — on and off the pitch. The players were forbidden to smoke cigarettes or drink alcohol, something many of them found hard to adhere to. This did not worry Jacky. He liked a drink, but could take it or leave it. The same went for cigarettes. Jacky only got to play three games for Woolwich Arsenal in the league as the season was coming to a close, but there were some friendlies lined up which Jacky was excited about.

Kate liked Jacky, even though he was very quiet when she was around. She was friendly towards him and did not seem to mind when he became tongue-tied or flustered. Gradually, Jacky was able to relax around Kate and Mary-Ann, and when Jim suggested they all went to the local music hall together one Saturday evening, Jacky jumped at the chance.

'We'll have to pay for the lasses,' said Jim. 'Mrs. Shoebridge has offered to stay at home with Agnes just this once, so Bertha can get out.'

As soon as Kate and Mary-Ann returned home from work that day they headed to their room and began preparing for their night out. The girls had never been to a concert hall before. They giggled and chattered excitedly, as they dressed and did their hair. Jacky was nervous but looking forward to an evening with the girls. There were no such places in Sacriston, and Jacky was not sure what to expect. He hoped he did not make a fool of himself in front of Kate. And what if Kate was fonder of Tim than of him?

The concert hall was not the grandest place in London, but to Jacky it looked magnificent. Jacky and Tim paid for Mary-Ann and Kate, and they entered the huge building. They were ushered to a table, and the six friends sat eagerly awaiting the first act. Food and drinks were brought round.

'It's amazing,' said Kate looking around at the high ceilings and fine drapery.

'Aye, it's like running out onto the Manor Ground pitch,' said Jacky.

Jacky's nervousness soon disappeared as he was caught up in the atmosphere of his surroundings. Jacky hung onto Kate's every word, and Kate laughed at Jacky's quips. The music started, and attention was turned to the stage where a rotund, bald man sang a lively, comical song. The audience was there to have a good time, and the song was well-received. His performance was followed by various acts, including a magician, a comedian and various musicians and singers. The conversation flowed as the group recounted and enthused about the entertainment. Jacky could not remember having had such a good night.

Jacky and Tim grew closer, and they spent a lot of time together. They went to the public baths, and Tim taught Jacky how to swim. They hired slipper baths and were able to relax in the tubs, without family waiting to hop in their water before it became cold. Jacky had never taken a bath for his own pleasure; baths were something to get the coal dust off, and the water was usually already black, as Jacky had invariably taken his turn after his older brothers had bathed in the same water. Tim also helped Jacky with his game. He had been with the team for some time so knew the players quite well. He told Jacky about each of the players; their strengths and weaknesses and their demeanour. Jacky's role in the team was to make darting runs up the wing and cross the ball to the centre-forwards, which he did with speed and accuracy that had not been seen before at the club. However Jacky's performances were inconsistent. At times he felt homesick and his mood dipped. This was reflected in his play and on many occasions he did not perform to the best of his abilities. At other times, when he was in high spirits, he played out of his skin and won the respect of the fans. Jacky had joined the team in April, and after just one month the season was coming to a close. Woolwich Arsenal had some friendly matches lined up at the end of the season; Jacky and his teammates would be travelling abroad to Europe.

Back at their digs, the boarders had all finished their evening meal, and the women were collecting the dirty dishes.

'What are you doing over the summer, Jacky?' Jim asked.

'Well, I'll be going back home. I've got a few handball matches lined up, so hopefully I can make a bit of money while I'm there,' said Jacky.

Kate could not hide her disappointment. She had grown fond of Jacky. Even though they were not courting, they spent time together in the group. She thought Jacky had feelings towards her, but he seemed happy to be going back home — even though they would not see each other for some time. She made her excuses and left the room, Mary-Ann in quick pursuit.

'Looks like someone will be sad to see you go,' said Tim as the door closed.

Jacky was taken aback and felt the colour rush to his face. He was fond of Kate but had not thought anything of it. He had been swept along by all the dramatic changes that had taken place in his life in the last month. When he went to sleep at night, his thoughts were about football, and what he needed to do to fit into the team and ways he could improve his game. He found Kate attractive but thought she was just being friendly — the same as she was towards the other chaps. She had a kindly, fun-loving personality. After his disastrous relationship with Mabel, Jacky did not feel ready for another romance. And had tried to put thoughts of girls to the back of his mind.

'I...I...I didn't think...' stuttered Jacky.

'Lad! Are you daft? You can see she's got a thing for you; she goes all giggly when you're around,' said Jim.

'She's always giggly,' protested Jacky.

'And that sparkle in her eye,' said Tim.

'I wouldn't do anything I shouldn't,' said Jacky. 'I just didn't realise.'

'Don't worry, Jacky. She'll still be here when you get back,' said Jim.

'But what if she thinks I don't like her? She might meet someone else while I'm gone.'

'Well, if you go off and leave her what can you expect?' said Tim stirring things up.

'What should I do? I can't start courting her and then go off and leave her, and I can't stay here.'

'Looks like you're buggered, pal,' said Tim, grinning from ear to ear.

Later Tim, Jim and Jacky played dominoes, but Jacky's mind was on Kate. He had been attracted to Kate as soon as he had set eyes on her but had not thought to do anything about it; he had only known her a few weeks. Now he knew that Kate had feelings for him, he could not get her out of his mind. Jacky knew he was on a tight schedule. The last game of the season was on the Saturday, then the team had just three days before heading to Europe on a Football Friendlies tour. After that, Jacky had to head straight up north to Sacriston, as he had handball matches arranged, and all hell would break loose if he did not play. Plus the fact that there was money to be won and the world championship to retain. Not going back was out of the question.

On the last day of the season, at the end of April, Woolwich Arsenal beat Derby County — finishing a respectable seventh in the league. Derby County were relegated. Jacky had mixed emotions as the season ended. He was keen to return home and see his family and friends, and play handball all through the summer, but he had just settled into life in the south and would miss his teammates and the football matches. He would also miss his housemates and the independence he felt living away from his mother.

The friends had arranged to go to the music hall that evening. Jacky made up his mind that he would speak to Kate then, and explain the situation, but Kate seemed to avoid him that evening, and he did not get a chance to talk. He did not get an opportunity to talk to her on the Sunday either.

The following morning, the team left for Europe. Jacky had never travelled abroad before and was thrilled to be given the chance to see a bit of the world. The team set off on the train to Harwich, from where they boarded a passenger steamer to Belgium. Thankfully, the weather conditions were good, and they had a fairly smooth ride across the sea. Jacky felt his stomach turning at the movement of the waves but managed to take his mind off the nauseous feeling in his stomach by watching the waves rolling in the distance, and taking in the salty air and the smells and sounds of the steamer.

As the team disembarked and Jacky stood for the first time on foreign soil, he was surprised at how similar to England Belgium appeared. The buildings were a little different from those in England, but not drastically so. Trams ran along the streets, and horses and carts transported goods and people through the Belgian streets — much the same as in England. The people looked and dressed like people in London, but when they spoke the words that flowed from their mouths were nonsensical. Jacky found himself staring at a couple who were holding an animated conversation. Their expressions and gestures looked familiar, but the words were meaningless. Jacky was fascinated.

The team made their way to the railway station and took a train to Brussels. The scenery looked similar to England, with green fields spreading into the distance. The landscape was flat and unremarkable but kept Jacky's interest. The players joked and chatted — excited at the prospect of playing a team of foreign players who they knew so little about.

When they reached Brussels, the team checked into a hotel. It was not a grand hotel, but it was more luxurious than anywhere Jacky had stayed previously. Parts of the city were clean and spacious, with tree-lined avenues adding greenery to the ornate brick buildings and cobbled streets. Although the day had been long and tiring, Jacky did not feel drowsy. His head was full of the sights and sounds of this foreign land.

Jacky shared a room with Jim. Finding it difficult to sleep, Jacky chatted and fidgeted into the night, until Jim lost his patience and told Jacky to be quiet and get some sleep.

Jacky lay silently, eyes closed, but it took him a long time before his head, full of thoughts, became a head full of dreams.

The following day, the Woolwich Arsenal went to the Stade du Vivier d'Oie — the ground of Racing Club Brussels. Even though the match was a friendly, both teams played with grit and determination. The Belgian players called to each other in their native tongue. This was disconcerting to Jacky, as he was unable to understand their cries. There was a fair size crowd cheering on the local team — eager to see an English team in action. Woolwich Arsenal went ahead, but the Belgians clawed back to 1 – 1. Towards the end of the second half, Jacky made a darting run up the wing and put in a brilliantly placed cross to Peter Kyle. Kyle ran past three defenders, before slotting the ball into the bottom left corner of the goal. 2 – 1 to Woolwich Arsenal. That was how the game finished. It had not been an easy game, but Woolwich Arsenal deserved the win.

The rest of the tour was demanding. The team would either be travelling or playing. From Brussels they went to The Netherlands, where they beat The Hague 6 – 3. Next it was Preussen, in

Germany, where they won 9 – 1. From there they went to SK Slavia IPS in the Austro-Hungarian empire, where they played twice, winning both matches. They then went on to Vienna and Budapest, and their final match was against Magyar TKK, where Woolwich Arsenal won 9 – 0. A satisfying end to their European tour. The following day the team took a train back across Europe and returned to Ostend to catch the steamer back to England.

Jacky did not return to Plumstead but instead took the train straight back to the North East, where he went back home to Sacriston. As the steam train travelled north, Jacky looked out of the window at the changing landscape. He was happy to be heading back to his hometown, but with thoughts of Kate filling his mind. He realised how much he missed her and considered alighting at the next station and catching a train back to London. But then Jacky thought about the games of handball he had lined up, and meeting up with Micky for a drink in the Robin Hood, and he settled back into his seat with a smile on his face.

Elizabeth was expecting Jacky and had spent the morning baking pies and tarts. The smell of baking hit Jacky, as he entered the back door. It was good to see his mother, and it was good to see the smile on her usually solemn face, as she welcomed him home.

'Good to see you, our Jacky. You look like you could do with something inside you. Get your boots off, and I'll get you a cup of tea and something to eat,' said Elizabeth fussing around Jacky.

Elizabeth gave Jacky a mug of tea and a large slice of pie and then took his bag, and was about to start unpacking Jacky's clothes, but the smell from inside the bag made her wince.

'Oh sorry, Mam. That's me football gear. It's a bit dirty,' said Jacky.

'It certainly needs a wash,' said Elizabeth taking the bag outside and emptying the contents in the back yard, away from smelling distance.

Elizabeth wanted to hear all about Jacky's travels around Europe and life in London. She wondered if Jacky might have seen the King.

'Eeh, a nice cup of tea. I couldn't get a proper cup of tea the whole time I was abroad. And as for the food…it was peculiar. Jacky hungrily tucked into his piece of pie. He was happy to tell his

Mother about his travels and the sights and sounds of London, but he was itching to see Micky.

'Do you know what shift our Micky is on this week, Mam?'

'He called by yesterday at about this time, so I reckon he must be on earlies.'

'I think I'll go and see him, Mam. That pie was champion. There's nothing beats your pies, Mam.' And with that Jacky put his boots back on and headed out of the house to see Micky.

Chapter 29

Jacky gave a quick knock on Micky's door, before entering and calling out, announcing his arrival. Micky was polishing his boots but quickly dropped what he was doing to greet his brother.

'By, Jacky! It's good to see you, man,' said Micky. 'I'll get me boots on, and we can go to the Robin Hood.'

Jacky said hello to Meg and the children. They were delighted to see their uncle and clambered over him. Jacky dug in his pocket and gave them each a ha'penny which seemed like treasure to them. He was introduced to George; the new baby in the family. Jacky dug in his pocket and found a sixpence, which he tucked into George's hand.

Jacky and Micky almost skipped to the pub together. It was as if they had not been apart. The beers flowed and the lads chatted, but Jacky was holding back; thoughts of Kate on his mind. He wanted to ask his older, and much wiser, brother for advice but did not know how to broach the subject.

Micky knew there was something on Jacky's mind and managed to get Jacky to tell him what was bothering him.

'Write to her,' suggested Micky. 'Otherwise, you'll be worrying about it all the time you are here. And you need to have your mind on retaining the championships.'

Micky was right. Writing to Kate would be easier as well. Jacky would have time to think carefully about what he was saying. But then he would not see what Kate's reaction was. Jacky could picture her and Mary-Ann giggling at the letter and thinking Jacky a fool. Maybe he could get Micky to write it? Micky was much better with words than Jacky. Micky dismissed that idea, so it was up to Jacky to put pen to paper.

Dear Kate,

I just wanted you to know that it is cold here in Sacriston without your sunny face to warm me up...

Dear Kate,

I love you and cannot wait to return to you...

Dear Kate,

Would you like to come to Sacriston and watch me play handball? I can really hit a ball...

Dear Kate,

I hope you are well. I am missing you and looking forward to my return to Woolwich in a few weeks' time...

Dear Kate,

I hope you are well. I am missing Woolwich and looking forward to my return in a few weeks' time.

The handball practising is going well, and my mother is pleased to see me.

Yours sincerely,

Jacky Mordue.

With the letter posted Jacky felt he had at least let Kate know he was thinking about her. If that was not enough to keep her from shunning any attention that may be paid to her in his absence, then she clearly was not worth his affection. Jacky was not in love with Kate. He found her attractive and would like to get to know her better, but now he was back home and there were handball matches on which to concentrate Kate was not his priority.

Jacky was able to practise for many hours on the handball court as most of the men in the village were working long hours. Youngsters gathered round the court to watch him practise. He had become even more well-known, now that he played in the football first division.

'Mr. Mordue!' called a boy who must have been about eleven. He had bare feet and cropped hair. 'I reckon I can give you a run for your money.'

'Do you now, son?' said Jacky, ready for a break as he had been running around the court for over an hour. 'Come on then.'

The lad was taken aback but was thrilled that Jacky had responded to him. Jacky threw the ball to him.

'You start.'

The boy's friends watched in amusement as he ran around the court as Jacky toyed with him. Jacky did not let him win a point, but he gave him a chance to play.

'Mr. Mordue would have to have one arm behind his back and his feet tied together for you to win a point,' quipped another lad.

But the boy did not care. He had had a knockabout with the great Jacky Mordue — world handball champion and first division footballer.

Jacky spent time with Micky. He was unhappy to see his brother living in such a run-down building, while he himself was living in respectable digs in London. He would always feel a tinge of guilt that it was him that was enjoying life as a professional footballer whilst Micky toiled below ground.

'Micky, I had a letter from Kate,' said Jacky.

'Oh, aye. What did she say?'

'Well, she said what she had been doing while I've been away and said she's looking forward to my return.'

'That's good. You'll be looking forward to getting back to Woolwich.'

'Yes, I miss the football matches. We should have a few cracking games this season and hopefully a good run in the F.A. Cup.'

'Well, yes. But I did mean you'll be looking forward to getting back to see Kate,' Micky smiled.

Micky and Meg were trying to make the best of things in their new home. It felt constantly damp — even in the summer, and a rank smell lingered in the air. The oven in the range never seemed to reach a really hot temperature, even though Meg thoroughly cleaned it and had the chimney swept. The nearest water pump was a ten-minute walk away, which was difficult for Meg when she had their young sons to contend with, as well as trying to carry pitchers of water back to the house. Neither of them complained; they had a place of their own.

There were many collieries in the area, but one of the most recently built was in Horden — near the coast. There was an opportunity for Micky to relocate there. Although he did not have any sons old enough to work at the pit, he had three young sons who may work there one day. He was also a very good footballer and the collieries were keen to entice good sportsmen to their pits.

Micky returned from his shift to find Meg, baby George tucked under one arm, hastily trying to boil water to put in the tin bath. Meanwhile, William was peeing into a potty in the kitchen, and Tucker was trying to pull it over.

'Tucker! No!' she yelled, trying to stop Tucker from creating even more work for her. Meg looked exhausted.

She smiled when she saw Micky. Micky saw to the boys and took the potty outside to empty it. He poured the hot water into the tin tub in front of the fire and removed his filthy clothes and stepped into soapy water — instantly turning it murky grey. Meg saw to the stew that was on the stove.

'Howay, come and sit down,' he said to Meg. 'I can wait for my dinner.'

Meg flopped onto the cracket at the side of the tub. Her ankles were slightly swollen, as she had been on her feet all day. She picked up a cloth and started to wash Micky's back. It wasn't a chore for Meg to rub the coal and grit from his back, revealing the taut skin and toned muscles below.

'How would you like a new house? Just built with a roof that doesn't leak and a back yard with a coal-house and a privy.' said Micky.

'A privy in the yard? Not shared with ten other homes? Now that would be something,' said Meg. 'Stop teasing, Micky.'

'I'm not teasing you. We could have a house like that. Just not here.'

'Where? On the moon?'

'Well not quite that far. Horden. It's by the sea. Less than twenty miles away. I can get a job at Horden Colliery and a house with it. They're still building them.'

'Oh, aye. Our Tom was saying something about that.'

'Well, what do you think?'

'Would you want to move there? Away from your family?'

'I asked you first.'

'Well, it would be hard leaving me Mam, but I want to get the lads out of this house, Micky. It should be pulled down.'

'If Jacky can go all the way to London, I'm sure I can go as far as Horden,' said Micky.

'When would you be able to get started at the colliery?'

'The sooner I say yes, the sooner we'd get a home. And as soon as we got a home I could start.'

The lodgers returned from work and the clothes horse was put round the bathtub to allow some privacy. Micky vacated it, and the two men took their turn in removing the coal from their bodies. Rain had been falling all afternoon, and it was beginning to drip through the ceiling. Micky put a bucket underneath to catch the drips. Meg continued to prepare the men's dinners, while trying to pacify George and keep William and Tucker out of mischief. She pulled the range door open, and it came loose in her hand, clanking to the floor, hitting her foot. She quickly pulled her foot away, but it had been burned and bruised. The noise woke George, and he started crying. Meg had to leave George to cry, as she was in pain. She quickly poured cold water over her injury. Her foot was throbbing, but thankfully the injury was superficial.

'That's it. First thing tomorrow I'm applying to get a move to Horden,' said Micky.

Meg, fighting back tears and pain, dished out the stew before seeing to George. Once he was settled she went about emptying the bathtub. She was at breaking point but struggled through. She tried to stay positive, and the hope of moving to a better place kept her going.

Chapter 30

Jacky was keen to return to Woolwich. He had his independence and found his mother's fussing irritating. The journey was long, but Jacky enjoyed looking at the changing landscape of the English countryside. Most people he knew had not travelled further than Durham.

It was good to see Jim and Tim, but Jacky was apprehensive about seeing Kate. He wondered if it was a good idea to become romantically involved with her, considering they had to share a house. If things went wrong, it could become very awkward.

The men stood as the girls came into the room at dinner time. On seeing Kate, Jacky felt his fears vanish. He had forgotten how lovely Kate was. Jacky beamed from ear to ear. Kate's face lit up when she saw Jacky. They remained formally polite whilst in company, but Jacky wanted to speak to Kate on her own and establish whether or not she would consider a romantic involvement. Kate and Mary-Ann wanted to hear what Jacky had been doing while he was away and were impressed when he told them he had retained the title of both singles and doubles World Handball Champion. They giggled and chatted throughout the evening meal.

Jim and Tim had decided to go to the local pub that evening, and Jacky went with them. It was not the kind of establishment Kate and Mary-Ann would enter, so they went for a short stroll together, before returning to their lodgings. Jacky wished he could spend the evening with Kate but enjoyed his night out with his friends.

The following week, Jacky managed to grab a moment alone with Kate. He fumbled with his cap as he asked Kate if she would like to court him. Kate was delighted and accepted without hesitation. They started their romance under the watchful eyes of Bertha and Jim.

The players were eager for the new season to get underway. There were a couple of practise matches to begin with, and then the league started at the beginning of September. Woolwich Arsenal had a slow start to the season; they drew their first game. Jacky did not feature in the game, and he was happy to have missed the match; the rain had fallen heavy and hard. The ten thousand spectators all held aloft umbrellas. The players could barely run on the waterlogged pitch and visibility was poor. The match ended in a 1 – 1 draw. Jacky featured in the next four games, all of which ended in losses. Their sixth game was against Manchester City, who they beat 2 – 1. It was a good result, as City had started the season well. Jacky's performances were inconsistent. Some days he played out of his skin, while on other occasions he could not make his mark on the game. It was obvious he had ability, but his erratic form resulted in him being left out of the first team a number of times, having to make do with playing for the reserve team. Tim was Woolwich Arsenal's star player. He had been at the club since 1902 when they were in division two and had helped the team earn promotion to the first division. In October, as a long-serving member of the team, Tim was given a benefit match. These matches earned the player a huge sum of money, which they could never earn from week to week on their meagre wages. It was a way of thanking the players for their loyalty to the club. Liverpool were to be the opponents — a great fixture to have as a benefit game. However, Woolwich Arsenal had decided to make the match a joint benefit game — Tim sharing the occasion with Roddy McEachrane, who had also joined the club in 1902. This meant the pot of money the players received would be shared between the two of them. Tim felt somewhat cheated. Jacky was disappointed to be left out of the team on that day; he had formed a good friendship with Tim and wanted to be part of the occasion. A crowd of eighteen thousand watched the match. It was a close contest, with chances for both sides, but, to the delight of the home supporters, Woolwich Arsenal won the match by two goals to one.

'I hope you'll be buying us a few drinks tonight, Tim,' said Jim after the match.

'You'll have to wait until I see the money, Jim, then I'll be more than happy to,' said Tim.

However, the weeks went passed and Tim and Roddy still did not receive their payment. The season continued with an even number of wins, losses and draws. There were rumours of financial problems at the club. With Chelsea being the only other first division team in the London area, there were few away supporters attending matches on a regular basis, and, with Chelsea playing in the top flight for the first time, Londoners could get to Stamford Bridge, Chelsea's ground, a lot easier than they could get to Woolwich Arsenal's Manor Ground at Plumstead. The munitions workers, who had supported the team thus far, were now suffering from financial hardships. Few had money to pay to watch a first division team. Woolwich Arsenal's ground was in the industrial area of the town, with few houses in the vicinity. Many watched other local teams, charging lower admission prices. Dwindling numbers not only affected the team financially; when they played away games, they had little or no support. This did nothing to boost the players' confidence or morale.

Tim was beginning to become disillusioned with the club to whom he had been committed. He, along with the club and supporters in general, went through something of a slump. There just was not the enthusiasm or optimism that had been there for the previous few seasons. Jacky played more games during December; he was still keen to prove himself in the top flight game, but never really played to the best of his ability. Players, such as Jacky, were still keen to make their mark and were excited to play opponents who they had previously read about in the newspapers. Although his play was inconsistent, Jacky's speed and ability to cross the ball were soon recognised throughout the league, and opposing defenders knew they had to up their game to stop Jacky from skipping past them time after time.

On Christmas Day, Woolwich Arsenal had a home game against Newcastle, which they drew 2 – 2. Following the match, Mrs. Shoebridge and Bertha laid on a festive Christmas roast, followed by Christmas pudding. The friends drank and sang around the fire but had to keep their celebrations to a minimum, as they had another match lined up on Boxing Day — being at home to Liverpool. Young Agnes played with the doll she had received for Christmas. Jacky missed his family, but he was happy to spend Christmas with Kate and his housemates. Jacky was comfortable in Kate's company. Kate laughed at all Jacky's jokes and hung on to his every word. Jacky did not feel as if Kate was trying to catch him out whenever he spoke. She did not have any ulterior motives; she was a genuine friend and accepted Jacky for what he was. Jacky now realised this was how a relationship should feel, and how wrong his time with Mabel had been. Kate was hard working.

Leading up to Christmas she had been spending long hours at the dressmakers, where she and Mary-Ann worked. Even so, she was happy to mend Jacky's clothes and darn his socks by the light of the candle in the evenings. Jacky wanted to treat Kate to nice things. He did not have a lot of spare money, as he always tried to send a little to his mother, but he saved up and had bought Kate a small brooch for Christmas. Kate was delighted with the gift; nobody had ever given her jewellery before. This was Jacky and Kate's first Christmas together, and one they would always remember.

The match against Liverpool on Boxing Day was a friendly, without anything riding on the game. There were just three thousand spectators present, and the game finished in a draw. Two days later, Woolwich Arsenal hosted Sunderland in a game they won 4 – 0. The Christmas schedule was busy. The team travelled up to Sheffield on New Year's Eve and then further north to Sunderland, on New Year's Day. Unfortunately for Jacky, Sunderland won by five goals to two, but Jacky had played well and the friends and family who had come to watch the match could be proud of him. Jacky also made a good impression on the Sunderland management. Following the match, Jacky made the most of being in the north east and called in to see his mother and his brothers. He stayed for a couple of days, but the next fixture was away at Bristol City. Jacky took the train straight from Sunderland to Bristol and played in a match they won 2 – 1, which was a good away result. The team had played six matches within a fortnight.

Chapter 31

As the winter closed in, it became increasingly difficult to keep any warmth in the home. Micky had applied for a move to Horden Colliery, but as of yet nothing had come up. Meg did her best to keep baby George warm, but it was hard in such squalid conditions. There was heat in the direct vicinity of the range and the open fire, but the rest of the house was cold and damp. Micky and Meg were worried about the health of their children. The bedroom was icily cold. Tucker developed a cold, which William also contracted shortly afterwards. Meg knew that putting them to bed in their cold, dank bedroom was not helping their health. They were breathing in musty air and could not keep warm. Micky moved the children's bed downstairs where there was some warmth. The children's bed and the sofa bed, in which Micky and Meg slept, filled the room.

'I'm going to chase up my application to go to Horden. This is no way to live, and I'm not having you and the bairns living like this,' said Micky.

'Aye, Micky. This house isn't fit to live in. I can't bear to see the bairns so cold and miserable. I'm trying my best — really I am,' said Meg.

'I know you are, flower. Don't blame yourself.'

The following day, baby George was taken ill. He developed a bad cold which then went to his chest. His health deteriorated rapidly. Meg sat up all night nursing George, keeping him warm. Micky fetched the doctor the following day. On examining the baby, he looked grave. George had double pneumonia. There was no proven treatment. Meg and Micky knew that the prognosis was not good. Meg could not bear the thoughts of losing another baby. George coughed and wheezed. He had a high temperature. He looked as if he was suffering but was too weak and tired to cry. Meg nursed her baby throughout the day and night, frightened to sleep, in case she should wake to find George had given up his fight for life. Micky did not like to leave Meg and George, but he had to continue to work. He felt helpless watching his baby struggling to breathe. He tried to comfort Meg, but all she wanted was for her baby to be well again. Words of reassurance were pointless, as

Micky knew the chances of George surviving were slim. As the days passed Meg was encouraged by George's determination to cling to life. He was still gravely ill, but he was not giving up. He began to sleep more soundly — coughing less. His breathing regulated. He appeared less distressed. George slept almost continually. He seemed to have got over the worst of his illness. Meg began to feel optimistic; George might just pull through. Days turned to weeks, and George became stronger. He still coughed occasionally, but his temperature was normal, and his appetite returned completely. But George was not the healthy baby he had been before his illness. His lungs had been permanently damaged.

At last a position at Horden Colliery came up for Micky, and they were allocated a new home.

They moved just two weeks later. Micky had help from Meg's brothers, Bill and Tom, loading up the cart with all their belongings and making the sixteen-mile journey along the tracks to Horden.

'Dad, are we nearly there yet?' called William from the back of the cart.

'Not long now, son.'

Their new home was on Ninth Street. When the houses were built, they were unimaginatively named First street through to Thirteenth Street. The Mordue's house was at the end of the street.

'I'll go and get the keys,' said Micky.

Meg stayed on the cart with the boys, eagerly awaiting Micky's return. The house looked amazing. The roof and walls were solid. There were no cracks or broken windows or tiles. She looked up and down the street, catching glimpses of neighbours peeping out to see who was going to move into the house. William and Tucker scrambled off the cart and ran up and down the street, eager to stretch their legs after the long journey.

'Stay where I can see you, pets,' said Meg.

Micky soon returned with the key to the house. He took hold of George, while Meg got down from the cart.

'Howay, let's get inside,' said Micky passing George back to Meg and opening the front door.

William and Tucker ran back to the house, eager to follow their parents into their new home. The front door opened straight into the main room of the house — with the range on the far wall. They walked through to the kitchen at the back, where there was another, smaller, fireplace, backing on to the one in the front. The back door led out to the yard where the coal house and outside toilet were at the far end — by the back street.

'Eeh, Micky, it's lovely. Look, our own netty, right outside the back door. And a yard. I can put a line up, just there. It's champion,' said Meg.

'Aye, it's grand. Let's have a look upstairs,' said Micky.

The narrow staircase was by the front door. Micky led the way up. There were two good-sized bedrooms; each with a small fireplace. The floorboards were new, and there was even a slight smell of paint. Everything was fresh and undamaged.

'There's no beds. Do we have to sleep on the floors?' said William.

'We've got to fetch the furniture from the cart,' said Meg. 'Your Da and Uncle Bill will make sure you've got a bed to sleep on tonight — don't you worry,' said Meg.

The empty rooms looked large, but once the Mordue's few possessions were brought inside, there was a lot less space. Meg lit a fire and put a kettle of water on to boil. Once the men had finished emptying the cart, Meg made them all a cup of tea and shared out the stotty and butter she had packed.

'By! This is a canny place,' said Tom. 'I wouldn't mind coming out here to live.'

'Aye, we'll have to bring Mam over to see you. She'll be made up to see you in such a lovely house,' said Bill. 'Haway, Tom. We better get back before it gets dark.'

Tom and Bill set off back to Kimblesworth with the cart, leaving Micky, Meg and the boys to settle down and get used to their new surroundings. Meg busily made beds and emptied boxes, while Micky set fires and moved furniture and rugs. William and Tucker played in the back yard, and George sat happily in a chair by the fire, watching his parents and taking in his new surroundings.

As the light faded, Meg took William and Tucker upstairs and helped them get ready and tucked them into the bed they shared.

'The potty is under the bed if you need to go in the night,' said Meg. 'Now go to sleep and if you're good we can have a walk down to the beach tomorrow.'

Meg wished she had not said that. It filled the boys with excitement, and they found it hard to get to sleep. They had never been to a beach before. Meg went downstairs and put George in his cot. Meg and Micky lay in the sofa bed, wrapped in each other's arms, listening to the boys upstairs who were chattering and giggling. It had been a long day, but Meg was still wide-awake thinking about their new home.

'I still can't believe it, Micky. It's like a dream. This house, it's warm and dry. It just feels different. It already feels like our home — something that that shack in Sacriston never did.'

Micky smiled and held Meg tightly in his arms. She looked happier than he had seen her look for a long time. The radiance in her face was returning. Micky loved Meg more than ever. He felt a lump in his throat and had to blink back tears that had formed in his eyes. He did not want Meg thinking she had married someone soft.

Micky started at the pit the following day, and Meg soon got chatting to her new neighbours, who were keen to meet the newcomers and find out as much as they could about them. Everyone meant well, but everyone knew everyone else's business in a colliery village. As the house was relatively spacious, and Micky had five mouths to feed, Micky and Meg decided to take in a lodger. Henry Emerson was a bachelor in his forties who had suffered from polio as a child. Subsequently, he was unable to work below ground at the pit and was a stone miner on the surface. He moved to Horden to work in the new mine but was unable to have his own house and was looking for lodgings. Micky understood he was an honest man and was happy to let him board with them. Henry moved into the smaller upstairs room, and Meg provided him with meals and did all his washing. Henry was no trouble and was friendly to the boys, keeping himself to himself much of the time.

Chapter 32

In the first-round proper of the F.A. Cup, Woolwich Arsenal played Hull from the second division at home but could only manage a goalless draw. The replay was in Hull five days later — on a Thursday. The trip to Hull was long and cold. There was barely any support for Woolwich Arsenal, but the Hull supporters came out in their thousands, hoping to see their side knock out a team from the league above. The Hull players were fired up for the match, and with the crowd behind them, they soon went ahead. Jim made what was a rare error and let in a soft goal. Once Hull were ahead, Woolwich Arsenal needed to attack, which left them vulnerable. Jacky made a few good runs, but his passes were not finding the centre players. The final score was 4 – 1 to Hull. Two days later, Woolwich Arsenal were scheduled to play Manchester City in the league, and so rather than heading back to Plumstead, the team travelled to Manchester and stayed in lodgings. The team morale was low. It was always disappointing to go out of a cup, but to lose to a team from a lower division was even more frustrating. The match against Manchester City did not go well. The players were not in the right frame of mind and were disorganised and made many silly errors. It was only when City went three up that Woolwich Arsenal started to play, but the ball was not running for them, and, leaving themselves exposed at the back, they conceded a fourth goal. The journey back to Plumstead seemed to take forever. There was a melancholy amongst the players. They had conceded eight goals in two games and only managed to score once. The train rattled past places where other big clubs played, travelling south on a journey that seemed to take an eternity. On arriving in London, they still had to travel further to the south of the river. Travelling home always seemed a lot quicker and more enjoyable after winning a match.

Everton put in a bid for Tim, which was accepted. Tim felt the time was right for him to move on. The financial problems at Woolwich Arsenal were beginning to take their toll. Their manager, Phil Kelso, also became disgruntled and resigned — leaving in the same month as Tim. Things were certainly changing at The Manor

Ground, and not for the better. Jacky and the team were sad to see Tim go; he was not only their key player but also lifted the mood and attitude of the others. Tim had helped Jacky settle in at Plumstead. The house would be a lot quieter without him.

As spring approached, Jacky heard rumours that other clubs were interested in signing him. He loved his time in Woolwich, and he did not want to leave Kate, but he missed his north-east home and was torn.

'Just tell them you don't want to leave the club,' said Kate.

'It's not as easy as that. The attendances have dropped here at Woolwich Arsenal. They wouldn't say anything officially, but it's clear the money isn't coming in. If they can get good money for me, they'll take it,' said Jacky.

'But they'd be worse off without you. You're their best player now that Tim has gone — well, you and Jim, but he's a goalie so that doesn't count.'

'Well, I don't know if I'm their best player, but they know they'll get a canny bit for me.'

'So which clubs are after you and what's going to happen to us Jacky?'

'Well, there's a few, but I know Sunderland have shown an interest. If I could go there, I'd be back near home. And I'd be playing for a team I've cheered on since I was a lad.'

'Sunderland? That's miles away. I'd never see you,' said Kate. Her face had dropped.

'Come with me then, Kate.'

'What do you mean? I can't give up my job — I'd have no money. I might find something, but I might not.'

'Then, let's get married. I'll look after you,' said Jacky.

'Are you asking me to marry you, Jacky? If you are, you should do it properly.'

Jacky had not planned to propose to Kate, but the conversation and circumstances had led to the situation. He did not have to think twice; he knew he could not bear the thought of leaving Kate, and he knew she would not go with him unless they were married.

Jacky got down on one knee. 'Kate, will you marry me?' he asked, holding her hand.

Kate's face lit up. She knew if she said yes she would have to move to a new part of the country, where she would know nobody apart from Jacky. But she would be with the man she loved. She could not contemplate being parted from Jacky.

'Yes, Jacky. I will.'

'Jacky leapt to his feet, and they hugged one another in an unusual public show of emotion.

When they returned to their lodgings, Kate and Jacky announced their news while everyone was eating dinner. Everyone was delighted for Kate and Jacky.

'There is just one problem. I haven't asked Kate's mother. She may not agree with another daughter marrying a footballer,' said Jacky.

'Yes, you'll have to get Mum's approval,' said Bertha. 'You're not twenty-one yet.'

'Jacky intends to write to her to ask her permission to marry me,' said Kate. 'I can't see her saying no. You're married to a footballer, so I can't see why she wouldn't let me.'

'Well, this deserves a toast,' said Jim. He went to his room and returned with a small bottle of whisky, which was far from full. He poured everyone a small tot, and they drank to Jacky and Kate.

'Well, sign up for Liverpool and I'm sure she'd be happy,' Jim joked.

'Could you, Jacky?' asked Kate. 'I'd love to go back to Liverpool.'

'I can't do that, Kate, and Jim knows it,' said Jacky.

Jacky was more worried about what his own mother would say. Elizabeth had not met Kate. But Jacky had just turned twenty-one, so he did not need his mother's permission. And he was sure she would take a liking to Kate. Why wouldn't she? And Kate was non-Catholic — that would help. Jacky wrote to his own mother and to Kate's mother. Kate also wrote to her mother.

They soon received a reply from Kate's mother; Bertha had previously written to their mother, assuring her that the man Kate was courting was of good character, so Kate's mother was delighted her daughter was to be wed.

Elizabeth was not so quick to respond. She was unable to read and write, which meant Dan had read the letter her. He also replied. Not with a message that his mother had dictated, but a personal letter. In it, he said how pleased he was for Jacky, and how their mother would soon come round to the idea of him marrying so quickly and without having introduced his bride-to-be to her. So, it was evident that Elizabeth was not happy.

Jacky and Kate were married a few weeks later — in Woolwich. It was a small gathering, and Bertha put on a spread for them back at the lodgings. Just a few close friends were in attendance, but that did not matter to the newly-weds. They were happy.

Woolwich Arsenal finished fourteenth in the league. Following their last league game, which was at home to Sheffield Wednesday, the team packed their bags and set off on a tour of Scotland. It was an intense tour, lasting just ten days, but including eight matches. Jacky played his last game for Woolwich Arsenal on Thursday 30th April against Kilmarnock. The team headed back to Plumstead.

The next time Jacky would see the team, he would be playing against them. A few of the team were moving on to different clubs, but Jacky was the only one heading to Sunderland. Jacky was sad to be leaving Woolwich Arsenal. He had had good times and made good friends, but he had been signed up for Sunderland for a record fee of £750 and would be heading back up north; back home.

Chapter 33

Back in Plumstead, Jacky and Kate packed the few belongings they had and said their goodbyes. Jim and Bertha were also on the move. Jim had been signed by Blackburn Rovers. Bertha was pleased to be heading back to the north-west, near her family.

'I'll write as soon as I can,' said Kate hugging her sister Bertha.

'And I'll see you on the pitch, when I'm putting the ball past you,' said Jacky to Jim.

'Howay, Kate. We've got a long journey ahead of us,' said Jacky.

Jacky and Kate were heading to Sacriston to introduce Kate to Elizabeth and the rest of the family. Jacky had wanted to stay in a hotel in Durham City, but his mother was appalled at the thought of his not staying at the family home. Elizabeth's already spotless home was swept, dusted and polished from top to bottom. Kate was terrified at the prospect of meeting Jacky's mother.

'Don't worry, Pet. Me Mam's bark is worse than her bite,' said Jacky.

'What if she doesn't like me, Jacky?'

'Stop worrying — it'll be fine.'

Even though it was a warm May day, Elizabeth was sitting in front of the fire, knitting. As Jacky and Kate entered the room, she put her knitting down and rose to her feet.

'Hello, Mam. Hello, Dan,' said Jacky.

'By, lad, it's good to see you,' she said, taking Jacky's hand and offering her face to be kissed.

'And you, Mam,' said Jacky.

Jacky and his mother started chatting about the journey and the weather, leaving Kate standing awkwardly, clutching her bag. It was as if Elizabeth wanted to pretend she wasn't there. It was Dan who sensed her uneasiness and saw how brutal his mother was being.

'And this must be the new Mrs. Mordue…' said Dan, gesturing towards Kate.

Kate blushed as the attention turned to her.

'Oh! Aye, this is Kate. Kate, this is my mother and my brother Dan,' said Jacky.

Elizabeth politely welcomed Kate into her home and family, but there was no warmth in her words. Jacky was her youngest child, and there was not a woman on earth who would be good enough for her beloved son. Kate did her best to smile and please Elizabeth with her conversation, but she felt intimidated and unwelcome. Jacky was oblivious to the situation and happily chatted with Dan about football, while Kate shrunk further into her shell. The following day, Kate was eager to leave and start the journey to Sunderland, where they would have their own home — away from her intimidating mother-in-law.

Jacky felt excited to be moving to Sunderland with his new bride, but the season would not get underway for a few months, and he wished they could stay nearer Sacriston or Horden — near his brothers and friends. The house they were renting was near Roker Park football ground. It was a four-roomed house; two up, two down. They could just about afford the rent without having to take in a lodger, and considering Jacky would often be playing away matches, leaving Kate alone in the home, it would have been inappropriate for a man to be in the house with Kate, while Jacky was away.

Jacky and Kate had never known such space. They had everything they needed. The house was also in close proximity to the seafront; just a ten minutes' walk to Roker Pier and even closer still was the beautiful park.

Jacky had a few handball matches arranged in order to retain his title, so he did not waste any time in heading to the handball wall in Sunderland and practising his game. At first Kate went along to watch Jacky as he practised, but Jacky ignored her, concentrating on his game — leaving her standing for hours on end, with nobody to talk to. Kate decided to spend her time turning their house into a home. Jacky was on a winning streak with his handball, retaining the World Championship. He made a decent amount of money from his winnings and gave Kate money to buy materials, and make soft furnishings for the house. Kate was also able to make herself new clothes. She was thrilled to be able to buy fabrics and have the time to cut and sew. However, with Jacky spending much time away playing matches and practising, Kate felt isolated. She was not used to being alone. She could not remember a time that she had ever been by herself in a house. Initially, it had felt as if she was privileged, but the novelty soon wore off. Kate was desperate for company. She busied herself with housework and sewing, but needed more. Kate began to explore her new surroundings and took a walk to the pier. She watched the waves crashing in on the shore. The clean sea air filled her lungs, and the breeze made her feel alive. But then she watched children playing on the beach and families chattering and laughing together. It was when she was amongst the crowds that Kate felt the loneliest. She longed to join in their conversations and share all her new experiences. When Jacky returned home, Kate would want to talk about anything and everything he had done. She wanted Jacky's constant attention, whereas Jacky wanted to read his newspaper in peace and quiet — winding down after a busy day.

Chapter 34

Micky and Meg settled into their house in Horden. Horden Colliery had been established just eight years earlier but was rapidly expanding — exploiting the abundant undersea coal. Tunnels and passages were being excavated, reaching continually onwards below the sea. The colliery was just a short walk from their home, and Micky soon settled in at the pit. He became friendly with some other men who had recently moved to the area. Wilf Belcher had worked at Sacriston Colliery and had also moved to Horden. He played alongside Micky for Horden Athletic — a local amateur team consisting of coal miners. They soon became firm friends. Wilf was a bachelor and lived with his brother and sister and their widowed father. Micky and Wilf worked together, played together and drank together. They frequented Horden Big Club; a welfare club built by the coal company.

One Sunday morning, Mrs. Coatman, Martha and Teenie paid Meg a visit. Teenie was excited to see her nephews and her big sister.

'Meg, we saw the sea. When we were coming down the hill, we could see the sea,' said Teenie. Although she was now eleven years old, she had never been to the coast before.

'Aye, we can have a walk there later. Would you like that?' said Meg.

Teenie almost burst with excitement.

'Mam, I need the netty,' she said, looking along the road for the communal privy.

'It's in the back yard, Teenie. Just pop out the back door, and it's the door on the left. Don't go in the other one — that's full of coal,' said Meg.

Teenie could not believe the house had its own toilet, and a flushing one at that. When she went back indoors, she was full of zeal.

'Oh, Mam, it's wonderful. It doesn't smell bad like the privy we have to use. Can we live here?' she enthused.

'Well, that's what I've come to tell our Meg; yes, we will be coming to live here. Your Dad and the lads are all getting jobs here, and we've been offered a house,' said Mrs. Coatman.

Meg, Martha and Teenie were all smiles, taking each other's hands and dancing around the kitchen. Meg felt like a child; she was so happy and excited at the prospect of her family coming to live close by.

'Meg, I'll be able to come and see you every day and look after George,' said Teenie.

The Coatmans, having seen Meg and Micky's home and the other new homes being built, had all decided to make the move to Horden. There were three working men in the family, and soon their youngest son, George Robert, would turn fourteen and be able to work at the pit. This made it a lot easier for the family to be taken on and given a colliery house. Within weeks, the Coatmans made the move and were given a relatively large house just around the corner from Meg and Micky. The Coatmans also had an outside flush toilet. Their house did not lead straight out of the front door onto the street, as most of the houses did, but had some steps and a small front garden. Meg was delighted that her family lived close by. Whilst Micky was rarely at home, his time taken with work or leisure, Meg spent almost all her time at home. There was always cleaning, washing, cooking, mending and various other things to do in the house. And with young children to keep an eye on, it left no time for anything else. George was never going to be as strong and boisterous as his brothers; he was always a sickly child. William and Tucker would play in the streets with older boys, running off to the dean or the beach. George could not keep up with his siblings and, being so young, was not allowed out on his own. He stayed at home with his mother. Some evenings, when the children were in bed, Meg set to work on her clippy mats. These were mats made from old rags. Sometimes her mother or sisters would visit, and they would chat away with hooks and scissors, cutting and progging. Meg was happy; almost every other woman in the village lived a similar life to her. Every working day, the men worked long and arduous shifts with accidents and injuries being commonplace, and a fatal accident a permanent threat. Micky had black scars all up his arms from the frequent times debris would fall and cut him, as he worked. The wounds would heal around the coal dust

142

ingrained in his skin. Men had problems with their lungs as they breathed in coal dust, and their knees and ankles would become arthritic as they toiled in water, crawling and kneeling in the narrow passages. Their wives and mothers appreciated the bleak existence the men endured and ensured that their homes and children were well cared for. Some wives were less fortunate than Meg, having husbands who were violent or frequently drunk, or who spent all the rent money at the pub or on gambling. Micky was a loving husband. Every Friday he handed his pay packet over to Meg. Meg gave Micky a set amount of pocket money and kept the rest to pay bills. Some weeks, if Micky had been working a seam that had been particularly poor, the money in his pay packet would not cover their expenses. The rent she received from Henry helped, but during those weeks, Meg would eke out the small amount of food she had available and make thin broths and bread to keep them fed. They would be hungry, and there would be no extras, but they got by. If Meg could afford meat, maybe a shin of beef or lamb, Micky and Henry would get most of the meat that was on the bones. They were the ones bringing in the money, and it was imperative they were well-nourished. Occasionally, if Micky had worked a productive seam, his pay packet reflected this, and Meg was able to put some money aside 'for a rainy day'.

Chapter 35

On September the 1st, Jacky had to sit and watch as Sunderland played their first game of the new season. Sunderland had signed two other new players; Charlie Thomson was recruited from Heart of Midlothian, and Arthur Brown arrived from Sheffield United, and the manager felt they were not ready to play together. The match was away to Manchester City. It was frustrating for the new lads to have to sit and watch, as their team battled hard but could not find the net. Jacky was keen to play alongside the Sunderland goalkeeper, Leigh Richmond Roose. Roose was not like any other goalkeeper in the profession, and he was not a professional player. He remained an amateur, in order to avoid any restricting contract, but was said to earn more in expenses than the rest of the team earned as professionals. Most goalkeepers stayed firmly in their penalty area, but Roose took advantage of the rule that allowed him to carry the ball up to the halfway line. Being a tall, formidable player, he would make a save in his penalty area and then run up the pitch in the manner of a rugby player — dodging opponents, before launching the ball to the forwards. He was a crowd-pleaser and an entertainer. At times, he would turn his back on the match and have a chat and joke with the crowd. Jacky soon realised he had to get to understand the team goalie; he was a very different player and personality to Jim Ashcroft, his old team and housemate.

Sunderland's third game was away to Middlesbrough, so the team did not have far to travel.

Jacky was hopeful that he would get a game. The Roker supporters were becoming frustrated seeing their expensive new signing sitting on the bench. Jacky's brothers, Micky, Dan and Jimmy along with Bill and Tom Coatman were among the spectators. They had managed to swap their shifts about so they could get down to Middlesbrough to watch what would, hopefully, be Jacky's first game for his new team. As Sunderland supporters, they would be able to cheer on Jacky, along with the rest of the away crowd.

The match started slowly. Jacky appeared nervous; he was keen to impress the crowd and his teammates and wanted to get a goal or a win under his belt. All eyes were on Sunderland's new £750 winger. Jacky didn't ease into the game at all in the first half — looking more like a spectator, but when George Holley shot from outside the area, lobbing the 'Boro keeper and giving Sunderland the lead, Jacky's nerves left him and were replaced with the excitement of the occasion. Jacky's confidence grew with each touch of the ball, and the crowd warmed to their new player. Jacky darted through the 'Boro defence. He laid the ball off to Holley, who then returned the ball to Jacky's feet. George Holley was a brilliant player, but he was not used to playing with someone as fast as Jacky. Once he got used to Jacky's pace, and Jacky understood George's way of playing — the two made progress and played well together. The defence was left off-balance, and Jacky was able to slot the ball past the 'Boro keeper and into the back of the net. The travelling Sunderland supporters cheered; this was Jacky's club, and he was their man of the moment. He felt he had come home, and this is where he belonged. Sunderland went on to score once more; a perfectly placed pass from Jacky on the wing was headed into the top right-hand corner. 3 – 0. Jacky and Holley hit it off, both on and off the pitch.

The season continued well, and at the end of October, Sunderland were away to Blackburn Rovers. Kate was to accompany Jacky on the journey to Blackburn, in order to see her sister, Bertha, and Jacky was keen to see Jim, and hopefully put the ball past him.

'Kate, you look a bit peaky. Are you sure you are up to travelling?' said Jacky.

'Jacky, I'm fine. I'm not missing the chance to see Bertha.'

Kate stayed at Bertha and Jim's home, while the men played their match, which was inevitably followed by a few drinks in the local pub.

'Kate, it's so good to see you. Are you keeping well? You're looking a little pale. Are you eating well?' said Bertha.

Kate stumbled on her words and then suddenly burst into tears.

'I think I'm carrying a baby,' she sobbed.

'That's good isn't it?' said Bertha.

'Well, it would be, but I haven't got a soul in the world to talk to — apart from Jacky, and he doesn't want to listen to me talking about sewing and cleaning, and anything else I do.'

'Have you not got to know your neighbours? How about the other players' families?'

'I don't know. I'm no good at starting a conversation, and I certainly wouldn't approach anybody I didn't know.'

Kate's neighbours had spoken to her as she had passed, but she had not had the courage to continue the conversation or go into their homes. Her shyness came across as rudeness. Bertha felt pity for her sister. Kate was such a lively and lovable person when you got to know her, but she was reserved and lacked confidence. Bertha and Jim were new to Blackburn, but Bertha had slipped easily into life here and had neighbours to talk to.

'I know it will be hard for you, Kate, but you need to start talking to people. Smile at them instead of looking away and running back into your house. You are a lovely person; the women in Sunderland would be lucky to have you as a friend,' said Bertha.

Kate wished she lived nearer to Bertha. It was difficult for a woman like Kate to move to a place with no family or friends.

'You're keeping well though, Kate? No sickness or anything?' said Bertha.

'No, I've been fine. Jacky doesn't know so don't go saying anything. I'll tell him when I start to show.'

The men returned in a jovial mood. Jim was pleased to say that none of the Sunderland team, including Jacky, had managed to put a goal past him. Blackburn had won 1 – 0.

On a cold December morning at the end of 1908, Jacky and the Sunderland teamed travelled the short distance to Newcastle for the local derby. Newcastle were doing better than Sunderland in the league. This was going to be a tough game for Jacky and the team. There was such a large turnout for the game that many supporters were turned away and had to watch the reserve match instead.

The game started slowly without much incident, but then on twenty-eight minutes, Sunderland took the lead. Sunderland just about deserved the lead, but the game was close. However, just on the stroke of half time, Newcastle were appointed a penalty for an alleged handball against Thomson. The Sunderland players were furious, as they felt this was a very bad decision. To add to their frustration, Sherman slotted the penalty home past Roose for

Newcastle to draw level at 1 – 1. In the dressing room at half time, the Sunderland team were livid at the injustice of the decision. Their manager, Bob Kyle, pointed out that the best way to make their point was through the game, showing Newcastle who were the better team, and who should be winning the game. The Sunderland players took this on board, and all eleven players came out onto the pitch, ready to start the second half. Ready to make a point.

It was a whirlwind twenty-eight minutes. Newcastle were not given any time to get back into the game or settle on the ball. The Newcastle supporters were stunned into silence as Sunderland mounted attack after attack. At 1 – 2, Newcastle were still hoping to even the match, but within minutes Sunderland had progressed their lead to 3 – 1. The Sunderland supporters could not believe their eyes as their team pushed forward once again and scored yet again. At 4 – 1 Newcastle were looking deflated, but Sunderland kept on applying pressure. It seemed as if every time Sunderland got the ball, it would end in a goal. Jacky was running up and down the right wing, passing ball after ball into the box. Bill Higgins and George Holley were amazing — reaching every ball and skipping round defenders. The goals kept going in, and the Newcastle goalie kept picking the ball out of the back of the net. Jacky managed to hit the target, adding to the goal tally, and Arthur Bridge scored twice. Higgins and Holley both completed their hat tricks, and on seventy-four minutes the score was 9 – 1 to Sunderland. It was the largest away win that the first division had seen, and it was against Newcastle — who looked on course to take the title that season. This was a game that would be talked about for years to come by Sunderland supporters.

The team were elated; it would be a day that Jacky Mordue would never forget.

Chapter 36

Kate and Meg were both expecting a baby, but their experiences were poles apart.

Meg did not have time to dwell on her pregnancy — she had three young boys to attend to, plus a home to run. There was endless laundry to be washed and dried, and with it being winter, this was a nigh on impossible task. Clothes were draped on lines and clothes horses near the fire. Their permanence made it seem like a part of the décor. Neighbours and family called in. When Meg walked to the shops, there was always someone wanting a chat. Family and lodgers had to be fed. When the children were in bed in the evening, Meg flopped in the chair and started on her knitting, before Micky urged her to go to bed as her eyelids were dropping — as well as her stitches. Kate, on the other hand, dwelt on her pregnancy. She did not have anyone with whom she could discuss the ins and outs of having a baby. She was used to younger siblings, but not babies. She did not know what to expect. Bertha sent letters, knowing Kate was lonely, trying to cheer her up, but Kate still had not managed to get to know anyone in her neighbourhood. She busied herself with making baby clothes. She enjoyed buying white material and ribbons and sewing tiny clothes. She could not imagine a baby could be so small; they were like dolls' clothes.

Both babies were born in March 1909. Meg had a very quick labour. William ran to fetch his grandmother, Mrs. Coatman, who boiled water and prepared the bed. The local woman, who assisted in many of the births, was summoned, but she had barely put a foot through the door when baby Hannah arrived. She was a beautiful, healthy baby. They called her Hannah after Micky's sister Hannah, who had played women's football in the 1890s before her premature death.

Meg, as was the custom, had to stay in bed for ten days following the birth; with Hannah by her side. Meg's sister, Martha, took over Meg's chores and helped look after the boys while Meg was in bed. Meg felt fine and wanted to get up and help; she hated feeling helpless and being waited on, but lying-in was deemed essential.

Kate, on the other hand, had a traumatic labour. Her younger sister, Ethel, had made the journey from Liverpool and was staying with Kate and Jacky while Kate was heavily pregnant, but Ethel had no experience of childbirth. The doctor was called to attend the birth, which was long and complicated. Baby Edna was born in the early hours of the morning, and Kate was fortunate to have survived the trauma. Fortunately, Edna was none the worse for her ordeal. Ethel had planned to return to Liverpool two weeks after the birth of the baby, as she needed to find paid employment herself, but it became evident that Kate would not be well enough to leave her bed for some time.

Jacky was over the moon to be a father, and he adored baby Edna, but he hated to see Kate so unwell. He blamed himself to some extent; he had brought her here, where she knew nobody, and he had carried on with his life and not helped Kate to adapt to her new surroundings. He had not helped her make friends, and now he had got her in this situation, and childbirth had almost killed her. It had not crossed his mind that Kate might be finding things difficult. She had not complained, but thinking about it, she hadn't been herself since they moved here. Jacky had been so wrapped up in his own change of life and surroundings that he had not noticed Kate struggling. He felt guilty, although he would never share these feelings with anyone. Now he had another dilemma. At the end of the season, which was fast approaching, Sunderland were to tour Europe, and Jacky was expected, and was very keen, to be part of the tour. He knew Kate was not well enough to be left alone with a new baby. The only solution would be for Ethel to stay on in Sunderland, whilst Jacky was away, and until Kate was well enough to care for Edna and resume domestic duties. Ethel was keen to get back to Liverpool to see her fiancé but knew Kate needed her there. Even if Jacky did not travel to Europe, he would be little or no help to Kate.

Jacky continued to play well for Sunderland, and they finished third in the league, behind Newcastle and Everton. Tim Coleman had settled in well at Everton and made a good impact on the team. As soon as the league finished, the team prepared for their tour of Europe.

Jacky was sorry to leave Kate and Edna but was excited to be heading off to Europe once again.

Sunderland travelled to Austria-Hungary, Czechoslovakia and Germany. The Hungarian crowds cheered every goal — whichever team scored. The standard of play by Sunderland was better than any they had seen. The Sunderland players felt relaxed and treated each game as a kick-about. However the European teams and supporters took each game very seriously. There was one hiccup, losing 2 – 1 to Vienna AC. Robert Kyle, the Sunderland manager, was livid. Temperatures had reached 90 degrees — something the players had not experienced before. The match had been gruelling, with brutal tackles flying in and atrocious refereeing, but Kyle felt that was still no excuse for being beaten by a vastly inferior team. From then on, Kyle made it clear to his players that they had to play to win.

Sunderland won the rest of their matches, finishing with an 8 – 3 win over FC Nuremberg, with Kyle refereeing the match and being a lot more competent and fairer than any of the previous referees mediating the tour games.

Jacky enjoyed every minute of the tour. He loved travelling and seeing the sights and sounds of Europe, and he loved playing football. He felt privileged to have such a gratifying job. His time at the colliery had made him appreciate his current position. Occasionally, he would think about the times he spent as a fourteen-year-old, down the pit, in total darkness, surrounded by stench and vermin. How glad he was to put those days behind him!

As the tour finished, and the team was on its way back to Sunderland, Jacky was looking forward to seeing Kate and Edna, however, when he returned, his reception was cold. Kate still spent much of her time in bed. Ethel appeared embarrassed by her sister's behaviour and moods and tried to make Jacky feel welcome in his own home.

'Here you are, flower,' said Jacky handing Kate a beautifully wrapped gift box.

'Thank you, Jacky,' said Kate. Her expression remained solemn, as she eased off the ribbon and opened the box. Inside was an unusual but charming brooch encrusted with turquoise.

'That's nice,' said Kate, hardly looking at the gift.

Kate did not even take the brooch out of the box; she just placed it on the bedside table. Jacky felt dejected. He was hoping Kate would be pleased with the brooch, but she looked unimpressed and miserable. He bit his tongue and quickly left the room. Jacky was beginning to lose patience with Kate. It had been over two months since Edna's birth, enough time for Kate to get back on her feet. Jacky could not understand why Kate was so unhappy; she had a new baby, a lovely home and a good husband.

'I'm sorry, Jacky,' said Ethel.

'What have you got to be sorry about?'

'I feel bad. That was rude of Kate. If I'd been given something as beautiful as that, I'd be made up. I don't know what's got into her. I've heard some lasses get down when they've had a bairn, but I'm sure Kate will come round.'

'I'll get the doctor,' said Jacky. 'He can check her over and see what's wrong.'

Ethel was worried; it was not unheard of for women to be locked away in asylums due to insanity caused by childbirth. Kate was certainly acting unreasonably; she had become miserable and quiet.

'Just leave it a few days please, Jacky. Let her get used to you being home. It's been hard for her with your going away with Edna so young.'

Jacky thought about it. He just wanted the old Kate back.

'Alright. But if she's no better by the end of the week, I'll call the doctor.'

'Thank you, Jacky,' said Ethel.

Ethel wondered how she could get Kate to snap out of her melancholia. She did not know what to do. The only thing she could think of was to write to their older sister, Bertha. Ethel put pen to paper and put baby Edna in her pram, and walked to the Post Office. Ethel did not receive a reply in the post from Bertha. Bertha arrived on the doorstep four days later, unannounced.

Kate was surprised and delighted to see her older sister. No mention was made of Kate's condition. The sisters rallied round her and encouraged her to leave her bed. Bertha insisted Kate show her around her home and the parks and shops nearby. They walked along the promenade, taking turns to push Edna in the pram. With the sun on her face and wind in her hair, it wasn't long before Kate was feeling, and looking, healthier and happier.

Bertha only stayed a few days, and Ethel was afraid Kate would once again become dispirited, but Kate continued to improve. She bonded with Edna and felt excited at the prospect of returning to her sewing and making tiny dresses for her baby. Kate and Ethel took trips to the shops and along the beach-front. Ethel chatted to people who Kate did not recognise, but who turned out to be her neighbours. With Ethel's encouragement, Kate started talking to women she passed on the street, whereas before she would have looked away, shy and embarrassed. Kate responded with warmth, rather than the self-conscious awkwardness that had made her appear aloof. Having a baby in a pram helped Kate's situation. Women would approach her and coo over baby Edna.

Two weeks later, Ethel felt she could stay no longer. Kate was well enough to resume her household duties and care for baby Edna. Kate did not want Ethel to leave; she offered to pay her to stay and work for her and Jacky, but Ethel's heart lay in Liverpool, where her fiancé lived and was waiting for her return. Ethel had to find a job in her home-town and build a life for herself. Ethel, who, as a very outgoing young woman, had chatted to Kate's neighbours, and knowing that Kate felt lonely and isolated, had hinted to them that Kate would appreciate their acquaintance. When Ethel left Sunderland, Kate's neighbours called in on Kate, bringing with them scones or tarts, letting her know they were there if she needed them. Kate busied herself with needlework, creating pretty tiny dresses and bonnets for baby Edna. Everyone was friendly when they knew Kate's situation, and gradually Kate made a few good friends and felt relatively happy in her new home. When a neighbour offered Kate money to make an outfit for her child, Kate was delighted to help. She had too many requests to keep up with but was happy to be kept busy doing the job she loved, while taking care of Edna, who was a good baby, and a joy to Kate.

Chapter 37

In January 1910, there was trouble at Horden Colliery. Following the Lloyd George budget, there had been non-payment of wages. At first, it affected just a few men, but as the miners supported each other, the colliery had soon come to a standstill. It was difficult for everyone in the village. Most families lived from week to week on the wages that were brought in, and if these wages stopped for any reason, for many there was no food or savings to fall back on. Meg tried her best to feed her family, but it was not long before she took Micky's only suit to the pawnshop, in order to buy food. The coal supply was dwindling, and she took the children to the beach to search for pieces of coal. Every family did the same, and there was little to be found. It was a dark time for the village; In the proceeding few years, miners and their families had been enticed with the promise of a good wage and improved working conditions; now there was no money coming in and life was embittering.

'Mam, is there anymore? My tummy is still empty,' said William lifting his empty broth bowl, trying to scrape out traces of food.

It broke Meg's heart to see her children hungry. Meg watered down the broth so that it went further, but it was becoming tasteless and held little nourishment. Baby Hannah was still at the breast but needed food to supplement this. As with the other babies when they were weening, Meg took a small mouthful of food, chewed it thoroughly, then took it out of her mouth and fed it to the baby. It was all Meg could do to stop herself from swallowing the food herself. Her stomach rumbled and cramped with pain, but she had to feed her children. Meg's milk dried up, so Hannah no longer had her mother's milk to supplement her diet.

Occasionally, Henry, the lodger, would produce a rabbit (Meg did not ask from where he got it — probably best not to know) which Meg would skin and prepare. The rabbit would provide meat for a week for them all, if Meg used it carefully. Micky hated not being able to provide for his family. He was willing to work his fingers to the bone for his wife and children, but that is just what the pit owners would demand of their workers. The miners and their families would toil and work in harsh conditions for long hours, and, even in the best of times, would have little to show for their labour.

As the days went by, unrest and frustration grew in Horden as conditions worsened, and the community was becoming desperate. Miners would hang around the streets, not knowing what to do to change their plight. Neither the miners nor the managers would give in. The situation was dire. On a cold, gloomy morning in late January, a number of miners gathered in Horden, as was becoming the norm. Micky was amongst them. Soon hundreds of hungry, desperate men and boys milled around the village. More and more men took to the streets, and in their hunger and desperation, it was decided that they would hold a demonstration —marching through Horden village towards Hardwick Hall, the home of Mister Priest, the colliery manager. Micky and his mates joined the march. Micky did not want to cause trouble but could not stand idle while his family went hungry.

Over three hundred men took to the streets, in what was intended to be a peaceful demonstration. Others stayed in the village, milling around the streets, aggression and dissatisfaction growing ever stronger.

As the marchers reached Hardwick Hall, Priest refused to come out and talk. He could see the anger in the miner's faces, and rather than face them he called the police. This made the miners even more frustrated, and it was not long before a small number of men became aggressive. They wanted Priest to do something about their plight — not just sit in his fine home, warm and comfortable, with an abundance of food, while his workers and their families were on the brink of starvation and freezing to death. However, before the police arrived, stones were being thrown and windows were broken. Micky did not want to be part of the violence. He knew it would be futile to try and calm his comrades, so he edged his way out of the throng to the rear of the mob. He could see that there was going to be trouble and did not want to be caught up in any violence, although he felt the anger surging in his blood. It would have been very easy for Micky to release his frustrations with the mindless destruction of property, but he used self-control and backed away. Very quickly, stirred by one another, many miners had become riotous. Priest was frightened for his own and his family's safety. He secured his family in a room at the back of the house, and as police arrived he took up a position on the roof of Hardwick Hall. Anxious for his own safety and that of his family, Priest fired warning shots over the heads of the crowd, in an attempt to disperse them. Protesters clambered up the building and his shotgun was wrenched from him and broken. In the scuffle, a fourteen-year-old lad received shotgun wounds to his leg. The number of police on the scene increased, allowing them to mount a baton charge, driving the rioters back, and finally dispersing the crowd. The boy and one man were badly injured in the incident and taken to hospital.

Meanwhile, with the police away from the village, a few opportunists seized their chance to break the law. Starting with the grocer's shop, they ransacked the store, helping themselves to food and anything else they could lay their hands on. Increasing numbers of men joined the pillage. Why should their family go hungry, when others were helping themselves to food? Violence escalated as the mob became frenzied, smashing windows and doors, out of control. Shopkeepers hurriedly locked their doors and pulled down their shutters, in an attempt to keep the looters at bay. The men were running wild, venting their frustration with destruction. They advanced through the streets, looking for their next target. Within minutes, the Horden Miner's Club, which just a few weeks previously had been their sanctuary, was ransacked, looted and set on fire. Cheers mingled with the billowing smoke, filling the air with menacing contempt. The mob calmed down, watching with satisfaction as the flames engulfed the building. Crowds gathered, watching in disbelief as the structure burned. It was a dark day for Horden. Soon after this, an agreement was made between the miners and the owners, and work resumed at the colliery.

Chapter 38

Nine months after the end of the strike, Meg gave birth to another baby. The baby had not kicked and moved inside her as much as the previous babies. The birth was quick and relatively easy; with Mrs. Coatman and the midwife present. There was a hush as the baby came into the world, and Meg caught the pair swap concerned looks. Meg feared the worse — memories of the loss of her premature baby returning to her. As her mother wrapped the baby in a towel it let out a muted whimper. The baby was alive, however, Mrs. Coatman's tone was sombre.

'It's a lass,' she said mournfully.

'What's up? Is there something wrong?' asked Meg, sweat pouring from her brow.

Mrs. Coatman found it difficult to look her daughter in the eye.

'Sorry, flower, she's not a well baby,' said Mrs. Coatman, shaking her head and handing the tiny bundle to Meg.

The tiny infant was perfectly formed. Her nose was tiny, and her lips were like cupid's bow. But they had a tinge of blue. The baby was pale, with an unnatural hue to her skin. She was small and weak.

'Oh, Mam, she's beautiful. But what's wrong with her?' said Meg, tears welling in her eyes.

'I'd say it was her heart,' said the midwife, 'But if you can afford it, you'd best get the doctor to have a look at her. I'm sorry lass, but I don't think she'll last long.'

Meg felt hollow. She cuddled the baby, holding it to her breast. She was unable to talk. The tiredness and emotion of the day had drained her. Meg sat in silence, rocking the baby in her arms, unable to take her eyes off her precious new-born. The doctor called within the hour and diagnosed a hole in the baby's heart. There was nothing to be done for her.

Martha Coatman ran to meet Micky at the colliery gates and bring him straight back to Meg. She explained the situation, as best she could. Micky ran all the way home and rushed to Meg's bedside. She still sat, babe in arms. The colour had drained completely from her. Micky saw the pair of alabaster faces mirroring each other in serene silence. His heart dropped, and he felt a lump in his throat as he sat on the bed, putting his arm around Meg's shoulder, and looking down at their helpless new baby.

'She's beautiful, Meg,' he said.

Meg said nothing. She just stared into the baby's face. Meg and Micky called their baby girl Elizabeth, after Micky's mother. The baby took to the breast without a problem, but she slept a lot and was small and pale. It was heartbreaking to watch this tiny mite cling to life, knowing she had no hope. They had the priest come to the house and christen the baby, but this was done without a fuss.

Following her confinement, Meg resumed her household duties. She had to leave baby Elizabeth in her crib while she attended to her other children and all the housework. Meg longed to cuddle her helpless baby. Elizabeth fought to stay alive for four weeks, finally peacefully slipping away, cradled in her mother's arms. Tears trickled down Meg's face as she clung to her baby's body, not wanting to let her go.

During the following weeks and months, the image of baby Elizabeth's tiny, blue-tinged face flashed through Meg's mind at unexpected moments, and tears trickled down her face. She was now expecting another baby but was unsure whether she had the mental strength to endure another loss. She hoped and prayed that this baby would be healthy. She would love to have a sister for Hannah, but the health of the baby was all that mattered.

As the months passed, Meg's belly expanded. and she felt the baby moving and kicking inside her. The baby was born quickly; a healthy little girl who they named Mary. Hannah was moved into the bedroom with the three boys, and Mary had the crib in the downstairs room with Meg and Micky. Meg's life revolved around her home and family. Her daily chores kept her on her feet from dawn until dusk, but she was happy.

Micky, like most men, did not spend much time in the family home. With the football season back up and running, Micky would either be playing for Horden Athletic or going to watch Jacky playing for Sunderland. The Horden football team were going from strength to strength, and became Wearside League winners for the first time in April 1912. It was a big boost for Horden, with many of the locals following their team. This gave them something to cheer about.

Conditions had improved at the colliery, and Micky was doing well as a hewer, however, pay was not steady, as Micky was on piecework. The team of men he worked with were all hard-working and fair, with two men on each of the three shifts. Some weeks, the coal would just fly out of the seam, the men filling tub after tub, and the pay would be higher than usual, but on other weeks the rocks seemed to want to hang on to their precious coal, and even though the miners worked harder than ever, the amount of coal extracted would be insufficient to provide six men with a decent week's pay.

Micky was strong and good at his job and always kept out of trouble. He worked with intelligence, and the managers saw that he would make a good deputy. Subsequently, Micky was offered the job of deputy down the mine, but before he could take on this role, he had to be trained. The job of a deputy was a responsible position, being in charge of the safety of the mines, and Micky had to be qualified to do the job. Deputies had to ensure the mine was well ventilated and that the roofs were safe. They would have to support the roof with props of wood, replacing old workings. They would also clear away any sudden eruptions of gas or fallen stone. The mine had to be safe, ready for hewers to do their job of extracting the coal. Deputies would do much of the work themselves or delegate where appropriate. They were in charge of a certain district of the pit. Micky's pay would be better than at present, and it would be a fixed rate — ensuring a regular income.

Chapter 39

In 1910, Leigh Roose had suffered a broken wrist and no longer played for Sunderland. The team missed Roose's skill and showmanship. The players had to adapt to a different, more traditional style of goalkeeping from their new signing. Frank Cuggy and Charlie Buchan signed for Sunderland in March 1911. They played up at the front with Jacky. The three men soon developed an understanding and a way of playing that was arguably the best in the league, becoming known as the Sunderland triangle. Jacky was thriving at Sunderland. Jacky had also made an impression on the England committee and was called up to play for England in February 1912. The International Championship was held every year and had been for the past twenty-eight years. The four home countries took part: England, Scotland, Wales and Ireland. The games were played in the respective countries, changing the home/away advantage each year. At its foundation, this was the first-ever international football tournament. This year, England had to travel to Dublin, Ireland, for the first game of the championship. Jacky travelled with his teammate, George Holley, who had also been selected for the squad. It was the first time Jacky had travelled to Ireland. Jacky felt proud and privileged to be selected to represent his country and was thrilled to be able to travel in the process. He had been selected to play on the left wing, which was not his favoured side, but still, he played well, as did the entire team. Bob Crompton, of Blackburn Rovers, led the team onto the pitch, and from the start they dominated the game. The final score was 6 – 1 to England, with goals from Holley, John Simpson, Bert Freeman and a hat trick from Harold Fleming, the Swindon Town player. Michael Hamill scored the consolation goal for Ireland.

Scotland and England both beat Ireland and Wales, and the deciding match was held between the two at Hampden Park in Glasgow, at the end of March. Jacky was disappointed not to feature in this game. A crowd of over one hundred and twenty-seven thousand watched the match, which ended in a one all draw, with Sunderland's Holley getting the England goal, and Andrew Wilson the Scotland goal. Goal difference was not taken into account, so the championship ended with England and Scotland as joint winners.

Later that year, in September, the 1912/13 season got off to a slow start, and Sunderland had not had a win in their first seven games of the season. The eighth game was at home to Middlesbrough. Bob Kyle, the Sunderland manager, had made expensive signings, purchasing Charlie Gladwin and Joe Butler for £3000 — a large sum of money. It was Butler's second match in goal for Sunderland and Gladwin's debut for the team. Inspired by the Roker crowd, the players were spurred on to play this game with renewed determination, wanting to beat their rivals. A goal from Harry Low gave the Sunderland side a surge of confidence, and Jacky Mordue, Holley and Hall all went on to score in the 4 – 0 win. The new signings of Gladwin and Butler had ensured Sunderland kept a clean sheet. This was the turning point of the season. The following game was against Jacky's old team, Woolwich Arsenal, and Jacky put two away — one a penalty, with Holley securing the 3 – 0 victory. Jacky was the regular penalty taker for Sunderland, having never missed a spot-kick for his side to date. Sunderland won their next two games easily and were soon climbing the table. In December, there was a crowd of just 10,000 present when Charlie Buchan scored an amazing five goals against Liverpool. Martin and Jacky Mordue added to his tally, making it a decisive 7 – 0 win to Sunderland. On Christmas day, Sunderland travelled to Sheffield and beat Wednesday 2 – 1, but the following day, Wednesday returned to Roker Park and managed to defeat Sunderland by two goals to nil. From that day, Sunderland did not lose a league game. They also had an amazing F.A. Cup run. The first quarter final was at Roker Park against Newcastle. The derby game was an uneventful 0 – 0. The replay was held just four days later, at St. James' Park. Once again the sides could not be separated, with a 2 – 2 draw. Sunderland travelled to Manchester and beat United by three goals to one in a league match, and then had to replay the F.A. Cup tie once more, at St. James' Park. On this occasion, Sunderland came out strongest, and Jacky Mordue slotted home the opening goal, shortly followed by Holley making it 2 – 0 at halftime. In the second half, Sunderland continued to dominate, and Newcastle became increasingly frustrated, giving away a penalty. Jacky Mordue blasted the ball into the net to make the score 3 – 0, and secure Sunderland's place in the semi-finals.

At the end of March, Sunderland played Burnley at Bramall Lane, home of Sheffield United, in the F.A. Cup semi-final. The game finished in a 0 – 0 draw and had to be replayed four days later — this time at Birmingham City's ground, St. Andrews. Burnley went ahead, and were leading 2 – 1 at half time, but in the second half Sunderland dominated, and Buchan put them level. Sunderland persistently attacked and frustrated the Burnley defence, who gave away a penalty with just five minutes of the match remaining. Jacky Mordue coolly struck the ball past the Burnley keeper, and Sunderland were through to the F.A. Cup final for the first time in their history. In the meantime, Micky Mordue's Horden Colliery team were dominating their league once again, and were also having a great run in the Monkwearmouth Cup.

Chapter 40

The nineteenth of April 1913 was a big day in the footballing lives of the Mordue brothers.

Jacky and the Sunderland team had travelled down to London to play the F.A. Cup final, at Crystal Palace. Their opponents were Aston Villa, who had won the cup on four previous occasions — the last time being in 1905, when they had beaten Newcastle 2 – 0.

Coincidentally, on the very same day, Micky's Horden Athletic were playing in the Monkwearmouth Cup final against Southwick — the match being played at Roker Park, Sunderland's ground, of all places. Micky was delighted to be in the team for Horden's first Monkwearmouth Cup final, but he was sorry to have to miss taking the train down to London to watch Jacky in the F.A. Cup final.

Both games kicked off at the same time, 3:30 pm.

There was a crowd of over one hundred and twenty thousand at Crystal Palace, eagerly awaiting the match between the two leading clubs in the first division. Thousands of Sunderland supporters made the trip on the packed trains, hemmed in like sardines for seven hours. This did not dampen their spirits; they were out to enjoy their trip down south. It was a beautiful sunny day, and many travellers took advantage of the latest innovation, the motor buses, which took them on sightseeing tours of London.

The Sunderland players had never been involved in such a big occasion, and they knew they had a real chance of taking the double: the F.A. Cup and league title. Some of the players were physically sick before the match, and Bob Kyle had a job to keep the players composed.

Jacky anxiously jogged out onto the pitch, wearing the red and white striped shirt of Sunderland; he had never, before, been so nervous. The noise and the number of people were incredible. He could feel his heart pounding and his stomach-churning. How was he going to play football, when he could hardly put one leg in front of the other? He so wanted to enjoy this day and make the most of his opportunity, however, he found it difficult to stop thinking about the importance of this game and put himself under a lot of pressure.

As the game started, the Sunderland player's nerves were evident; they did not play their usual game and made many mistakes — giving the ball away all too easily. Sunderland's Scottish player, Charlie Thomson, was out to unsettle Aston Villa's Harry Hampton, who in a recent Scotland versus England international had bundled the Scottish goalkeeper over the line. Their exchanges were the most prevalent incidents in the first half of the match.

Both sides were playing the long passing game, but Villa were distinctly better than Sunderland. Their forwards made more runs, and their defence played with energy and determination, if not skill. Jacky Mordue did manage to make one terrific shot, but it hit the Villa crossbar. Villa were awarded a penalty for a trip on Stephenson in the area. Wallace stepped up to take the penalty but thumped the ball well wide of the target. It was a let-off for Sunderland. Thomson, Richardson and practically the entire Sunderland team, were having a bad day. They were overcome with nerves and could not get into their stride and play to their potential. Buchan and Martin missed shots that they had been putting in the back of the net with ease in the run-up to the final. Even though Aston Villa dominated, the teams went in with the match goalless at half-time.

Back at Roker Park, Horden were playing well. Micky Mordue and the rest of the team were passing the ball with confidence and putting together some lovely moves. Southwick stayed solid in defence at first, but as soon as Horden went a goal ahead, Southwick tried to push forward and left gaps at the back. Horden punished them, scoring two more goals before half-time. Southwick continued to attack in the second half, not giving up, and they managed to penetrate the Horden defence, making the score 3 – 1, but Horden kept breaking, and the final score was 6 – 1 to Horden. They were the Monkwearmouth Charity Cup winners for the first time. Their captain, Tucker Miller, lifted the trophy.

At Crystal Palace, the F.A. Cup final was becoming quite a memorable game, but not due to the standard of play, but the battles that were occurring on the pitch. Thomson and Hampton continued their feud, and at one point Hampton was down injured for several minutes. He retaliated, kicking Thomson when he was down. Neither player was sent off during the match. Thomson played what was probably the worst game of his season. He was never comfortable on the ball and appeared to be overcome with nerves and preoccupied with his dispute with Hampton.

To make things worse, Hampton netted the ball from a free-kick. Thankfully for Thomson and the rest of the Sunderland team, the Villa crowd's celebrations were thwarted, as the goal was disallowed for offside. It was a scrappy game which never flowed or did the teams justice. Hardy, the Villa goalkeeper, had to leave the field for ten minutes with a sprained ankle. Harrop took his place in goal, during which time Sunderland failed to exploit the situation. When Hardy returned to the pitch, his ankle was heavily strapped. The Villa followers loudly cheered, uttering their support. This seemed to lift the Villa team, and they continued to surge forward. The attack forced a corner, which Wallace placed with accuracy into the box, enabling Tom Barber to neatly head the ball into the back of the net. A thunderous roar went up from the Aston Villa supporters.

The Villa defenders took no chances from then on, kicking the ball into touch at any sign of danger. Their forwards did not ease up and continued to press the Sunderland defence.

Sunderland made a promising attack, but Martin's shot struck the post; it seemed that Sunderland were destined not to score. The allocated match time drew to a close, but the referee kept the game going, as there had been so many stoppages. The unusually long period of extra time flew by for the Sunderland supporters, whereas, for the Villa supporters, every minute seemed like an hour, as they anxiously held onto their lead. Eventually, the referee blew his whistle. Aston Villa had won the F.A. Cup.

Jacky Mordue and the rest of the Sunderland players were devastated. They fell to the floor, heads in hands, while the Villa team celebrated their victory.

Back at Roker Park, a deathly hush fell over the crowd as news came through that Sunderland had been defeated.

Thomson and Hampton had remained on the pitch until the end of the match, but they both received suspensions following the game. The referee was also disciplined for allowing the game to deteriorate so badly and allow seventeen minutes of extra time. The spectacle that was to have brought the game much good publicity had had the opposite effect.

Jacky and his teammates were utterly dejected. They knew the cup had been theirs for the taking and were disappointed at the way they had lost the game. They could not hold their heads high and say they did their best; their performance had been a shambles. The long journey home was subdued.

Just four days after the final Sunderland, had to travel down to Birmingham and play Aston Villa once again, this time in the league. With just three games left of the season, the title was still undecided. It was another battle between Sunderland and Villa. Sunderland had the advantage and just needed to beat Villa to finish top. A crowd of 70,000 watched the match at Villa Park. Sunderland wanted revenge, but Villa had confidence, knowing they could beat their opponents. The Sunderland players rallied round. They were determined Villa would not beat them for a second time. It was a much better game than the F. A. Cup final had been; both teams playing the exciting, flowing football that had taken them to the top of the division. Villa took a first-half lead, but the Sunderland player's nerves held up, and Walter Tinsley scored to make the score a one, all draw. The title was still undecided, but Sunderland had the advantage.

Sunderland won their last two games of the season, beating Bolton Wanderers and Bradford City. They won the league for the fifth time in their history, after a gap of eleven years. The players received their medals and lifted the trophy. Jacky and his Sunderland teammates were elated. This was another momentous occasion for Jacky.

Back in Sacriston, Dan Mordue read the newspaper report to his mother. The Sunderland trio of Mordue, Buchan and Holley were much acclaimed — even appearing in an Andy Capp cartoon. And Dan was thrilled when he opened a packet of cigarettes, only to find his youngest brother's face staring up at him, from the cigarette card he pulled from the packet. He gave the card to his mother, and she carried it in her purse from that day on.

At the end of the football season, Sunderland went on another tour of Europe. The team left Sunderland on 1st May and travelled to Hungary, Austria and German. The players were met with the same enthusiasm and admiration they had received on their previous tour. The matches were gritty, and the conditions were difficult. There were twenty thousand people in Budapest watching the first match, which was against Ferencvaros. Jacky and teammate Charlie Buchan played out of their skins and enthralled the spectators who cheered every goal. Sunderland won 9 – 0, but it would have been more; the referee turned down three penalty shouts in the first half, not wanting Sunderland to score their opening goal from the penalty spot.

In the second match, the referee oversaw the match from the side-lines; he refused to referee from the pitch, as he did not want to get his boots muddy.

A later game was played in Budapest, against Blackburn Rovers, who were also touring. This was the most difficult game of the tour. Sixteen thousand spectators watched the match. The referee was a Manchester man, who was now coaching in Austria. Sunderland had to come from behind to win the match and were presented with a handsome, grand statuette bronze figure, valued at £25 — with each player receiving a medal worth £2.

When the team was travelling from Vienna to Berlin, they were on the same train that conveyed Princess Victoria of Prussia to Berlin, for her marriage with Prince Ernst of Hanover. They also visited the cathedral where the wedding took place. They were fortunate enough to greet King George and Queen Mary in the streets of Berlin. The royal couple had travelled to Germany to attend the wedding, along with other royals and dignitaries, including Tsar Nicholas II of Russia.

The Austria-Hungary legs of the tour had been enjoyable and well-natured, but in Germany it was a different story. The crowd and players were full of anger and aggression. In Berlin, the German players were unhappy with the Sunderland players using their shoulders to edge players off the ball. In return, the Germans kicked everything that moved. Sunderland won seven goals to nil but were tripped and abused as they left the field.

Jacky enjoyed his time off the pitch in Germany; the team being treated well. They spent an enjoyable day at Potsdam, the residence of the Kaiser. The tour was organised at a slower pace than previous tours, thus allowing the players to see something of the countries they visited.

The final match was in Hamburg. This was another fierce battle, with Sunderland winning five goals to nil. Richardson was pleased to get himself sent off in the last ten minutes, having retaliated following a nasty tackle. Charlie Buchan followed him off the pitch, not wanting to be kicked any longer. He felt he would be safer in the dressing room than on the 'battlefield'. As the Sunderland players left the field, the crowd threw missiles; umbrellas were used to protect the players.

Off the pitch, the mood was more relaxed, and the team enjoyed their leisure time, before returning to London on Saturday 24th of May. Jacky headed back up to Sunderland with some of his teammates. He was pleased to see Kate and Edna, who was now four years old, and becoming a very confident and independent little girl.

Jacky spent time with his family but also made time to play handball and see his brothers and mother.

Chapter 41

Four months later and the Sunderland team were looking forward to another season. Their first match was away at Preston North End. Jacky was fired up for the game, eager to play competitively after the summer break. The match did not start well, with Sunderland going behind, but the team soon got into their stride and drew level. Jacky's pace was too much for the Preston defence; he flew past them time and time again, crossing the ball to Charlie Buchan. The Preston defenders' frustration was evident — culminating in a rash tackle. Jacky's leg buckled and twisted under the challenge, as he crashed to the ground. Jacky did not get back to his feet. The pain was excruciating; he thought he may have a broken leg. The Sunderland players ran across, some gathering round Jacky and others laying into the Preston defender. A twelve-man brawl ensued, while Jacky writhed in agony on the turf. Once the players had calmed down and Jacky had regained his composure, he was helped off the pitch, his face white and contorted with the pain.

Jacky was seen by a doctor, who concluded that the leg was not broken, but the knee was badly damaged. Jacky had his leg encased in plaster and had to stay in hospital, leg raised. Jacky was mortified and highly frustrated. He could do nothing but lay in bed, under the instruction of the doctor.

'If you put your weight on that knee you might cause even more damage. As it is, it's unlikely that the knee will ever be the same again,' said the doctor, matter-of-factly.

Jacky was devastated. He relied on his body to carry out his job. His life was sport. Jacky could not imagine a life without football or handball. There was nothing he could do to help himself. He just had to lay there with his leg raised. Jacky was cheered by the visits of his teammates and Kate. They broke the monotony and tried to reassure him that he would soon be back on his feet. However, as the days passed, and it seemed that Jacky's knee would never get better, Jacky's spirits sunk ever lower. When his friends visited, he pretended he was sleeping. He could no longer bear to hear about the matches he had missed. When Kate visited, he was abrupt with her. She could do no right.

After three long weeks, the cast was removed, and Jacky was able to leave hospital, but his leg was far from mended. He lived under a cloud, which Kate could not disperse. The doctor remained pessimistic, in reality knowing little about such injuries and referring to archaic treatment procedures. Kate did not know what to do. Edna had been excited to see her father and ran to him. Jacky, seeing that Edna was oblivious to his injury and about to propel herself at him, yelled at his daughter. Edna jumped and recoiled from Jacky, bursting into tears. Kate gathered Edna in her arms, but Jacky admonished Kate for not restraining the girl. Kate and Edna left the room, leaving Jacky feeling worse than ever. He was angry with himself and angry with everyone. Rather than lifting, the cloud was beginning to engulf the whole family. They were fortunate that Sunderland were still paying Jacky's wages, as he was in contract until the end of the season, but if Jacky did not recover, his contract would not be renewed, and there would be no money coming in. Jacky was frightened to put weight on his leg, fearing he would do further damage, but he knew he needed to get back on his feet. He began to stop caring. Maybe he would just lie back and go to sleep and not wake up. That would put an end to his worries. Unbeknown to Jacky, Kate wrote to Micky. She did not know who else to turn to. Jacky adored Micky, and if anyone could get through to Jacky, it would be Micky.

Micky did not hesitate in coming to visit Jacky. He was on a night shift the week he received the letter. Following his shift, he returned home, bathed, ate and then headed to Sunderland to see his brother.

Jacky was startled when Micky walked through the door. It shocked Micky to see Jacky looking so pale and melancholy. He could see through the forced smile on Jacky's face.

'Well, I was ganna buy you a pint, but if you're not going to get out of that chair, I'll have to go on my own,' said Micky.

'I can't get out, Micky. I'm finished,' said Jacky.

'Says who?'

'The doctor. He said if I put weight on my knee, it might never be the same again.'

'So, you're just going to sit in that chair for the rest of your life?'

'What if I can't walk properly again, Micky? What am I going to do?'

'You won't find out unless you get out of that chair, Jacky.'

Jacky bowed his head. He was scared.

'Come on, lad. Get to your feet. I'll give you a hand,' said Micky.

Jacky wanted to fall into his brother's arms. He wanted Micky to make things better. Micky always made things better.

'You're going to have to do this, Jacky. I can't do it for you.'

The brothers sat in silence for a few minutes. Jacky was summoning up the will to attempt to stand unaided. Without a word, he pushed on the arms of his chair and stood up. Jacky was slightly shaky, but he was surprised at how easy it had been. His legs, even though they had not been used for a few weeks, were strong enough to support him.

From that day, Jacky did not look back. He gradually used his legs more and more. Once Jacky made up his mind that he was going to be alright, he exercised and worked through pain to build up his muscles and regain fitness. Jacky tried to rush his recovery, as he could not wait to play again, and regretted the time he had already wasted moping in his chair. After two months, Jacky was running and kicking a ball and training with the team. In mid-November he travelled with the team to Goodison Park to play Everton. He found it difficult, and as the game progressed the pain in his knee worsened, but Jacky would not let anyone know the discomfort he felt. He was not as sharp as he had been before the injury, but his skills had not left him. Jacky knew he would have to rely more on his prowess than his speed to get past defenders, but hoped his speed would return the more he played. The game went well, and Jacky scored a goal, as Sunderland won by five goals to one.

Chapter 42

Meg and Micky's fourth son, John, was born at the beginning of 1914. He was a bonny lad. Now, with four sons and two daughters to look after, Meg was on the go constantly, but she was very happy. Micky was a deputy manager at the pit, with a steady, reasonable wage. They rented their own house and had six lovely children — although George would always be frail. Meg's family lived close by, and her younger sisters, Martha and Teenie, were often calling by to help out with their nieces and nephews and chat with Meg, as she carried out her chores. Micky was a good husband and, although he enjoyed a pint, he did not spend his wages on gambling or excessive drinking. He spent much of his free time playing football and handball, as he had always done.

It was the beginning of August when William, their eldest son, who had just had his eleventh birthday, came hurtling through the back door — tangled with the washing hanging on the line.

'Da! Da! The Germans have invaded Belgium.'

Micky jumped up from his chair and pulled on his boots, and he and William went back down the street to find out more about this shocking news.

On the 4th of August 1914, Britain declared war on Germany. It was not long before posters were put up asking people to join the army. Coal was in demand, so miners were not required to go to war, but as the weeks dragged on, the call for volunteers grew stronger.

At the beginning of September 1914, as the new football season got underway, Sunderland played away at Aston Villa. There was a major recruitment drive at the ground, with the French and Russian national anthems being blasted around the terraces. Many of the Sunderland players, including Jacky, were eager to sign up, however, the football league continued, and the players were in contracts, so unable to go to war. They were sure that one day, they would be able to do their bit for their country, so every weekday an army instructor came to the ground and put the players through military training, using broomsticks instead of rifles. The players found it hard to concentrate on the game and were unhappy and frustrated as the war progressed, and they could do nothing.

Bill Coatman made the decision to join up. He was a single man of thirty, and this was his chance to serve his country. Tom was not as keen as Bill — he was not the fighting kind, so was happy to stay and work down the pit. Micky felt torn. He wanted to enlist with his brother-in-law, but things were different for him, having a wife and six children. At the big club, there was talk of who had signed up. At first it was thought that the war would be over by Christmas, but it soon became evident that this was not going to be the case. Micky sat at a table with his friends, Wilf and Bobby.

'There's a lot of lads joined up who have never lifted more than a pen. How are we supposed to beat the Huns with a bunch of office boys?' Wilf quipped.

'Well, they canna do much else with their fancy educations when there's a war on. You try telling the Germans that the pen is mightier than the sword,' said Micky.

Bobby fished out a leaflet from his pocket. It was the propaganda that was being handed out to any suitable young men, after the last cup-tie at Roker Park.

'What did you keep that for, Bobby? You're not thinking of signing up, are you?

'Haven't made me mind up yet, but, aye, I'm considering it.'

'But we don't have to go. The need for coal is greater than ever, now.'

'I've been stuck down that pit ever since I left school. I'm thirty now and still living at home. Maybe it's time I did something else. They'll be plenty of people to man the pits.'

'Aye, you've got a point there, Bobby,' said Wilf. 'Maybe Sheila Kelly would look twice at me if I wore a uniform.'

'You'd need more than a uniform to win Sheila Kelly's affection,' laughed Micky.

'A few medals pinned to my chest; how could she say no?'

The friends laughed and chatted, but the idea of joining up was growing stronger.

'Well, if you two are in so am I. I'd have nobody to sink a pint with if you two go,' said Micky.

'It's different for you, Micky; you've got Meg and the bairns.'

'Aye, I'd make them proud of me. Our Jacky plays football for England. I'll fight for England.'

As the weeks went by and the war continued, Micky felt increasingly frustrated. They had been told the war would be won quickly. Micky would not be away from his family for long. Meg had her parents living close by; she would cope without him. The thought of being injured, or worse, never crossed Micky's mind.

At the end of October 1914, Micky and his friends decided once and for all that they would like to fight for their country, and chose to sign up for the Yorkshire Regiment, whose nearest recruitment centre was in Sunderland. They set off on the train and joined the queue outside the recruitment office. There were men and boys of all shapes, ages and sizes. Some looked like they would struggle to tie their shoelaces; others looked like they were still at school. The smell of stale human sweat filled the air. The three friends filled in their application forms with details of their address, age, occupation and religion. When they were finally called in, they each had their eyes tested and had to strip for their medicals. When this was all successfully completed, they each had to swear an oath and that was it. The recruiting sergeant took his sixpence per man. Micky, Bobby and Wilf had taken the King's shilling. There was no going back; they were now soldiers.

Two days later, the joining instructions arrived in the post, including a travel warrant.

'Looks like they want me,' said Micky to Meg.

Meg had to hold back the tears. It was a brave and honourable thing that Micky was doing, and she knew it would be hard for him, but it would also be hard for those he was leaving behind. Many a wife was glad to see their husband going off to war — with regular money arriving and none of the demands made upon them in their loveless marriages. But Meg and Micky were still deeply in love, and it was at night-time, when all the children were sleeping and she found herself alone in her bed, that she knew she would miss Micky most. Despite the fact she had had eight babies, and spent her days with her sleeves rolled up, pinny on, toiling for hours on end —at night-time Micky made her feel like a woman. He had only to wrap his arms around her, and her cares would melt away.

His kisses healed her weary mind and body, and the touch of his hands still thrilled her. She knew Micky would be a good soldier; he was brave and strong and had a sharp mind. It was difficult to know what to say to Micky. She wanted to plead with him not to go, but knew she must support his decision and not let him see how truly worried and upset she felt.

'How could anyone not want you?' she said kissing the top of his head as he sat staring at the letter.

Meg's sister, Martha, moved in when it was time for Micky to go away. It was not that Meg would be unable to cope on her own; Micky was the breadwinner — not a housewife. It was that Henry still lodged there, and it would be unheard of for a woman living on her own, or with just young bairns to have a male lodger in the house.

When it was time to leave, Micky hugged and kissed all his children — something he seldom did. It was not through lack of love, but it just wasn't the way. Lastly, he held Meg in his arms, holding back the tears. They had said their goodbyes in the privacy of their own room the night before.

Wilf Belcher, Bobby and Micky boarded the train and waved, as the whistle blew and the engine hissed. The train slowly moved along the tracks and in a puff of steam, Micky was gone.

Meg could see the pride in William's face, as he said farewell to his father. It took all her strength to hold back her tears. Micky's mother had not come to wave off her son. She knew she would not be able to hide her emotions.

Mary and Hannah skipped back down the road. The excitement of seeing their father onto the train had passed, and they were too young to comprehend the reality of the situation. Baby John started to cry, and it was a relief for Meg to be distracted by her young one. She had no time to dwell on the departure of her husband; her days would carry on as before, but her nights would be long and lonely.

Micky, Wilf and Bobby arrived in Richmond in their civilian clothes, and it would be a long time before they received their khakis. Micky and Wilf were put in the same tent, but Bobby was separated from them. It was cold and damp, and the ground moved in mud. They were given just one blanket each, which was alive with unwanted inhabitants.

Twenty-two men had to squeeze inside one bell tent. The men had to squat in the tents, as there were no ground-sheets or seats, and the floor was thick with mud. The air in the tents was dense, thick with the smell of human odours and cigarette smoke. Some of the men pissed in their boots at night-time and then tipped it outside. The urine allegedly helped the leather soften; making the boots more comfortable for the long marches ahead. The food was not fit for a dog. It was served in a mess tin, and was fatty meat, swimming in a watery broth. The best way to eat it was with the hands, fishing out the gristle and bone from the greasy water. And the portions were meagre. The men felt constantly hungry.

Luckily, they only stayed at Richmond for just over a week, before being moved to Belton Park Camp near Grantham. Here they joined the 6th Battalion of the Yorkshire Regiment: the Green Howards. Conditions here were just as bad until the end of November, when all the trainee soldiers were put into newly built huts. These felt luxurious in comparison. Micky and Wilf were issued with a temporary blue uniform as the khaki uniforms were still unavailable.

The training was hard and constant, but Micky had no problem with it. His work as a miner and his long arduous games of handball had kept him at the peak of physical fitness. There were many men, office clerks, and the like, who had never put their bodies through such physical tests. It was a slow and painful process for these men, but they increased in strength and stamina by the day. The day started with physical exercise from six until seven in the morning. Drill, bayonet and tactical training followed this, and also a great deal of marching. At first the marches were about eight to fifteen miles, weighed down with a full pack, but they increased in length to over twenty miles at a time. At night-time, there was often trench digging and emplacement construction to be carried out.

There was relief from the gruelling training, in the form of more physical exercise: sports. Micky was chosen to play football for his company, and inter-company matches took place on Saturday afternoons. Even though there was a shortage of uniforms and weapons, there was a plentiful supply of footballs, quoits and other sports equipment.

Micky kicked a ball around at any spare moment; there was always someone happy to join in. Even though it was gruelling and incessant, Micky enjoyed the physical challenges he was put through, but not the repetitive drills and inspections. He missed his family: the children and Meg. He missed having a pint with his mates at the club. He missed the smell of freshly baked pies that filled his home, and the broth bubbling in the cooking pot by the fireside. On Sunday afternoons, they were given a few hours off, and he and Wilf would walk to the local pub for a pint, or to a local farmhouse which sold tea and cakes and had a huge open fire at which to sit.

Even though many men from the village had gone to war, life went on much as it always had in Horden. There were stories in the newspapers, but the realities of war were difficult to envisage. That was until December the 16th 1914.

The day started the same as any other day in Hartlepool, a busy dock seven miles down the coast from Horden. People were going about their business as usual until, without warning, shells were fired from three German heavy cruisers, just off the coast. The targets were the shore batteries and the lighthouse, but residential areas in close proximity were also hit. The bombardment lasted some forty minutes, with over a thousand shells raining down. Screams were heard, as people ran frantically through the streets, separated from loved ones. Coastguards tried to evacuate the area as quickly as possible, but communication lines had been broken, and the scene was chaotic. The gasometer was hit, causing an almighty explosion. Over one hundred people were killed, including nine soldiers — the first to die in battle on British soil, in almost two hundred years. As well as those that lost their lives, many more were injured.

The Royal Navy was aware of an imminent raid, and had placed their warships at sea in order to trap the retreating German fleet, but a misunderstanding among the British allowed the Germans warships to escape. Hartlepool was left reeling, with many churches, public buildings and hotels damaged — as well as over three hundred homes. There had been a simultaneous attack on Scarborough, which had also caused much destruction, and an attack on Whitby, which had damaged the abbey.

The attacks, being so close to home, rocked the residents of Horden. Tom Coatman visited his sister, Meg, telling her the news.

'Cold-blooded murder, that's what it was. Bairns killed in their own homes, without any warning. And where was the bloody Navy while all this was going on? That's what I'd like to know.'

'The Germans wouldn't attack Horden, would they, Tom?'

'Well, I wouldn't put it past them. We're by the coast and we've got coal.'

'I wish Micky was here.'

'Well, he couldn't do out if a shell landed on the roof. Nobody could. Anyhow I don't suppose those Huns will be back in a hurry. It was unexpected this time, but we'll not get caught like that again.'

'What's the world coming to when folk aren't safe in their own houses? I must admit, I thought Micky was daft going off to fight, but now I can see why he's doing it. The sooner we beat them Germans the better,' said Meg, fighting back the tears.

Tom was tempted to say that without coal, the war would soon be lost, but he held his tongue. He did not want to undermine his brother-in-law's war effort, and knew that Meg needed assurance that Micky was doing the right thing.

'Aye, well, Micky will help have this war won before we know it, but until then I'm just up the road; I'll be round at the first sign of trouble.'

Chapter 43

Back at camp, the days turned to weeks, and the weeks to months. Micky and Wilf missed their families and their homes. They thought they would be making a difference, but here they were doing neither one thing nor another – just training, with the reason they joined up, going into battle, eluding them.

Finally, on the 5th of April 1915, the battalion left Grantham and began the march to Rugby. The number of men on the march was immense; the line must have stretched for over a mile. They marched for twenty miles a day, via Scalford, Thrussington and Whetstone. At night-time, they slept in schools or public buildings, packing in like sardines. On the Wednesday, they marched through Leicester, where they were met by incredibly generous support. All work had been suspended, and the streets were lined by a cheering, enthusiastic crowd, showering gifts and good wishes on the troops, as they marched through the town. It lifted Micky's spirits to see so many people giving them so much respect and support. Their tired limbs found renewed strength, as they proudly proceeded past the masses.

On 8th April, they reached Rugby and then took the train to their new training camp at Witley. Their spirits were lifted further, as they viewed the countryside and open heathland. The weather was glorious, and the mood was upbeat. At Witley, intensive training at brigade and divisional levels began in earnest. On the first of May, His Majesty King George V, accompanied by Lord Kitchener, inspected the Division. As they passed by, Micky noticed how bloated and red-faced Kitchener looked. Far removed from the imposing figure portrayed in the propaganda posters, Kitchener had a glazed, detached look on his face — like a man in a mask. In contrast, the King looked as regal as Micky had imagined him and exuded an air of importance. Micky brought to mind how, not so long ago, Jacky had told him of seeing the King and Queen in Germany. How circumstances had changed since then!

The following day, it was reported that the King wanted to convey to the troops his appreciation of the splendid appearance and steadiness of the men on parade the previous day, and that he had very great pleasure to see such a splendid body of men. His majesty also remarked on the good condition of the horses.

A couple of days later, Micky received a letter from Meg saying their three youngest children, Hannah, Mary and John, had all gone down with the measles. Micky wished he could go home to be with his wife and family, knowing how worried Meg would be. Having lost her sister, Susannah, to measles, Meg dreaded her children catching the disease, although she knew it was almost inevitable.

Micky received another letter from Meg three days later. She was writing to say that the girls seemed to be over the worst, but baby John was in a bad way. Micky was devastated. He knew Meg would not have wished to worry him needlessly; things must be very serious. Micky longed to return home and see Meg and the children. He wondered if he should approach his superiors to request leave, but knew it would not be permitted. He quickly wrote a letter to Meg, acknowledging the family's plight, and sending his love to her and the children.

The following morning, Micky was summoned to see his Commanding Officer.

'Take a seat, Mordue,' said the officer.

Micky knew it was bad news and dropped himself into the chair.

'I'm sorry to have to inform you that we have received a telegram, informing us that your son, John, has died. You will be allowed home immediately but must return in seven days.'

'Thank you, sir,' replied Micky, shell-shocked. John was just fifteen months old, and Micky only knew him as a babe in arms. He had not seen him taking his first steps or heard him utter the word 'Dada', although Meg had written and told him John had said it repeatedly. Micky had not been there for Meg or for baby John.

In a trance, he returned to his room and packed a bag. He took out the recent photograph he had of John. He was a bonny baby with chubby cheeks and strong limbs. He was not under-nourished or neglected. John was a thriving baby boy, who weighed more than most babies brought up in the village. Micky tucked the photo in his breast pocket and set off to return home to Horden.

Chapter 44

John was laid out in a tiny white coffin on the dining table, surrounded by flowers. Micky found it hard to comprehend that this peaceful-looking child was not simply sleeping. Micky had an urge to pick up his young son and shake him so that he would wake up. Surely it was all a mistake? John was merely asleep and would stir and call for his 'Dada' at any moment. Micky stroked John's cheek. It was icily cold. Micky turned to Meg. Her eyes were red with the tears she had cried. Micky took her in his arms and the tears returned. Meg's body shook with silent sobs as she clung to Micky.

'I nursed him the best I could, Micky. I'm so sorry,' wept Meg.

'Lass! Don't even think about apologising. I know you are the best mother a child could hope for, and I know you would have done everything possible to help our John. He looks like a little angel lying there. God must have reckoned the only place for him is in heaven.'

Meg had sat and nursed her three children day and night. Her sister, Martha, had helped with the other children and the chores. John had been a bonny baby; it seemed incredible that his life should be cut short so cruelly.

Hannah and Mary were still poorly but on the mend. They did not understand what had happened to their little brother. When Meg had tried to explain that he had gone to heaven to be with God they were not happy. They wanted John to be there with them.

The funeral took place the following day. Meg stayed at home with the girls, while Micky and the older boys went to the funeral. John's tiny white coffin was placed across his father's lap, as they made their way to the church. John was placed in the same grave as baby Elizabeth. Following the burial, close family and friends went back to the Mordues' home for the wake, the women doing their best to comfort Meg.

Meg was in a daze, trying to stay strong in front of her other children. Losing John, her youngest son, when he had not long since celebrated his first birthday, had knocked her for six. She had had a soft spot for her youngest; his bright nature had filled her with joy.

Now all that remained was the photograph, which had pride of place on the sideboard.

It was extremely hard for Micky to say goodbye a few days later, when it was time to leave. He hugged his family and did not want to let go. A few months earlier, he had said goodbye to John, aware of the dangers he, Micky, himself faced, but not imagining that it would be John whose life would come to such an abrupt end.

'I'll be home as soon as I can. Take care Meg,' said Micky, swallowing hard.

Meg could not speak, but slowly let Micky's hand leave her own as her lips quivered.

Micky was soon back with his unit and the realities of camp life. With their recent move to Witley, the soldiers thought they would soon be going to see some action, but the training continued for a further eight weeks, and the men were becoming increasingly agitated, wondering when and where they would be going next.

Chapter 45

The football season finished with Sunderland finishing eighth. Almost all of the Sunderland team headed straight to the Sunderland war recruitment office and signed up.

It was hard for Kate. She had made friends, but she depended on Jacky for support. Edna was now five years old, and Kate doted on her.

'I cannot continue to play football, while men are fighting for us, Kate,' said Jacky.

'I know, Jacky, but I don't know what I'll do without you,' said Kate.

'It won't be for long. I'll be back before you know it. And I'll write.'

Kate broke down in tears. She could not hide her emotions and was unable to put on a brave face. It made it difficult for Jacky, but he knew what he had to do.

Jacky and his teammate, Charlie, were recruited into the Royal Garrison Artillery and were sent to Ripon in Yorkshire to start their training, receiving their uniforms and spurs. Jacky soon learned that the horses took priority over the men. Every day, the horses were groomed, fed and watered, before the men were given their breakfast. All the men in the unit respected and got to love the horses they cared for. Each one had its own personality; it took the men a while to get to know the different horses, but they soon had an understanding of their individual characters. It was much the same with the other men in their groups. They were all living in such close quarters and on top of each other, night and day, that they soon knew one another very well. Jacky knew that it took Charlie a while to wake up and face the day; he did not like early mornings. Whereas Jacky was happy to be up with the lark and leapt out of bed full of energy, ready to start the day. However, Jacky was like a bear with a sore head late in the evening, when all he wanted to do was hit the sack.

Getting up early and seeing to the horses was Jacky's favourite part of the day. He had never had much to do with animals, but found the company of these giant beasts relaxing — although they could give a nasty kick; Jacky made sure he kept away from the horses' rear ends. There was one horse that he felt particularly fond of, and Jacky was happy to muck out the stable and feed the magnificent creature.

'You care more about that horse than you do about me,' said Charlie.

'Well, he's better looking and got a better kick than you that's for sure,' said Jacky. 'I think if I hadn't been a footballer, I could've been a jockey.'

'Aye, they're fine animals. Best not get too attached to any of them though; you don't know where they'll end up...or us for that matter.'

'That's right enough. I just can't get over how big he is. You could put three pit ponies on top of each other, and he'd still be taller than the lot of them.'

'Come on, time to get our own breakfast before we start on fatigues. Let's just hope it's not peeling potatoes. I think I'd rather have hooves like him than peel any more potatoes.'

Jacky and Charlie headed back to the mess room for their breakfast, before starting their fatigues — peeling potatoes, dishwashing and other daily chores. This was the part of the day Jacky did not enjoy, but he was happy polishing his boots; he had swapped his football boots for army boots. There was a lot of marching. Some men complained about the amount of exercise involved in the training, but Jacky enjoyed the physical exertion. Jacky and Charlie were used to training routines and keeping fit. Although most of the men were fit, none of them came close to Jacky and Charlie when it came to football, and the pair were put on opposing teams when friendly football matches took place. The men spent just a few weeks at the camp in Yorkshire, before being moved. It was hard saying goodbye to the horses they had come to know, but it helped Jackie to soon realise that becoming too attached to anyone or anything when at war was not a good idea. He said farewell to the horses, before packing his bags and marching with Charlie and the other recruits to the railway station.

Chapter 46

At the end of June, the khaki uniforms Micky and his company had been waiting for, finally arrived.

'You look like a proper soldier now, Wilf,' remarked Micky.

'About bloody time! I've had enough of being a Kitchener Blue. The least we deserve is a proper uniform and decent weapons.'

'Well, I reckon we should see some action before too long; we've been in here for seven months now.'

'Aye, France I reckon. About time an' all; I didn't sign up just to sit about training camps for months on end.'

When the order to leave was finally received, it was all systems go. There was no warning and no time to prepare. On the 1st of July, the battalion was informed that they would be leaving that day, marching to Farnham railway station and taken by train to Liverpool.

'They're keeping us in the dark about where we are going. I don't reckon it's France; not if we're going up to Liverpool,' said Wilf.

'I don't care where they send us; I just want to get away from the training camp and get this war finished.'

Just then Micky was called in to see his commanding officer once again.

'Sit down, Mordue,' said the officer, in a less sympathetic voice than before.

Micky was worried; as far as he knew everything was fine back home, so what was this all about?

'It's your wife's father. We've had word that he died yesterday.'

Micky was shocked that Mr. Coatman, who had suffered from breathing problems for a while, should die so suddenly, unless Meg had chosen not to tell him his health had deteriorated. Micky had seen him when he had returned to Horden for John's funeral, and he seemed fine at that time. Micky was stunned. Mr. Coatman had treated Micky like a son for the last eleven years and, having lost his own father when he was young, Micky had grown very fond of his father-in-law.

'Unfortunately,' the officer continued 'you cannot be granted leave for the death of your wife's father. If it was your own father that would have been different.'

'But, sir, my wife has been through a lot recently and I feel I should be there for her,' said Micky boldly.

'We can't make any exceptions, Mordue. We're leaving this afternoon, and you will be coming with us.'

Micky walked outside, stunned. He wanted to be with Meg. She adored her father, and this would be devastating for her, following the death of baby John just a couple of months before. Micky knew he had no choice. He could not see Meg. A rushed letter would be the best he could do. If only he had been home by Christmas as Kitchener had promised.

The battalion arrived in Liverpool, in the early hours of the following morning. They consisted of 944 rank and file: 30 officers, fifteen four-wheeled carts, four two-wheeled carts and nine bicycles.

The following day, R.M.S. Aquitania got underway from Liverpool, escorted by two destroyers to a point between the Scilly Isles and Cape Ushant. At about 5 am on the fourth of July, South of the Irish Coast, the destroyers departed. Just ten minutes later, the alarm sounded: a German submarine had been reported. The Battalion stood to boats. A torpedo was fired from the German submarine and passed close under the stern of the boat. A lucky escape.

As the Aquitania headed south, the temperature rose. All was quiet for a few days, as they passed Gibraltar, until on the seventh of July the alarm sounded, and the battalion stood to boats once again. Another submarine had been reported, but it appeared that no torpedoes had been launched, and the boat continued, on course to Malta.

The heat increased. The men had never experienced such temperatures. The pitch in the seams of the boat bubbled, as it was so hot. There was a constant sickly smell of steam, grease and oil from the engine room. Micky had never seen water as clear and blue as the Mediterranean Sea. Porpoises swam alongside the boat, playfully weaving in and out of the waves. Micky looked longingly at the crystal water all around. He would love to feel the cool water about his skin. At night-time, there were strange shapes and glows hovering in the sky above the water, and the sea itself seemed to hold wondrous mysteries of changing light and colour.

The food on the boat was poor, and there was very little to drink. The men felt heat fatigued and blinded by the glare of the sun. When the boat put in at Malta, they had to stay on board. Fruit boats were rowed out to meet them, selling tomatoes, pears, apples, chocolate, Turkish delight, cigars, cigarettes and lace. Bronze-skinned boys dived into the deep blue sea around the boat, salvaging pennies and bully beef thrown into the water by the soldiers. They left Malta and continued on their journey. The landscapes were like none they had seen before. Greek islands shimmered in shades of pinks and mauves. Some were lush green, covered in vineyards. A strange, sandy-looking island came into view, with lines of what looked like volcanic peaks. This was the Island of Lemnos. It wasn't until the following day that the men could disembark with the baggage being unloaded the day after — the twelfth of July.

Lemnos Island was very exposed with little or no shade. The men had believed they would disembark and move straight into battle, but instead they were put on this remote island with its oppressive silence. Troops from Australia and New Zealand had previously passed through the island, before being dispatched to the Ottoman campaign, but the British troops, who were now landing, knew little of this. The heat was intolerable; there were countless flies, green and black, and sweat and sand. A strong wind blew, blowing sand in its path. There was sand everywhere. After the arduous journey, packed onto the boat in the unbearable heat and smell, gearing themselves up for battle, the men were overcome with despair. After just one day on the island, the Battalion was struck down with stomach cramps and diarrhoea. Some suffered so badly that they had little choice but to sleep near the stinking, fly-ridden latrines. It was a one-and-a-half-mile trek to the nearest water. Carts were used to fetch the water, which was warm and tasted stale. In contrast to the insufferable daytime heat, the nights were bitterly cold. The atmosphere was gloomy. Almost everyone felt bodily sick. To make things worse, there were no letters — no escape from this hellhole. On leaving British soil, the soldiers had felt enthused and strengthened by the prospect of finally being able to fight for their country. Now they were miserable shadows of their former selves.

A soldier from one platoon, who just weeks earlier had been a strapping figure of a man, had been one of the many who had been afflicted, and was now weak and a poor excuse of the man he was. The effects of dysentery had made him too weak to crawl to the latrines, and he lay, trousers and underclothes round his ankles, covered in his own excrement. Two of his comrades, themselves languishing, wrapped his arms around their shoulders and managed to drag him to the latrines, where they lowered him down next to the stinking pit. As soon as their backs were turned the soldier rolled headfirst into the ditch and was completely unable to move. His friends struggled to pull him out but did not have enough strength left in them. In a matter of minutes the soldier was dead, having drowned in the foul excrement and waste. Following months of training, and never having fought a battle, he died a deplorable death.

Greeks appeared selling watermelons, which the men had never seen before. Sinking their teeth into the sweet, juicy red flesh was heavenly. At this moment, this tasted better than anything they had ever eaten in their lives. The sea was clear and swimming with fish. The men had to avoid the dozens of sea urchins scattered over the seabed. The water was cool and refreshing, and the only place on the island to escape the flies. The men could have been on the moon for all they knew, such was the alien nature of their surroundings. They did not know where in the world they were; they had never heard of Lemnos.

In the heat and with the terrible sickness the men endured, they felt like doing nothing more than resting and cooling themselves in the sea, but this was not possible. Every morning at 5.45 am. the men had to go on parade. Drills followed this. There was little time to rest, before the night attack practise started at 7.30 pm and continued through the night until 3 am. It was not enough to put the soldiers through the heat and disease they had to endure. The men were pushed so hard in these unforgiving conditions that some collapsed from exhaustion. A cemetery was created on the island. Men were dying before they made it to the battle-ground. To the other soldiers, this was a crushing waste of life. On the sixteenth of July at 9.30 a.m, the Battalion was inspected by the Army Corps General. Micky and Wilf supported each other through this period of fatigue and despondency.

On the 20th of July, the battalion left their bivouacs and embarked on the H.M.S. Harpy and H.M.S. Savage and travelled to Imbros, another island. They were continually worked hard — practising boarding and embarking from lighters, which were landing craft, with a ramp at the bows, known as Beetles.

On the 24th of July, there was an inspection by Sir Ian Hamilton, who remarked on the good physique of the men. The following day, the men were given the first of two inoculations against Cholera. The injection left them feeling as if a mule had kicked them. Still they were expected to carry on with little rest.

Two days after the second of their inoculations against cholera, orders were received that the battalion would embark that afternoon. The men were relieved that they would finally be getting involved in some real action, but they felt physically weak and fatigued by the heat and effects of their injections. This was it. The time had come for them to play their part. Instructions were given to the commanders, but everything was to be kept so secretive that the lower ranks were not told of the battle plan. They were simply told that they had to attack and gain ground without firing any shots. They were to use only their bayonets.

They had had little sleep the previous night, and as instructions were received that day, they had been up and on parade at 5.45 as usual. The men were given two days of iron rations, which they would have to make last for four days. They were also given two empty sandbags and two bottles of water. They had instructions not to drink the water through the night, as it was not known when they would be able to refill their bottles. They were also given two hundred and twenty rounds of ammunition. They had to travel light, leaving their heavy packs behind, and just carrying a light haversack on their shoulder. A triangular piece of tin, cut from a biscuit box, was tied to the corner of the haversack. This would show up like a heliograph; enabling gunners to support the attack. They also had two white armbands.

During the afternoon, the men had to march to the destroyers and lighters which were to carry them from Imbros to the Turkish mainland with the lighters in tow. Once again, the men had to endure cramped conditions on board the vessels. They were already fatigued, and the fighting had not yet begun. It would be a long night ahead of them. As they slowly crossed the water, the sun began to set, and night drew in. Before long it became pitch black. The night seemed darker than any they had experienced. There were searchlights on the Turkish coast, and these seemed to pick up the craft. It was impossible to know if they had been spotted at that time. As they approached the coast, the lighters were set adrift from the destroyers and headed to the beach under their own engines. Micky and Wilf, along with five hundred other troops, were aboard the first lighter to head to the beach.

The beach area at Suvla Bay stretched in a semi-circular shape, for approximately three miles. About a mile ahead, lay the higher ground. An area known as Salt Lake was within the area, but during the summer the lake was dry, with a fifteen feet gully connecting it to the beach. A relatively small number of Turkish troops held this area — mostly on the heights surrounding the bay. Some were stationed on Lala Baba hill and other small hills, near the shore. The plan was to take the beach and smaller hills, and then the higher ground beyond while there were relatively few Turks defending the territory. It should then be possible to link up with Anzacs, who would be simultaneously trying to break forward. However, the troops had not been informed of the overall plan and had not been shown maps of the area. They had only their immediate orders to follow, and having never before been into battle, were inexperienced. They had no choice but to blindly carry out the orders of their commanders. It was now 11 pm, and they were just about to disembark, knowing that a night of warfare lay ahead of them. The men, consisting of 25 officers and 750 other ranks, embarked on two lighters.

'This is it then, Micky.'

'Aye, God help us, Wilf.'

As they neared the beach enemy rifles, firing out of the blackness, greeted them. Micky and Wilf's regiment was the first to land. The ramp from the lighters was narrow, and the men had to disembark in single file — bullets whizzing past on both sides. As soon as the first officer stepped from the lighter, he was shot through, blocking the way of the ensuing soldiers. Faced with a hail of bullets from the waiting Turks, the following soldier had to step over the officer's groaning body and pull him out of the way. There was no time to waste; they had to get off the lighters as fast as they could, as they were like sitting ducks on a shooting range — picked off one by one. As soon as the men got off the lighters, they grouped in sevens or eights and followed the order to charge. The Colonel and Captain were shot immediately. Micky and Wilf ran with five other men, charging through the darkness — bayonets in hand. The bullets rained down through the darkness. Flashes of lights and flares momentarily lit up the side of the hill, but the men could not see the Turks hidden among the scrub, as they ran in full view across the open beach. The soldiers were like lambs to the slaughter, unable to fire back at the Turks — having orders to use bayonets and not to shoot. The men ran as fast and as far as they could. Wilf and Micky were amongst those at the very front of the assault. Their commanders were shot, so it was up to the privates to keep going. Wilf, Micky and the men ran forward in the darkness as best they could, stumbling on gorse and stones, but one by one they fell. The screams of the soldiers being shot to pieces around them were sickening and unnerving, but Wilf and Micky knew they had to keep going. After just twenty minutes of action, without having fired his gun, Wilf was hit. The bullet went straight through his head, and mercifully he was dead before he hit the ground. Micky knew he could not stop; he had to keep running. By the time he had reached the scrub at the bottom of the hill, he was the only man left standing out of the seven who had charged together. Blood rang thick and sweet over the pebbles and sand. Piles of bodies lay where they had fallen, never even making it across the beach. The blood-red waves washed onto the shore, hats and boots bobbing around on the water, gently nudging the bodies by whom they had so recently been worn, as if trying to stir them into life — to put them back as they had been just minutes before.

The adrenaline pumping through Micky's veins kept him going. The surviving men kept running up the small hill, and in the darkness ran across a narrow trench — unaware of the Turks hiding within. As they ran further up the hill, the Turkish soldiers shot at them from behind. They reached another trench, but this time they attacked the waiting Turks and managed to take the trench. It was narrow — only just room for one person to stand. It was impossible to avoid standing on the dead and dying that lay at the bottom of the trench. They had still not been given the order to fire, and some soldiers were wrestling the enemy to the ground, unsure whether they should shoot. By midnight, after a great deal of bloodshed, the Yorkshire Regiment had taken the small hill, Lala Baba, and occupied the trenches to the north. The assault had cost the battalion dearly, and all but two officers and a third of the troops had been killed or seriously wounded. Elsewhere, in and around the bay, there was little or no cohesion between the groups of men, who were inexperienced in battle, and had no idea what they should do next. They did not know if they should continue to press forward or dig in to where they were.

The lack of leadership was all too apparent. The few surviving officers tried to gather the men together and restore some momentum, but the soldiers were barely able to move and did not know if they should follow the commands of officers from different units, or wait for instructions from within their own group. The remaining officers tried to organise an advancement onto Hill 10, but with troops scattered, and darkness still prevailing, it was difficult to achieve any cohesive operation. It was only after sunrise that Hill 10 was eventually taken. The situation became more confusing and muddled as the day passed. Many of the lighters of the other regiments had landed in the wrong places, some hitting sandbanks and being stuck in the bay, with the troops having to wade to shore, up to their necks in water and under fire.

Micky had never felt so thirsty. The sun was relentless; there was no shade, and the air, thick with flies. The small hills next to the beach had been taken, but none of the surrounding hills. There were heavy casualties and a distinct lack of officers. The secrecy that had surrounded the landings had resulted in the remaining troops having no information or instructions as to what they were to do once they had taken Lala Baba. The battle plan had indeed been kept secret, but they were now virtually on their own. Even the two remaining officers of Micky's Battalion were unclear of the exact details of the plan; however, they managed to rally their troops once more, and made an attack on the lightly defended Scimitar Hill. After more bloodshed and loss of life, the Battalion took the hill and dug in. The men had shown incredible courage and determination, suffering from hunger and thirst in unbearably hot conditions. Those that were still standing were now dead on their feet. They had not slept for almost two days.

In the distance, to their left, it appeared that a small number of men had even made it to the Tekke Tepe ridge and were holding their ground. As the night turned to morning, hundreds more troops landed in relative safety and remained on the beaches. Micky had not had time to reflect or think about his actions. Everything had happened so quickly. Now he could not get the image of Wilf's torn and bloodied head out of his mind. His eyes wide, staring up at Micky through the darkness. Flashes of blood, flesh and bullets waved through his subconscious, drowning him in a sea of horror. Micky thought about the soldiers he had punctured with his bayonet. The sharp steel piercing their clothes before sinking into the soft flesh below. And the sudden lightness as the blade was retracted, red with blood. His boots had trampled on bodies, sinking and crunching their way through trenches lined with death.

During the night-time landings and offensive, Lieutenant-General Sir Frederick Stopford stayed aboard the HMS Jonquil — sleeping, as men fought and lost their lives under his command. Having no experience of such warfare, Stopford was content with the progress made and simply wanted to consolidate the position they held on the beaches. He had no intention of pushing ahead and taking the higher ground, even though British intelligence had estimated it would be thirty-six hours before the Turkish reinforcements would arrive. That would be on the evening of the eighth of August. General Ian Hamilton had sent Captain Aspinall, accompanied by Lieutenant-Colonel Hankey, to assess the situation. When they found a fairly relaxed atmosphere on the beaches, they initially assumed the offensive was going to plan. It was only when they realised that the higher ground had not been taken that the gravity of the situation emerged.

Hamilton was outraged and ordered an immediate attack on Scimitar Hill, as a preliminary to an advance on the high ground to the east: a ridge called Tekke Tepe. Unbelievably, the brigade staff, having little idea of the location of its formations, ordered them to concentrate at the Sulajik wells. At 4 am on the ninth of August, Micky and his battalion, not knowing that the plan was to take the very hill they already occupied, withdrew from Scimitar Hill, as all formations had been ordered to converge and regroup back at the wells. Another advancing battalion had to halt its successful ascent of the ridge, and also head back to Sulajik wells. The battalions that had made good progress were now, inexplicably, being ordered to leave the strong positions they had gained. The men that had been spotted by Micky, on the Tekke Tepe ridge, were not instructed back to Sulajik; those in command did not even know they were there — in spite of the group sending back communications. They were left stranded on the ridges with no support, and with the Turks reinforcing in great numbers. The lack of communication was pitiful and would prove disastrous. In the meantime, the Turkish reinforcements arrived and, without any confrontation, regained control of Scimitar Hill and increased their control of the higher ground.

Finally, later that same day, the British attempted to recapture Scimitar Hill, but by now it was too late. Micky and his battalion were being ordered to attack the exact area they had earlier that very day been ordered to leave. The hours that had been wasted had allowed the Turks to reinforce, and what could have been a relatively simple manoeuvre to capture the lightly defended higher ground, was now another bloody failure. More lives were broken and lost in the futile attempt to capture the hills. It emerged much later that all of the men who had been left on the Tekke Tepe ridge, without support or orders to withdraw, had been either killed or captured. Micky, and what was left of his battalion, dug out in the trenches for the next few days. There was no let-up from the heat, and the flies were a constant irritation. Micky could not take his eyes off the tin of bully beef he opened — knowing that the hundreds of flies that were eager to land on it were the same flies that had been feeding on the dead bodies and the latrines. Micky's throat was as dry and coarse as the landscape. Water was still in short supply. The Turks knew where the wells were located, and kept a constant watch — with snipers picking off easy targets. The Turks were on the high ground — spectators at a game. The allied forces had few places to hide. Micky had to keep down in the cramped, stinking trench.

Chapter 47

On Thursday the 12th, the battalion was given some relief. They were to leave the trenches and return to the beach. This was easier said than done, with snipers trying to pick them off as they crept through the scrub, trying to keep their heads down, but with nowhere to hide. Micky felt utter relief as he reached the relative safety of the beach. At last he sat and wrote to Meg.

'Just a few lines hoping you are all keeping in the best of health. I am pleased to say that I am all right myself, thanks be to the Lord. We left our camp to go into action last Friday, August 6th, and I shall never forget it. We had to make a new landing on the Peninsula. Arriving about 10 o'clock at night we found the Turks were waiting for us. They rained bullets at us as we were coming off the boat. Our Colonel and Captain got shot straight away. I am sorry to say that Wilf Belcher got killed about 20 minutes after we landed. We got our orders not to fire but use the bayonet only. It was just like facing certain death, but our regiment, who were the first to land, never faltered. We got the order to charge, and we did not forget to either. I am the luckiest man alive. I was with Wilf Belcher and another five of our section, and I am sorry to say all of them were shot by my side. How I escaped the Lord above knows. You can tell Mr. Bob Belcher that Wilf died like a hero. We have never faltered since Friday night until today (Thursday), when we are back out of the trenches. I have not much more to tell you. Only tell my mother how I am getting on. Keep your heart up, because I think I am sure to pull through now after the escapes I have had. So now I shall conclude. Give my best love to all.'

Micky lovingly placed the letter in an envelope. Meg would soon know that he was well. He did not want her to know the harsh realities of his experiences; maybe, he would never tell her. Micky drifted dreamily into a welcome sleep; his thoughts anywhere but here. But the respite was short-lived, and Micky had to return to the trenches that evening. The situation was a stalemate. The Turks held the hills. The Allies held the beaches. This went on for over a week, with very little to report, but those in command knew that they had to make a move. It was decided to make another assault on the hills, and attempt to link up with the Anzacs, further south. They would simultaneously attack and drive the Turks back. 29th Division was to attack Scimitar Hill, whilst the 11th Division, of which Micky was a part, was to attack W Hill and the Anzacs were to take Hill 60.

Chapter 48

The 21st of August 1915 was unlike every other day Micky had experienced in this barren land. Today, of all days, there was a mist in the air. The sun was hidden behind a haze of clouds. The Allies had counted on the fact that the sun would be blazing bright as usual, dazzling the Turks as the Allies advanced, but today this was not going to be the case. As this was such a major part of the battle plan — to time the battle with the sun blinding the Turks as they were being attacked — it was assumed that the battle would be delayed until the following day, but those in command had other ideas. During the morning, the Roman Catholic Priest preached to the waiting troops, warning them that they were about to meet their maker, and advising them to confess their sins, before it was too late. This did nothing to boost the morale of the already apprehensive men. At 3 p.m. the battle commenced, but once again it did not go to plan. The attack on Scimitar Hill went well, but Hill 60 was more heavily defended than expected. 11th Division was confronted by an Ottoman strong-point and heavy artillery fire. Their navigator was killed within minutes, and there was no one else with a compass. The men were scattered by the bullets and shells that rained down on them, losing their direction, and heading north-east instead of east. The troops on Scimitar Hill were exposed to fire from all sides, with 11th Division unable to support them. The groups found themselves scattered over the hillsides — disjointed, and, once again, without instructions as to what to do next. The Turks had a clear view of the events and were able to control the situation, while the Allies had no sight of their targets — being hidden by smoke, mist and the advantage of the higher ground. Once again the men did not falter, and all fought with selfless bravery. As hard as they tried, with bodies falling around them, the battalion could not make progress. The fighting continued all through the night.

The following day, it was decided to retreat back to the beach once more, but this would prove difficult. Turks were dotted all over the hillsides, picking off their targets. It was impossible to move without being spotted. Micky and a few of his comrades fought as they retreated, the bush tearing their skin, as they battled through the scrub. Men fell as snipers picked them off. Not clean shots, but blasts of flesh and blood that left them scrambling and crawling — gaping wounds dragged along the dirt. It was then that a shell blasted amongst them. A few of their number died instantly, but Micky saw that his leg was drenched in his own crimson blood. As he tried to move, he could feel the boot on his foot dragging behind him. It was a mangled mess of blood and leather. The pain was excruciating, but Micky knew he had to get away. He looked at the heaps of bloody meat that moments before had been his comrades. Screams and groans filled his ears. Only two of the men were still in one piece. They tried to help the others — rushing from man to man — assessing the damage. Micky then noticed the crackling flames licking the dry scrub surrounding them. The two survivors removed their jackets and tried to blanket the blaze, but it was soon evident that they were fighting yet another losing battle. They returned their attention to the men and attempted to drag them from the blaze. Micky stumbled and crawled for all his worth, but it was difficult enough to navigate through the terrain without having a foot hanging off. The screams of the men were haunting, as the crackling fire engulfed them. The smell of roasting flesh and leather filled the air.

Micky did not make it back to the beach.

Chapter 49

Meg received a telegram. She feared the worse as soon as she heard the knock on the front door. Nobody knocked on people's front doors. Apprehensively, she slowly opened the door a fraction — peering round the gap. She knew it would be the telegram boy. The young lad stood sheepishly on the front pavement. He could barely look Meg in the eye, as he handed over the piece of paper. Meg thrust it in the pocket of her apron and slowly closed the door. The longer she left it in her pocket, the longer she could believe that Micky was well. She was on her own in the house, with just three-year-old Mary. The other children had started back at school after their summer break. Meg sat at the kitchen table and took the letter from her pocket — staring at it — not wanting to open it. She looked at it for some minutes, oblivious to everything going on around her. There was a knock at the back door and Meg's mother, Mrs. Coatman, entered the house.

'What's it say, lass?' she asked grimly.

Word had already reached The Coatmans that the 'angel of death' had knocked on Meg's door.

'I can't open it, Mam,' said Meg.

'I'd read it for you, if I could, Pet,' said Mrs. Coatman. 'Shall I take the bairn for you?'

'No, Mam. Stay here please. I'll look at it just now.'

Meg took a deep breath and revealed the words she had been dreading.

Private Michael Mordue…died…sympathy…

Meg felt too hollow to cry. She felt an emptiness that she knew would never be filled. First it was her baby, then her father, and now her husband — all within six months. She was still wearing mourning clothes from her previous losses; now she would be forever in black.

Chapter 50

Jacky and his companions had moved to Weedon, near Northampton, to continue their training, when Jacky learned of Micky's death. It hit him hard. Jacky hoped that there had been a mistake; Micky could not have been killed. Jacky felt angry; Micky had not needed to go to war; he could have stayed at the coal mine, where men were needed. The authorities had said the war would be over in no time, but it had already dragged on for over a year. Jacky thought about Micky's sons — all young lads who no longer had a father. He thought about their mother and Meg — the women who loved Micky, and would be lost in grief. He thought about Hannah and Mary, Micky's daughters — so much like his own daughter, Edna. Now they would never know their father. Would Edna ever know Jacky? Jacky wanted the training period to be over, so that he could fight for his country and help to finish the war that had taken his brother. Jacky found it difficult to concentrate on the mundane tasks he was expected to perform; his mind continually drifted to thoughts of his brother, Micky. The daily routine of feeding the horses, taking breakfast, polishing boots and spurs, parade and fatigues did not require a great deal of concentration, so his mind would wander and repeatedly return to thoughts of Micky. There was a new side to the training here, which incorporated a large number of gun drills. This required speed and concentration and involved teamwork. Jacky's mind had no time to stray; he needed to stay focused. A six or four-man team would man a gun, and each take their part in the aiming, loading and firing of the gun. This had to be practised, over and over again, so that the gun team built up speed and proficiency in their duties. Jacky liked being part of a team; it was something he was used to. Each man playing their part, not wanting to be a weak link or let their colleagues down. Jacky found the training mentally and physically exhausting, but was happy to be able to throw himself into it — a welcome distraction. The men were also expected to learn each element of the gun team, in preparation for front-line action, being able to take up the role of fallen comrades.

As the weeks and months went by, the torment of Micky's death became less intense, and Jacky was able to manage his pain, although it would never completely disappear. Jacky continued his training. Although he played football with his army comrades, he missed the excitement of the professional matches and the sound of the crowd. Although league and cup football had been suspended on a national level, they were replaced with regional leagues. Clubs were short of players as they signed up to serve their country. When he had leave from duties, Jacky grabbed the opportunity to play for Fulham football club, as a guest player — putting in some great performances and scoring goals for his adoptive team.

At the beginning of 1916, Jacky and Charlie were sent to France, where they faced the realities of battle. The initial excitement of completing their training and being able to take part in the real action was soon extinguished. As well as the unpleasant living conditions, the threat of attack, and the trudging through mud, they saw and smelt death for the first time. They experienced battles on the front line, but nothing prepared them for the horrors of war that they endured in 1917. In January, the unit was posted to Colincamps in France where they joined the 1st Highland Battery — a unit that was made up of kilt-clad Scotsmen. The weather was icy cold, and the conditions were bleak. The days and weeks passed slowly, as guns were dragged into place, horses tended to and steady bombardment took place. Jacky and another five men were expected to man their gun, for up to forty-eight hours at a time — constantly under the threat of enemy fire. The guns would be loaded, aimed and fired, while explosions went off all around them. The gun barrels became red hot with their breech blocks jamming. Jacky used a pickaxe to open the gun ready for the next round, oil and smoke belching into his face. He slammed home the shells ready for the next discharge — the men and gun becoming part of the killing machine. Ammunition and air temperature variations meant that each fuse had to be set by hand, and the elevation adjusted by sore, tired eyes. The Germans intermittently used gas to bombard the gunners. Gas masks were effective against such attacks, but constantly wearing a gas mask during the gruelling physical effort of firing the gun proved extremely uncomfortable, and vision became restricted, making the task much more difficult. There was a constant threat of enemy fire — shells exploding around them. At first, Jacky flinched and cowered, but very quickly learned to ignore the loud explosions nearby, trying to ignore the fact that his life could be cut short at any moment.

The men made a shallow dugout near the gun, where they would shelter while the gun cooled down, or the few times when the gun was not required. The dugout provided very little shelter. Jacky went from working up a sweat and feeling uncomfortably hot while manning the gun, to shivering uncontrollably in the ineffectual dugout. The men were surrounded by filth, and their uniforms crawled with lice. At the end of their stint at the front, they were filthy, hungry and exhausted. On being relieved by another six men from the unit, Jacky would trek back from the front line to camp, rest and sleep before returning to the front line. This pattern continued, week in, week out.

At the beginning of April, plans were put in place for an attempt to advance. The soil around Arras was chalky, which enabled tunnelling to take place. The allies created a network of tunnels that allowed advancement and protection for the troops. The guns were moved into position. The battle raged. Jacky and his team worked tenaciously, keeping up a constant barrage of attack, while under fire. The initial push was a success and ground was made, but this was not followed up. The fighting soon returned to a bloody stalemate, with a huge loss of life on both sides. Jacky's division fared relatively well, with just one soldier being killed and another nine wounded in the initial attack. However, the enemy attacks on the guns increased and became more accurate. Shell and gas attacks were recurrent. Jacky had a narrow escape, when a shell exploded nearby, killing three of his comrades and injuring more.

'Charlie, you've got blood on your back,' said Jacky as the assault quietened down.

Charlie had felt the pain in his shoulder, but had continued to carry on his duty manning the gun. His uniform was coated in sweat, oil and mud; he had not realised there was blood in the mix. The wound was deep but did not appear to be life-threatening. The pain, which Charlie had ignored, was now acute. Charlie needed his injury to be cleaned and dressed.

'Looks like you'll have to get that sorted, Charlie.'

Charlie reluctantly left the fighting and was taken to the field hospital. It was only when Jacky was taking some rest that he thought about the consequences, should the shrapnel have hit Charlie just inches higher, in his neck. Charlie had had a lucky escape, but infection was still a threat. Jacky and Charlie had come to know every facet of one another. At times they wanted to distance themselves from each other, driving the other one crazy with their moods or irritating habits. At other times, they wanted nothing more than to spend time in the other one's company — a comforting familiarity in the hostile world that surrounded them. They shared experiences which nobody else would, or could understand; they had formed a bond that could never be broken. It was also something they would never talk about; it was a mutual understanding. Jacky longed for Charlie's safe return.

Charlie had not returned to the unit, when the ever-present onslaught of gas attacks finally took its toll on Jacky. He had not taken the brunt of the gas, which would have been fatal, but it lingered in the air, and the effects seeped into his airways. Although his stomach was not full, he was physically sick. He felt a burning sensation and swelling in his stomach. Along with three other men from his unit, he was taken to the Canadian Stationary Hospital at Le Havre. The Canadian medical personnel took great care of Jacky and the rest of the patients. Jacky recovered and felt relaxed and rejuvenated, for the first time in months. He spent just two nights in the hospital and then had to return to his unit at the front. On his return, Jacky was delighted to see Charlie back with the unit. The two men would have leapt into each other's arms in a demonstration of friendship and relief, grinning from ear to ear, but as it was, they just looked at one another, and nonchalantly acknowledged each other, keeping up their constrained exteriors, while inwardly rejoicing.

The battery continued to support the infantry and pound the enemy line, whilst themselves being fired at. In the middle of May, the unit moved once again. The men and horses trudged through the night, hauling the weaponry and supplies. Rain had made the chalky soil very slippery, and a caterpillar had to help with the manoeuvrers. At Agny, Jacky and the other gunners were sent forward to prepare the position. Jacky was coated in mud and exhausted by the time everything was in place. The guns were, once again, put into action, and Jacky had to summon up all his strength to continue assisting with manning the gun. When he was finally allowed some rest, he trudged back to the camp and rested his weary body. The next stint came all too quickly, as once again Jacky returned to duty. Every now and then, the unit would be moved, and the weaponry hauled through the slippery mud once again. Manoeuvrers and firing continued, with little advancement from either side.

June and July were relatively quiet, and the sun shone brightly in the sky. There were occasional thunderstorms, but in the main the weather was warm and bright. Fighting continued sporadically at the front, but not in the same relentless waves as on previous occasions. At the wagon lines, away from the front lines, sports were encouraged and arranged to occupy the troops. Batteries competed against one another in organised events. On June 23rd, Jacky's battery was up against the 113th battery. Jacky was able to compete, and won all the events in which he took part — being the fastest man present. Several group commanders were present to watch the events. Jacky enjoyed competing and being cheered on by his teammates; it made him realise how much he missed being on a football pitch, in front of a huge crowd, with the buzz and excitement of a game. This light relief did not last, and the following day Jacky returned to duty, but he could look forward to his next break and the chance of a game of football or cricket.

Following this lull, the battery moved from Arras to Ypres. There was to be a major offensive and preparations were underway. General Haig was keen to damage German defences, and advance as far as Belgium, in order to attack German submarine bases on the Belgian coast. There was also a probability that Russia would withdraw troops from the east — freeing up German troops to move to the Western Front, strengthening their forces. There had been opposition to the plan, especially by General Currie, in charge of the Canadian Corps. He thought Haig's plan would be a futile waste of life. Haig would not be diverted from his objective, and single-mindedly stuck to his strategy. Another negative factor against the mission was the weather. Heavy rain was predicted for the month of August, and this would have a detrimental effect on any advancement. This did not deter Haig; it was decided to go ahead with the plan. The heavens opened, and rain fell continually; more rain fell in the area than had fallen in the previous thirty years. As shells were fired, and horses, men and machinery trampled over the ground, it soon turned into a quagmire. Within days, men and horses were becoming stuck in the viscous mud. It was impossible to pull them out, as they slowly sank beneath the surface — slowly and painfully drowning. Bodies could not be recovered, and bombardments were continuous. The Germans had foreseen the attack and had counter plans in place. Jacky and his group were called upon to man the guns, day and night, with little rest, and under constant fire. The attack to the left was successful, but on the right, the Germans held out against the onslaught, firing from strong concrete emplacements. Ground could not be made, as it was nigh on impossible to cross the terrain. Seeing how futile a continued attack would be, General Gough left the battleground and met with General Haig, explaining the complications and hopelessness of the situation, and the impracticalities of continuing with the plan. Haig refused to listen, giving Gough no choice but to return to the battle scene and oversee the slaughter of his troops. Over the next two months, very little ground was made, but the number of casualties was immense. Haig continued to stubbornly refuse to back down, and exaggerated the numbers of enemy casualties, whilst underplaying allied losses. Many Australian, New Zealand and Canadian troops lost their lives alongside British and French soldiers. The mud and blood continued to flow.

On November the 6th, Canadian and British forces managed to advance and occupy the village of Passchendaele, just five miles north of Ypres. It was only then that Haig called off the offensive, claiming success.

Jacky had survived the battle, but his mind was as tattered as his body. Having battled in the shadow of death, surrounded by explosions, filth and carnage, Jack was as empty as the shells he had fired. Images of comrades' broken, and blood-stained bodies repeatedly flashed through his mind. His sleep was fitful and fraught: sleep opening up nightmares that he tried to push to the back of his mind, during the time he was awake. Many of the men had similar tormented dreams, but they were with other people who had shared the experience and understood the horrors which haunted them.

The war continued. In March 1918, Haig secured the appointment of the French general, Ferdinand Foch. The two worked well together and learned from past mistakes. With support from the United States of America, a one-hundred-day offensive was mounted. Following more battles and bloodshed, Germany's allies withdrew, and eventually Germany admitted defeat, and a ceasefire was announced on the 11th of November 1918.

Jacky and Charlie returned to Le Havre, along with thousands of other troops, making their way home.

'Well, Charlie, we made it,' said Jacky.

'Aye. Mind, I still can't believe it. I'm half expecting a shell to come flying over my head at any minute,' said Charlie, looking up at the clear, blue sky.

'I reckon there'll be a part of us that will always be thinking that Charlie.'

A young soldier approached them.

'I've been told you two are footballers, is that right?'

'Yes. Why is that? Have they changed their minds, and they're going to play a football match to see who wins? That would have saved a lot of time and lives, if they'd thought of that in the first place,' said Charlie.

'They're organising a match between the Belgians and the British, and heard you two were up here, so they want you to play.'

'Yes! I've got to like those Belgians; it'll be a shame to give them a hiding, but all in the line of duty,' said Jacky.

The match took place in a relaxed and jubilant atmosphere. It was a celebration of unity and freedom. Jacky concentrated on his game, and for the first time in years, really enjoyed the football match. He had liked playing the matches that took place during the war, but there was always a cloud over him. Now, that cloud had lifted. It was with relief that Jacky played this momentous game, with a spring in his step and a weight off his mind. He would soon be returning to England and playing the game he loved, for the team he loved. He would soon see Kate and Edna. His daughter would be nearly ten years old. He had missed a big part of her childhood. And he would soon be able to sleep in his own bed once more, with Kate beside him.

Chapter 51

When Jacky returned home, it was with a mixture of relief and trepidation; he had barely seen Kate and Edna in the past four years. As he walked through the door of their home, Kate smiled at him, and he kissed her on the cheek. But her eyes were distant; he could not read her expression. Edna looked at her father in the same way she would have looked at a stranger. Jack approached her. He wanted to give her a hug; something he had not done before, as he was never a demonstrative man, but he could not. He felt dirty. He felt that he was soiled by the atrocities he had endured.

'Give your Dad a kiss, Edna,' said Kate.

Edna reluctantly planted a kiss on Jacky's cheek.

Jacky had looked forward to this moment for years; the time he could return home to his family, knowing that he would not have to leave them again. Now that he was home. it did not feel like home at all. He felt as if he was intruding. He did not feel comfortable in his own home. Kate did her best to welcome him back, but it was strange for her too. She had coped on her own and built up an independent life, without Jacky around. Kate and Edna had become very close and were used to being the centre of each other's lives. Edna was worried that her mother would pay her less attention, now that Jacky was home. She was happy with things as they were and did not want the dynamics of the household to change. Jacky was like an outsider. Not only had he been absent for a large part of Edna's life, he was not the same man as he was when he signed up and joined the war effort in May 1915. It would take time to readjust to life, as it was before the war. Jacky ate the meal Edna had prepared for him, changed his clothes, and went to the pub.

Chapter 52

Jacky slowly tried to come to terms with his damaging wartime experience, but when he lay in bed, or sat in his armchair by the fire, his mind wandered. He had seen his friends and comrades fall around him. Some made it home, but with missing limbs. Some were shell-shocked. He pictured the horses, with their wide crazed eyes, slowly sinking to their deaths in the entombing mud. The image of the horrors of war were etched on Jacky's brain. And his beloved brother, Micky, would not be returning home. Why Micky? Micky who was only thirty-one years old, when his life was cut short. A lot older than most of the young men who had lost their lives in the war, but still in his prime — with five young children, and a wife who adored him. Micky, who had always been there for him, always encouraged and supported him. Why Micky? Why? And then it was rumoured that he had been burnt to death, unable to escape the flames. Flames that had been lit by Turks; Turks that had been warned by Churchill that an offensive was going to take place. Allegedly, Churchill had bragged and boasted, convinced the allies would destroy the Turkish defence, but incompetent leadership had ruined any chance of success for Micky and his comrades. Jacky repeatedly went over these thoughts in his mind. Anger grew within him. He felt guilty that he had lived, and Micky had not. At night-time, Jacky dreamt he was back on the front line. Every unexpected noise made him shoot out of bed. If Kate brushed against him, he would instinctively push her away, thinking vermin were crawling over him.

Edna continued to look at Jacky with distant eyes. He longed to have back the innocent little girl who looked forward to seeing her Daddy and sit on his knee. He had never spent a lot of time with Edna, but she had paid him excessive attention, when he had been home. Now she kept her distance and eyed him warily. And, to make it worse, at times when Edna would try to approach her father, Jacky was often lost in thought and was completely oblivious to her presence, until he stirred himself out of his detachment, by which time Edna had tired of being ignored. Edna did not understand her father's spasmodic reveries.

Jacky returned to Roker Park. It was great to see his teammates once more, but as the men looked around and shook hands, it was evident there were a few faces that would never be seen again. The players had parted almost four years earlier — all keen to do their bit in this 'great' war — enthusiastic and innocent. Those who returned were changed men. Some were more subdued, saying little and seldom smiling. Others were brash, making out they were unaffected by their experiences, whilst inside they were scarred and broken. Some got over their experiences better than others. Jacky gave the impression that everything was fine. He put on a brave face, not admitting to himself or anyone else, that he was suffering. Men were not supposed to show weakness. Jacky resolved to put his ordeal to the back of his mind, shutting a door on it. Jacky would not talk about the debilitating thoughts that crept into his head. Instead, he pushed them away — letting them haunt him for the rest of his life. Football was his saviour —the teamwork, objectives and discipline involved were what he was used to. He was surrounded by men who had the same mindset; he felt comfortable when he was with his teammates; it was a distraction.

Sunderland played in the Victories League. The 1918/19 football season would have been well underway by that time, so it was impossible to restart the fixture list with just a few months to go. Therefore, it was decided that local Victory Leagues would be played. The football league proper commenced the following September. Jacky had lost his concentration and speed. Although still top class, Jacky was not the player he had been before the war. In his early years at Sunderland, Jacky had been the making of Charlie Buchan. Their teamwork, along with Frank Cuggy, had been unrivalled. Now Jacky and Frank had lost their edge slightly, but still Sunderland finished fifth in the league.

When Middlesbrough approached Sunderland, at the end of the season, Sunderland were happy to take a large fee for Jacky. Jacky played for 'Boro for three seasons — finishing above Sunderland in the first two. At the end of the 1922/23 season, at the age of thirty-six, Jacky was approached by Durham City — a team that had been formed just four years earlier. They had finished bottom of the Third Division North the previous season, but had been re-elected to stay in the league. Jacky was brought in as a player-manager, to turn the tides of the team. Unfortunately, Jacky was not cut out for management. He found the pressures of expected success hard to cope with. He was used to being part of a team and ensuring he played the best he could in each match, but having the responsibility of the performance of the rest of his team on his shoulders did not suit Jacky. He found it hard to tolerate the lack of dedication and discipline of some of the players in the team. The ones who had not experienced the trials of war; their flippancy and immaturity irritated him. Anger and confusion boiled beneath his skin. The team lost more games than they won, and Jacky felt responsible for their lack of success. The feelings of failure added to the haunting memories that never left Jacky's subconscious. Jacky started to drink. It took away the pain. At the end of the 1924 football season, Jacky was relieved of his duty as player/manager of Durham City A.F.C.

Kate and Jacky had spent the money he had earned playing football as quickly as they had received it. This meant that Jacky needed to find work, which he did at a pit near Newcastle. He worked as a stone sorter once more. The job he had carried out as a fourteen-year-old boy. Jacky and Kate had to give up their relatively spacious home and rented a small flat above a shop in Newcastle. On many occasions when Jacky collected his pay on a Friday, he headed straight to the pub and drank himself unconscious. He was on a poor wage, and could ill afford to spend money on liquor, but he did. The lure of the pub and the mind-numbing effect the alcohol had on his brain were too much for Jacky to resist. Without football, Jacky's life was hollow. He still felt detached from Kate and Edna, so he excluded them from his life, which suited him. Kate ensured there was dinner on the table and clean clothes for Jacky to wear, but that was as far as it went. Edna was now sixteen. She was an extremely bright and independent young lady, and did not want to follow the path of domestic imprisonment, which was the norm for women. She had seen her mother, a football widow, giving up her life to run a home and bring up a child, seeing very little of Jacky as he followed his sporting dreams. Edna had found a job in an office, and was training to be a secretary. The money she earned enabled Kate to pay the rent. That was now her priority. Jacky gave Kate most of any money he had left, which was very little, but he always kept some by to see him through the week.

This was now Jacky's life — working, drinking and sleeping. His downward spiral was slow and constant. Jacky's brothers and other family tried to pull him out of the abyss, but no matter what they did, Jacky was unresponsive and wallowed in his pain and misery. Jacky had lost confidence in himself and the void that football had left was filled with stark memories of war. He could not, and would not, tell anyone how his nightmares had become part of his waking life. The traumatic images and feelings he had witnessed when in France and Belgium oppressed him and would not go away.

Kate was unable to find a way to help Jacky. He did not tell her what was haunting him; he did not want to reveal the things he had witnessed; he did not want to appear weak.

One Saturday morning in September 1928, Jacky's brother Jimmy called by and gave Jacky no choice but to come with him to Hartlepool. Jacky protested; he was tired and had a sore head. Jimmy lured him with the promise of a pint when they got to Hartlepool, and reluctantly Jacky accompanied his brother. Jacky's mind was muddled from drink and depression, and he was unaware why Jimmy was taking him so far from home. The brothers arrived at Hartlepools United's Victoria Ground.

'Well, let's get that pint now we're here,' said Jacky.

'After the game, Jacky.'

'Who's playing?'

'Hartlepools against Doncaster. Should be a good game.'

'What are you doing bringing me here, Jimmy? I've got no time for football now,' said Jacky.

'There's a few lads that want you to watch them play, Jacky,' said Jimmy.

Jacky was confused. He had tried to avoid all contact with the sport since leaving Durham. Reluctantly he went with Jimmy into the ground, and Jimmy purchased a programme as they went through the turnstiles. There was a fair size crowd gathered to watch the imminent match.

'Who are the lads that want me to watch the game, Jimmy?' asked Jacky, with diffidence.

Jimmy showed Jacky the programme. There on the team sheet were three Mordues — William and Tucker, Micky's sons, and Jack, Jimmy's son, who he had named after his brother twenty-one years before. It took a while for Jacky to register what was going on. He had no idea that his nephews played football. Well, he knew they played, but not at such a level.

'Your Jack and our Micky's lads?'

'Aye, Jacky. And they'll be made up you're here.'

'But why? Look at me…'

'Jacky, you're one of the best players in the history of English football. You were unstoppable on the wing, and you played for England on both wings. The lads are proud of you. You're their inspiration.'

Jacky pondered Jimmy's words. Failing as a manager and losing his speed and skill had hit him hard. He had lost sight of the player he had once been.

'Our Micky should be here, not me,' said Jacky.

'Aye, we all wish our Micky was still with us, Jacky. But that doesn't mean you shouldn't be here. Meg has always told the lads what a great sportsman their father was, but she also told them about their Uncle Jacky.'

Just then the teams came out onto the pitch. Jimmy pointed out the Mordue lads to Jacky. All three played up front. It was uncanny watching the three cousins — like turning back the clock and watching the three brothers, Jimmy, Micky and Jacky, playing for Spennymoor. It was a good game — end to end. Hartlepool had more possession and looked the better side. Just before half time, William crossed the ball, and Tucker slotted it into the back of the net. 1 – 0 to Hartlepool. The home supporters cheered — including Jacky. It was a long while since Jimmy had seen his younger brother show any signs of happiness. The half-time whistle blew, and Jacky and Jimmy chatted about the game, dissecting each attack, and reliving the goal. Jacky was looking forward to the second half. Once again, Hartlepool had most of the possession, but Darlington made the occasional break. The ball deflected to Jack, and he made a darting run up the centre, weaving in and out of defenders, before slotting the ball in the back of the net. 2 – 0 Hartlepool. Once again, cheers went up, and Jacky and Jimmy watched with pride.

'That could have been me out there,' said Jacky.

'He's got a canny left foot,' said Jimmy 'But none of them will be as good as you were Jacky.'

211

'Get away!' said Jacky, but he knew it was true.

After the match, Jimmy and Jacky met the lads in the pub. Jimmy was apprehensive about giving Jacky a drink; Jacky had started to return to his old self, and Jimmy did not want to jeopardise his progress. But he need not have worried. Jacky sipped his pint, but had hardly time to drink it, as he was answering all the lads' questions, and reliving stories of his days as a professional footballer. The lads also played handball and were amongst the best in the country. Jacky told them how he and Micky had been unbeatable, and what a fine player Micky had been.

Jimmy was worried that Jacky would slip back into his usual routine once he had taken him home.

'Will you be coming to the next match, Jacky?' Jimmy asked.

'Oh, aye, I'll be there,' said Jacky.

Jacky felt privileged to see Micky's boys play football, knowing that Micky could not be there. He owed it to Micky to support the lads and become part of their lives. He had wasted the last few years and missed his nephews turn from boys to men.

Jacky carried on working at the mine, sorting stones for very poor money, but he stopped drinking to battle his mental pain. He had seen what alcohol had done to his father. His father had never seen Jacky play football because he had drunk himself to an early grave, following his own battle with physical pain. Micky had never seen his sons play football because he had fought for his country. Jacky owed it to Micky to be there for the lads. Jacky could no longer play football, but he could take an interest in his nephews' careers. Reading match reports, and watching his nephews play would at least take the place of some of his dark thoughts — if not entirely. It would be difficult; Jacky could not change the last few years, but he could do something now…and he would.

The End

Printed in Great Britain
by Amazon

75090717R00129